GONE AND DONE IT

A DREAMWALKER MYSTERY

GONE AND DONE IT

MAGGIE TOUSSAINT

FIVE STAR
A part of Gale, Cengage Learning

GRMC -1

GALE
CENGAGE Learning

Farmington Hills, Mich • San Francisco • New York • Waterville, Maine
Meriden, Conn • Mason, Ohio • Chicago

F
104

LIBRARY OF CONGRESS CATALOGING-IN-PUBLICATION DATA

Toussaint, Maggie.
  Gone and done it : A dreamwalker mystery / Maggie Toussaint.
    pages cm. — (A Dreamwalker Mystery)
  ISBN-13: 978-1-4328-2813-4 (hardcover)
  ISBN-10: 1-4328-2813-4 (hardcover)
  1. Gardeners—Fiction. 2. Human remains (Archaeology) 3. Psychic ability—Fiction. 4. Paranormal fiction. I. Title.
  PS3620.O89G66 2014
  813'.6—dc23   2013041354

First Edition. First Printing: April 2014
Find us on Facebook– https://www.facebook.com/FiveStarCengage
Visit our website– http://www.gale.cengage.com/fivestar/
Contact Five Star™ Publishing at FiveStar@cengage.com

Printed in the United States of America
1 2 3 4 5 6 7 18 17 16 15 14

This book is dedicated to Savannah and Abe.

ACKNOWLEDGMENTS

I am so very grateful for all the friends and fans who have encouraged me along this journey. Critique partners Polly Iyer and Melody Scott helped sharpen this manuscript. Thanks also goes to Margaret Fenton, who invited me to participate in Murder on the Menu a few years back, which is the first time I'd ever heard of Wetumpka, Alabama. Lastly, I'd be remiss if I didn't mention my brainstorming team of Ginny Baisden, Marianna Hagan, and Suzanne Forsyth. Without you ladies, this series wouldn't have nearly the texture it does.

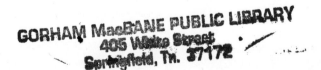

CHAPTER 1

My shovel bounced off a monster root. Tremors vibrated up my aching arms, jolting my knotted shoulders. I swore under my breath. Just my luck. The last installation for this landscaping job, and now I'd hit the mother lode of obstructions.

I leaned on the shovel and wiped my brow on my sleeve. Planting this weeping cherry should have been an easy installation. Should. What a crock. Should implied a promise, but it was an outright lie.

God, I was so tired of pretending everything was fine. Between bureaucratic red tape, enhanced sensory perceptions, and the odd jobs I worked, I felt decades older than my twenty-eight years.

Mosquitoes swarmed my neck and hands, feasting on the unexpected banquet named Baxley Powell. Sweat trickled down from the brim of my ball cap. Not a hint of a sea breeze reached this forested clearing off Misery Road. Instead, the air smelled of pine and decaying leaves, of dancing sunshine and brooding shadows.

At the rumble of an approaching diesel, the birds overhead quieted. Carolina Byrd's builder and realtor had been trouble-shooting the faulty exterior lighting at her new mansion, Mallow, which graced the other end of this winding driveway. Automatically, I checked that my mental shields were in place.

I didn't want any psychic readings off these bozos.

"Hey, pretty lady." Realtor Buster Glassman leaned out of

the driver's window, right overtop the blood-red Glassman Realty logo. "Whatcha up to?" Behind him, builder Duke Quigley bobbed his shiny head in greeting.

I groaned under my breath. Buster could talk the ears off a toadfish if he wanted something. I didn't have time to waste on idle gossip.

"Digging a hole." I jerked a thumb toward the shallow hole. "I'm all done once this weeping cherry is in."

"Beats me why the boss would want anything that cried." Buster grinned, laying on the charm.

Annoyed, I explained, using small words. "It doesn't actually weep. The leaves spill down instead of reaching up. Carolina loves the pink blossoms."

"You know that, dummy." Duke joined the conversation and punched his pal's shoulder. "Your mama has a weeping willow in her yard."

Buster bolted from the truck, rubbing his bicep. "Yeouch. I was gonna dig the hole for the little lady, but you'll do it now that you smashed my arm."

Duke followed Buster. The men tromped up to the hole, their waffle-tread soles leaving deep impressions in the sandy soil. "Got some trouble there, don'tcha?" Buster said.

The idea of help with the root extraction gleamed like a shiny Christmas package. But there'd be a catch. There always was a catch. "Nothing I can't handle."

Buster studied me. "That why you leaning so heavy on that shovel?"

"You got a chainsaw in there?" Duke nodded toward my vintage truck.

I wish. "Forgot it this morning."

His sigh was worthy of Scarlett O'Hara. "Bummer. What else you got?"

"My axe." That should send the slackers running for leather

seats, surround sound, and air conditioning.

Duke tsked. "Man, that's old school. Too bad we don't have a generator out here still. I could use my power tools."

Trust a man to think that a power tool solved all problems. "Nope. It's just me and the bugs out here. No electricity. No generator."

"I'll get the axe." Duke's chest puffed out, and he strode toward the truck.

Man, I did not want to owe Duke a favor. I stepped forward. "Really, I can do it."

Buster tapped my arm. "Let Dairy Queen fix your problem. Besides, I wanna talk to you about something. I heard you figured out Maisie Ryals held up the liquor store. I bet you got your daddy's woo-woo stuff going on in that pretty head of yours."

My simmering irritation amped to a rolling boil. Buster's good old boy nickname for Duke Quigley reinforced that I was an outsider here. Was it any wonder I was protective about the very thing that set me apart from others?

"Um." My lips compressed, sealing in further words. I didn't talk about my extrasensory talent with near strangers.

The thud of metal on wood filled the air. Buster steered me away from the manual labor. "I would consider it a personal favor if you could help me out with some picks."

The hair on the nape of my neck snapped to attention. "Picks?"

He lifted one shoulder with a negligent ease. "I do a little online betting. I figure you could help me up my winning percentage."

Even though I was shielded, there was a violent rumble in my senses. I knew trouble when I heard it. My ability to predict a person's truthfulness was darned near one-hundred percent, except when the person believed his lie.

Buster's voice changed timbre when he spoke about gambling. It became thinner, less resonant. He had a whiff of desperation about him, too.

Interesting.

Why was he lying to me?

My ponytail waggled from side to side as I shook my head. "I don't do that."

His fake smile ramped up a bit. "What could it hurt? I'll show you the ropes, teach you how to place the bets, and the next time you can keep the winnings for yourself."

I frowned. "Even if I could see the future, I wouldn't gamble."

His dimples faded. "Tell you what. You get back to me on this." He pulled out a golden case from his shirt pocket and extracted a crisp business card. "Call me after you think it over. This is a once in a lifetime opportunity. I've got the system down pat. You've got the woo-woo vision. It's a match made in heaven."

It was easier to take the card than to argue with him. I peeled off my leather work gloves to pocket the card. The thudding stopped. I glanced over my shoulder at Duke. He dropped the axe and hefted his battered trophy skyward. The root chunk was fatter than my thigh. I'd've been here for hours chopping that out. "Thanks." I meant it.

When the men left, I sighed in relief and lowered my mental shields. The sky seemed bluer, the breeze fresher, the greenery more vibrant. Birds called to one another from the forested canopy, filling the air with lovely trills and chirps. What a beautiful January afternoon.

My energy surged.

There was no one else at Mallow, no inhabited property for a couple of miles. I could relax. I rolled my tight shoulders in large circles, easing the tension.

The landscaped beds I'd installed this past week near Mallow had been darned near effortless because Duke had bulldozed the soil near Tara South, as I'd dubbed the fake tabby mansion. A century ago, tabby buildings were layered with a lime, sand, shell, and water mixture inches at a time and were thick walled. Solid, too. Today's tabby was a concrete block wall with a veneer of shell-spattered concrete. Nothing says classy and grand in my book like concrete block. Might as well roll in a whole fleet of rusty mobile homes, too.

I snorted at the thought.

Carolina Byrd would have a conniption if trashy trailers were located near her highbrow Mallow Plantation. She'd pointed out the place name in a local history book. A worthy name for her fancy estate with a grand entrance. She'd selected this weeping cherry for the entry because the pink blossoms complemented her sign's blue background and fancy gold lettering.

I thought the gilded sign was tacky, ostentatious, and a dangerous lure for thieves. She might as well have put up a flashing neon sign that said "Rob me." I hoped the crackheads and ne'er-do-wells left her and her special-needs child alone.

Not my problem.

Last month a former client had referred Carolina Byrd, of Macon, to Pets and Plants, and I'd been grateful for the work. I'd suggested native plants to Carolina and then I'd agreed to install the high-maintenance stock she wanted. The client was always right.

Dropping to my knees, I widened the bottom of the hole with a smaller spade. When the hole was large enough for the cherry tree's root base, I'd lime the soil to neutralize the acidity to suit the cherry. Another reason I wouldn't have chosen this plant to go in next to pine trees.

I was making good progress, opening the hole and deepening it when my shovel glanced off a hard object.

Something rock-like.

In coastal Georgia, we had few rocks. Granted, an early settler might have placed a rock here, but what were the odds of me digging it up? No rocks had been unearthed near the big house, and they'd pushed mounds of dirt around, evening up the land, filling a natural swale where Carolina wanted the house sited.

I could pry the rock out of there. But there was something about the distinctive gray color that riveted me. Something barely detectable on a sensory level. Unease rolled through my gut, weighing me down, making it hard to breathe.

Should I touch the object?

Whatever it was, the energy coming from it was minimal. Was it plant matter from the roots I'd exhumed? Possibly. But I doubted that explanation.

More likely, it was a gray rock I'd found. Rocks had found their way to the Georgia coast as ship ballast during Colonial times. This could be a ballast rock.

Despite my logic, my unease mounted. After learning the hard way to trust my instincts, I respected them. Something about this hidden object tripped all my senses.

I could call someone. But who? And what would I say? I dug up a rock and it might be important? Who would believe that I was scared to touch a rock?

Get a grip, Baxley. It's probably just a rock. I fetched my new trowel and knelt beside the hole. I held my gloved hands about a foot over the object and concentrated, hoping that the closer proximity would give a stronger signal.

No change.

Only a faint wisp of energy.

Self-preservation wouldn't let me dig unshielded. I fortified my senses with sturdy imagery and moved sandy soil away from the object, bit by bit. With each pass of the trowel, my nerves pinged.

The exposed shape was rounded like a summer melon. It didn't resemble a polished rock. The smooth texture seemed bony.

I shivered. Was this the remains of something or someone? A lump formed in my throat. *Let it be an animal,* I wished silently. Let it be something other than human remains.

I lowered down on my belly and brushed away the remaining dirt with my gloved fingers. Stroke by stroke until the empty orbs of twin eye sockets stared back up at me.

There was no mistaking the species.

I'd found a human skull.

CHAPTER 2

Senses reeling, I staggered away from the sandy hole toward the safety of my truck. I'd dug up a person. A dark shadow passed through me, icing my blood, disorienting me. The whine of insects had me cringing; the strength of the sunshine had me squinting.

I bolstered my mental barriers, dampening my extra senses, bringing my reaction to the skull back down to normal, if there was such a thing. Icy lightning coursed through my veins, and I panted like a pup.

Stop that. You'll get light-headed and pass out, and there's nobody for miles and miles. I glanced at the tangled woods swathed in unrelenting shadows. What secrets did they hold?

My sweaty clothes blanketed the chill in my bones. I couldn't fall apart now. I had to be strong. Help. I needed to summon help.

With trembling hands, I peeled off my leather gloves and fumbled for my cell. I went the wrong way on the alphabet until I found the sheriff's contact information. I mashed the Send button so hard it was a wonder it sprang back out again.

Birds chirped.

The sun shone.

And those sightless eyes swam in my head.

When the sheriff growled his name into the phone, I nearly swooned with relief. "Wayne? I need you."

"Babe, those words are music to my ears," Sheriff Wayne

Thompson's voice roughened with delight. "Your place?"

My stomach clenched with disgust. Why was he trying to make this into something it wasn't? I stroked the green pendant at my neck and felt better. "Get your head straight. I'm out on Misery Road. Out at that new place Carolina Byrd built."

"Oh, yeah. What's it called, Meadows or something? Wait. That's not it. The Marshmallow place."

"Mallow. She named it Mallow. I'm doing her landscaping, and I dug something up." The penetrating image of the sightless eyes flashed into my head, triggering another glacial blast down my spine. I shivered. "Correction. I dug someone up."

I listened to the thick silence with growing trepidation. My grip tightened on the phone. "Wayne? You there?"

"Dang, Baxley, my boy's got a big basketball game tonight. Why do you keep making work for me? Can't you cover it back up, and we'll look at it tomorrow?"

His callous remark burned all the way down my throat. Tears blurred my vision. "Get real."

He sighed. "I hate real. Real cuts into my hunting and fishing."

My gaze stopped on the weeping cherry tree. I'd hoped to be finished with this job today. Carolina had made it crystal clear I wouldn't get paid until the job was done. I needed this money. "Do your job, Sheriff. Or would you rather I call in the state boys? I'm sure they'd be happy to come take a look at my dead person."

"Hell, no. Don't do that. A man's got a right to moan and groan a bit. I'll do my job." He swore again. "My wife's gonna skin me alive. Hold on a minute while I have Tamika dispatch patrol units to your location."

I sagged against the side of my truck, wishing Carolina Byrd had put her entryway in a different location. What were the odds that the one place she wanted her tree planted was right on top of a dead body? And the body had been down there a long time. Those stout roots overlaying the skull hadn't sprung up overnight.

"Baxley? You there? Virg and Ronnie are on their way. They're out by the four-way stop."

Exhaling a shaky breath, I blinked the tears from my eyes. Ten minutes and help would arrive. Ten minutes and I wouldn't be responsible for this dead person. I could hold on for ten minutes. "Okay."

"What can you tell me? Can you identify the body?"

Shadows lengthened around me. A marsh hen cackled eerily. "There's not much left. And I only exposed part of the skull. I don't know what else is down there."

"That means visual identification won't work. We don't have any local missing persons except for the Gilroy kid, and I doubt she'd be planted out there. It might be someone who was passing through. Say, do me a favor. Use your psychic mojo stuff and get me an ID."

My knees trembled. "I don't want anything to do with this. Plus, soon as I get involved, you'll tell me I'm interfering with police business."

"Go for it. I don't see the harm here. If we're down to bones, it's more than likely a cold case. Probably not a homicide, or we'd have heard about it while we were growing up."

I gripped the phone tighter, wishing it was as easy to control my knee-jerk reaction to the naïve sheriff. "This isn't something I do on command. I'm not a parlor trick people trot out at their convenience."

"Don't get your panties in a knot. I just thought you could save us all some time and money."

A few months back, Wayne had asked me to become a deputy. I'd refused the job because being surrounded by the negative energy of criminals wasn't how I wanted to spend my workday.

I much preferred the good vibes from plants and animals.

But that was before my well pump starting acting up, before I noticed that my daughter's new-last-fall school pants were too short, before the dentist said Larissa needed braces. Any one of those expenses would break a single parent's budget.

The idea of receiving a steady paycheck had been worming its way deeper in my thoughts. With my deceased husband's Army benefits tied up in governmental red tape because there was no body, I had to be creative to pay the bills. December had been a good month, chock-full of pet-sitting jobs, but January, February, and March stretched out before me like winter doldrums.

I cleared my throat and jumped in head first. "Speaking of my special talent, I've been thinking. What are the chances of me hiring on as a consultant for the sheriff's office?"

"We don't employ any consultants."

Despite his flat tone, I forged ahead with my idea. "This could benefit both of us. I need money; you need help solving cases. So? If I help you with cases, you'll pay me?"

He hesitated for a moment. "I'll think about that. You could run up a lot of hours, sitting on your tail, in the name of trying to solve a case. Even if I used discretionary funding, it would eat up money the department could spend on equipment or supplies. You'd have to close cases before I paid you, and we don't have many murder cases."

Way down Misery Road I saw flashing lights on two vehicles. Sirens blared. I huffed out my displeasure. "Dang. This doesn't bode well for my checkbook balance. You can't promise to pay me unless I close the case for you. I can't promise that kind of result."

He sighed heavily. "That Virg and Ronnie comin'?"

The warbling sirens were louder now. "Yeah."

"You okay?"

I took inventory. My heart rate was back to normal. My stomach wasn't threatening to erupt. My hands weren't dripping with sweat. "I'm good." I meant it. "Look, why don't we do a test run? If I contribute to solving this case, you'll hire me as a consultant."

"What benefits come with a test run?"

"You'll get the benefit of a closed case." My eyes narrowed as another implication hit home. "Get your mind out of the mudhole. I'm not offering fringe benefits."

He laughed, a low sensual caress in my ear. "That's the Baxley I know. Do your woo-woo show for Virg and Ronnie. I won't have to stay out there very long if you solve the case, babe."

I had to be crazy to voluntarily spend more time around this oversexed man. "And another thing. Stop treating me like your next sexual conquest."

"A tiger shark can't shed its stripes." He hesitated. "At least with me you know what you've got."

The line prickled with silence. The hair on the back of my neck stirred. "What does that mean?"

"It means what it means."

CHAPTER 3

I could do without Wayne's sexual innuendos. I could do without his condescension about my extrasensory abilities. But I couldn't walk away from this potential income stream. Once this landscaping job here at Mallow wrapped up, I would be hurting.

I'd handled Wayne fine in high school. I could handle the man he'd grown into as well. I wouldn't cave because this was difficult. I'd show them all. Life may have socked me in the teeth, but I was coming up swinging.

The sirens stopped. Car doors opened. Boots clomped on pavement. The presence of two deputies should have filled me with relief, but my insides knotted at the coming ordeal.

Virg Burkhead was thinner than Ronnie Oliver, but both of them hadn't missed a meal in years. Virg was a few inches taller than me, about six feet in all, while Ronnie Oliver's brown eyes were level with mine. Both deputies wore khaki-colored uniforms with dark brown trim and snazzy gold accoutrements. And guns, of course.

Couldn't miss the firepower strapped to their generous waists.

"Hey, Baxley." Virg hitched up his sagging pants as he approached. "Heard you dug up a body. Didn't your mama ever tell you not to do that?"

I'd had an atypical childhood, growing up in an aging hippie and free-love household. The rules were few: be kind to your karma, love everyone, live each day like it was your last. Even so, I played along with Virg. "Don't get me started on my mama. And I don't know as I found a whole body, just a skull." I motioned toward the hole in the ground.

Ronnie leaned over the hole, spat tobacco out the side of his mouth. "Wouldja take a look at that? Holy Mother of God, we've got a dead person on our hands. Why is this happening? I didn't sign on to work around dead people. The cap'n assured me we didn't get any dead people."

"Wayne don't know everything." Virg pushed his way in front of Ronnie and peered in the hole. "Lookee there. You're right. It's a deadie. I wanted to go to the game tonight, too. My wife will be pissed."

"Your wife is going to kill you, and that's a fact," Ronnie said. "We need to cordon off the area. If this is a crime scene, we need to know who had access."

"Everyone had access, knucklehead. We're right beside the main road." Virg chucked Ronnie in the head and scowled at me. "What is it with your family and dead people? You some kind of a witch of somethin'?"

If I had superhuman powers, I would have tossed him across the road for insulting me. I hated labels of any kind. But I knew things I couldn't explain. Like I knew Virg was scared of me. His fear leaked through my shields. An acrid stench wafted from his armpits to my nose.

I doubled my protective barriers and moved toward him. "You've known me your whole life. I went to school with your sister and tutored your brother. I'm no more a witch than you are. I'm unlucky enough to have been told to dig this hole in front of that wall. I didn't set out to find any dead body. It found me."

My outburst seemed to surprise him. He rubbed his chin. "Well, dang. The sheriff is right. You are one feisty woman."

I jabbed a finger in his chest. "What is it with you men? Am I a threat to you? All I'm doing is trying to earn a living. I don't understand why men see that as aggression. Should I sit home and wait for the welfare fairy to find me? Should I hope a big strong man sweeps in to take care of me?"

"Sorry, ma'am." Virg backpedaled toward his cruiser. Ronnie, too.

It was my turn to curse. "Ya can't leave."

Virg and Ronnie crabbed away from me. "No, ma'am. We're going to update dispatch and summon the investigator and the coroner. Then we'll secure the scene."

God help us. If this was the state of our crime-solving force, Sinclair County was in big trouble. Two grown men running from one puny woman. They each had me by a hundred pounds, maybe more. Plus they were both armed with guns and pepper spray, and if I wasn't mistaken, Virg had a Taser on his belt, too.

The deputies holed up in Virg's cruiser. Anger and disgust rolled through me in waves. I kicked the ground with my boots, sending a spray of loose sand toward the skull. The men were acting like idiots, but fear made people stupid.

So did anger.

Anger made me react first and think later. Not a good plan for someone with something to hide. Only who was I hiding from? The world? Or myself?

I let out a string of cuss words.

The unexpected sound of my voice startled me. I had to pull myself together or my career as a psychic consultant to the sheriff would be over before it started. Trying to find out who this person was from the bare bones would be a first for me. For years I'd denied having anything other than intuition. I'd recently found out how my *intuition* worked, or at least one aspect of it.

The whole of it had not been explored. One thing at a time. That was all anyone could do. One thing at a time.

I touched the green pendant at my neck, the moldavite necklace that had been a gift from my late husband. I didn't believe Roland was dead, despite what the Army said, and this touchstone reminded me of his love. A sense of calm washed over me. I didn't understand how the stone soothed me, but I was grateful for order coming to my thoughts.

I scrubbed my face with my hands and stepped closer to the skull I'd unearthed. How would I do this? I'd already tried reading above the hole, and hadn't learned anything. Way I saw it, I had two choices. I could lower my shields and touch the skull. Or I could meditate and seek out the soul of the deceased. I hadn't tried dreamwalking in some time, but going into a trance out here in the woods was dangerous. My physical body would be unprotected, which is why dreamwalkers worked their craft in their home environment.

With Virg and Ronnie sitting on guns and Tasers, and God only knew what else, the vulnerability of a dreamwalk was too great a risk.

That meant I had to touch the skull.

I shuddered and edged closer to the hole.

Fast. Just do it and get it over with.

Doubt edged into my thoughts. What the hell had I gotten myself into? I'd sold myself and my abilities like a carnival sideshow freak. But then, people like Virg and Ronnie thought I was a freak anyway, so what did it matter? Especially if using my perceptions garnered me the income I needed to pay my bills and take care of Larissa.

The sun clouded over as I dropped to my knees beside the hole. Behind me I heard car doors open.

"Ma'am," Virg hollered. "Walk away from the hole."

I waved him off. "It's okay. The sheriff asked me to examine the bones."

Virg crept closer, his hand on his weapon. "Step away from

the deceased."

"I'm doing my job. Call the sheriff." Taking a deep breath, I turned my back on Virg and lowered my chest to the ground so that the skull was within arm's reach. Memories flashed in my head of the last time I'd touched an object belonging to a murder victim.

Horrifying, gut-wrenching, nauseating memories.

My body chilled. The smell of the freshly dug earth wafted up through me as if I wasn't even there. I splayed my hand above the empty eye sockets, focusing my awareness to my trembling fingertips. Virg muttered something else, but his words didn't register. I was doing this. For me. For Larissa.

I dropped my mental shields and reached for the skull. Light flared around me as if I were at the center of an orb, brighter than I could stand. I squinted into the glow. Energy pulsed above me, but only a faint trace ebbed through my hand. There was a soft sound, mournful, the way the wind sighs through the pines, but fuller. Like restrained weeping.

Hazy images flashed into my thoughts.

A man and a woman burying a child. A daughter. The man held his hat in his hand; the woman clung to an infant and wept as if her heart were cleaving in two. The image shifted, and I saw the same grieving man throwing dirt on two bodies in a hole. The sun hung low in the sky. He shoveled fast, with a grim expression and terse movements. A name slipped from his lips, too soft for me to catch.

The image winked out. Darkness filled in behind the image. Dismay roared through me. I was so close. I almost had it. I fumbled for the skull, but I flailed in vain.

Suddenly my back arched as excruciating pain shot from head to toe and back again. Screams ripped through the air. My screams.

CHAPTER 4

Fragmented voices drifted through the void. Voices raised in anger. Voices quivering in fear. I strained to hear the words, but they faded without warning.

I floated in the nothingness, bobbing along, blindly bumping into unfamiliar objects. I tried to reach out to steady myself, but my arms wouldn't work. Legs either.

What was wrong with me?

Was I dead?

No! A soundless roar erupted from my lips. This wasn't right. I had a daughter to rear. I couldn't die.

A pinprick of light appeared. Was that heaven? I edged toward the shadows. I couldn't leave now. Larissa needed me.

I fought the tide of the light, but its purity drew me forward. My head refused the call, but I was drawn to the beam, a hapless steel shard in a strong magnetic field. Panic rose in my throat; my pulse thundered through my ears.

This is not what I wanted. I want to live.

A voice threaded its way into the darkness. *Let go, Baxley. Don't fight it. Let go and let fate guide you. You can do this. Release control and listen to the sound of my voice.*

I recognized that voice. "Mama?" I craned my neck up, cursing my sightless eyes. "Mama? Where are you?"

It's all right, dear. Listen to my voice. Follow the sound of my voice. You can do this. Come on, Baxley. Do this for your family. Listen and let go.

I didn't want to let go, but I trusted my mother. I angled toward the sound of her voice. The light was brighter now, the air cooler on my skin. "I'm coming, Mama. Keep talking."

My fingertips tingled. My legs twitched. A nauseating sense of disorientation swept through me. I'd been there before. The gate between the living and the dead. I'd gotten trapped at this passage after Uncle Emerald died and again when I'd tried to find Roland on the night of his funeral. Mama had talked me back to life both times.

Blurred shapes moved in the gloom. I dialed in the sight, keeping Mama's beacon of a voice as my focus. Muscle spasms wracked my limbs, but I persisted. One foot in front of the other. I couldn't get discouraged about how far I had to go. Just one little step at a time.

That's my girl. Come on, Baxley. You're doing great. Listen to the sound of my voice. Listen and follow it to the light.

"You killed her, Virg." Ronnie's concerned voice wafted past my ears.

"She should have come around by now," Virg said. "Three seconds. That's all anyone stays out when we nuke 'em."

"Good thing I answered her phone," Ronnie said. "How you reckon her mama knew to call her? You think it's that hinky woo-woo stuff going on? Think them Nesbitts got their own psychic hotline?"

"Who the hell cares, long as I didn't kill her. Look at her eyelids. They're twitching now, and look at that. Her finger moved."

The darkness lifted from my head and my shoulders, then cleared from my waist and feet. I strode confidently on a well-trod path toward the light. I recognized this veiled place, and I knew my way home from here. I wasn't dead. I was very much alive.

My steps hastened. I raised my head to the warmth of the

light, hugging my arms to my hollow belly. Summoning energy into my core, I stepped through the thin veil.

White light ebbed into the glare of sunshine. Overhead, a solitary hawk soared in a cloudless blue vault. Beside me, oaks and fragrant pines stretched high toward the sky, bending the rays of the setting sun. Two round faces orbited over me. Virg and Ronnie. The sheriff's deputies.

"She's back." Ronnie's toothless grin brought warmth to my heart.

But his words confused me. I glanced over at Virg's grim face. "I'm back? I didn't go anywhere."

"You went somewhere, 'cause you shore weren't here," Ronnie said.

"Is Mama here?" I lifted my head up to peer around the wooded area. I saw the two cops, two police cruisers, my truck, and the gilt-edged sign on the tabby wall. Understanding dawned. I was at Carolina Byrd's new place, Mallow.

"Nope." Ronnie removed my phone from his ear and flipped it shut. "She called on your phone and insisted on talking to you."

Warmth flooded back into my limbs. Wonderful, life-giving warmth. Mama had known I was in trouble, and she'd come to my aid. I would definitely thank her later. I pushed myself up on my elbows. I may be a weird Nesbitt, but I wasn't entirely without resources.

"Hold it right there," Virg cautioned. "EMS is on their way."

A jolt of panic shot through my singed nerves. No doctors. I wasn't a lab rat. One experimental animal in the Nesbitt family had been enough. "Stop 'em. I don't need medical attention. I feel fine now. What happened to me?"

After Ronnie relayed that I'd refused medical attention to dispatch, I breathed easier. The muscles in my legs twitched as if they'd animated themselves. I stared at the odd sight, trying to understand what had happened. My distress returned full fold, and I glared at Virg.

He retreated. "Uh, I'm sorry, ma'am. I'm trained to protect the crime scene. I didn't know you were operating under the sheriff's authority."

"I told you it was okay."

His head bobbed in agreement. "Yes, ma'am, ya did. But people lie to us all the time. Noncompliants have to be subdued. Rule ninety-eight ten. I was within my rights as a LEO."

My brow furrowed. "You're guided by your astrological sign?"

"No, ma'am. LEO that's L-E-O. It means Law Enforcement Officer."

Heat rose to my face. Note to self: brain doesn't work well after passing out. Virg must be quoting from a policy manual, and I was on the wrong end of the law.

Just another crazy Nesbitt.

Hell, I'd always be a crazy Nesbitt. I couldn't change that, though Lord knows, I'd prayed for it often enough when I was a teen.

I sat all the way up, flexing my feet, stretching my arms, realigning my ponytail and ball cap. My back stung. But I was whole, which was more than I could say for my frayed senses.

The sunlight was too bright, Virg and Ronnie a little too loud. I tasted blood. Feeling around in my mouth, I found where I'd bitten my lip.

I tried to piece together the events before I blacked out. I'd come here to plant the weeping cherry tree. I'd dug the hole, had help removing the big root, and found a human skull. I'd called the cops. I had no recollection of passing out. "I don't get it. What happened?"

"Virg shot you with the Taser. You got tased, Baxley." Ronnie slapped his thigh and laughed as if it were the funniest joke he'd ever heard. "Yessiree, Bob. He shot fifty-thousand volts through your body."

That explained a lot. My emotions crested and surged dangerously. I glanced up at Virg. "Why did you shoot me?"

"I was protecting the scene." His hand rose from a pocket to hover above his weapon.

Was he going to shoot me now? My voice rose an octave. "From me? I'm the one who found it in the first place. You wouldn't have a scene if it weren't for me."

"You didn't follow orders. I had no choice."

If only my head didn't throb, I could make sense of this conversation. My fingers curled into fists, nails digging into my palms. "What orders? And who are you to order me around?"

"Once a LEO is on the scene, civilians must respect their authority."

"Or else you shoot them?" At the sound of a siren approaching, I winced. The sound magnified within my head, echoing through pain sensors at the speed of light. I clutched my head and rocked into a fetal position. "Oo-oohh. Make it stop. Make it stop."

"She's gone crazy, Virg. Should we cuff her?"

"You moron. She was okay a second ago. Somethin' changed. Look at the way she's holding her ears. Do you think she got a bug in there?"

"I ain't scared of no bug." Ronnie dropped down beside me and tried to move my hands.

I cupped my fingers tighter. I tried to focus on his rounded face. "Noooo," I whispered urgently. "The siren. Make it stop."

Ronnie flipped the switch on his com unit. "Cut the siren."

Blessed silence followed. Even so, it took a few seconds for my hypersensitive nerves to relax. Cautiously, I removed my hands from my ears. My gaze flitted around the area, assessing the next threat. My heart tried its darnedest to escape from my chest. Oh God, I needed to be far away from here.

"Better?" Ronnie leaned over, concern etched on his round face.

I swallowed hard and nodded. I wasn't okay, but I was better. My senses were too jacked up. That was the problem. I tried to dampen my senses, but nothing happened. The Taser had scrambled my electrical system, which is where my protective shielding originated.

I heard the ants marching over the sand, the whir of mosquito wings, and the slide of air over each leaf. I pressed my hands to my throbbing temples, but it didn't help. Biting down on my lip, I sought a way to protect myself from sensory overload.

I wanted to go home, to curl up in my bed in a dark room, and sleep until this mistake was corrected. What was I doing? This wasn't a mistake. This was life. Sleeping too much didn't work when Roland was declared dead by the Army, and it durned sure wouldn't work now.

I tried to stand. Ronnie planted a beefy palm on my shoulder. "Don't get up. We got to check you out first."

That should have put the fear of God in me, but my circuits were crossed and I laughed until I cried. How the hell could these idiots check me out when I didn't know what was wrong?

I was still rolling in the sand, laughing with tears streaming down my cheeks, when the sheriff and the coroner arrived. Great. Dr. Sugar.

Would he pronounce me dead or insane?

CHAPTER 5

I shrank back from the skinny coroner. Even though he routinely dealt with dead people, Dr. Bo Seavey, aka Dr. Sugar, had quite a womanizing reputation. His natty pants and bright shirt didn't fool me. The dark places I'd glimpsed inside his head on occasion made me shudder. I didn't want to know more about him, and in my hyperaware state, his personal information could leak across any physical contact we might have.

I felt along the ground for a weapon. Where was a sharp stick when you needed one? Too bad I'd chucked that fat root in the woods. "Don't touch me."

"Sounds like she's back to normal, Doc." Sheriff Wayne Thompson strutted closer, a gold badge gleaming at his trim waist. He was handsome as sin, with dark hair, bedroom eyes, and a muscular build. Trouble was, he knew precisely his effect on women. "She's breathing fire, and she's got two fists full of dirt."

"I'm fine." I hoped I was. Without warning, my left hand spasmed, and the sand slipped through my fingers.

"Interesting." Dr. Sugar approached with his black medical bag in hand. Beady eyes peered through his horn-rimmed glasses. The odor of death preceded him, a tainted blend of laboratory chemicals and cheap cigars. I winced at the pungent odors.

"Keep your distance." I released the other wad of sand and hid my trembling hands in my lap. With jacked-up senses, I was a sponge for Dr. Sugar's intellectual curiosity and Wayne's sympathy and lust cocktail.

The coroner's academic scrutiny unnerved me. No way would I submit to being a subject for a scientific paper.

And he wasn't going to feel me up, either.

I had standards.

With that, I mentally dismissed the coroner and focused on the sheriff. His sympathy could be the leverage I needed to get out of there unmolested. Besides, he owed me for being his math tutor back in high school.

I pointed at Virg. "Your trigger-happy, mullet-headed deputy tasered me." My voice quivered, but I didn't care. "I'm gonna sue him, you, and the entire sheriff's department."

"Ooo-wie, Virg." Ronnie grinned. "She's gonna nail your hide to the wall."

Virg's eyes rounded, reminding me of a frenetic happy-face image on the Internet. "No need to get all riled up. I said I was sorry."

"Sorry doesn't cut it. Hand me the Taser and let me fry your gonads. That's being sorry."

Virg blanched and backed away. His hands cupped protectively over his fly. Wayne stepped in front of him. "Nobody's going to taser anyone. How'd this happen?"

Curious. Wayne asked me instead of his deputy. Before I could get a word out, Virg answered. "She wouldn't back off the scene. I told her to leave it alone."

I glared a tree-sized hole through Wayne to Virg. "I told him that I had your permission. He shot me anyway. In the back. Let's hope no little old ladies or children get in his way. He'll shoot them, too."

Virg struck a warrior's pose with his weapon. "I am a lean, mean, fighting machine."

"You're another redneck with a gun." I reached for my

pendant and came up empty-handed. A gasp of surprise slipped through my lips. No wonder my senses were haywire.

"What? What now?" Wayne asked.

"My necklace. It's gone."

"And this is important?"

I nodded, tears springing to my eyes. "Roland gave it to me." Which was true, but that wasn't the only reason I needed my jewelry. "It must have fallen off over there."

"Stay put. I'll get it."

Wayne dropped to one knee and retrieved it. He tossed the pendant to me and stared into the gaping hole. "Cripes. I'd hoped this was a bad dream."

"Thanks." I rubbed my thumb over the cool green stone. Moldavite, I'd been told. Roland had been pleased that I favored his gift.

Very pleased, until he'd gotten himself declared dead by the Army. Now I had no idea where he was or what had happened to him.

A calming sensation flowed through my veins, and with it came a sense of profound relief. The green stone wasn't just a sentimental favorite. It had restored me after I'd had a brush with serial burglar Maisie Ryals, and now it was soothing the frazzle out of my nerves. My senses calmed, and I barricaded myself inside the safe zone.

The sheen fell off the day. Light waned to tolerable levels. Sounds muted. Emotional bombardment ceased. The sharp tang of men and death and forest receded. My tongue touched the place where I'd bitten my lip. I still tasted blood, but the taste no longer thrummed like hoofbeats through my thoughts.

I breathed easier.

"This isn't a dream, but it isn't a nightmare either." I had information he wanted, information that Wayne didn't expect me to have obtained. The corners of my lips turned up. The

Taser may have shorted my circuits, but it didn't erase my memory. I might land a job as a police consultant in spite of this disaster.

"Say what?" Wayne turned to face me, his dark brows beetling over his eyes. It should be illegal for men to have long, thick lashes like that.

"You remember our bargain?" I asked.

His features hardened. "What about it?" He waved the coroner over to the skull.

Virg and Ronnie inched forward on Dr. Sugar's shiny heels. I guess Virg was worried I'd snatch his Taser and zap him because he kept Ronnie between us. As much as the thought of tasing Virg pleased me, the idea of additional income glittered brighter. I could do this psychic investigator gig as long as Virg wasn't nearby with his Taser.

"You said if I helped you solve this case, I could work as a consultant for the sheriff's office," I said.

"You serious?" Wayne asked. "You got something on this victim?"

"Indeed I do. But I need assurances before we proceed. First off, no more tasing the consultant."

"Done."

"You could apologize for your staff."

"Like hell. Virg was doing his job. All you had to do was wait until I got here for confirmation. This person's been in the ground a long while. This isn't an urgent matter. This case is cold. Very cold."

He was right. I'd hurried because I was afraid I'd lose my nerve. I would be more patient next time. "It's my professional opinion, as your consultant, that this woman wasn't murdered."

"You know it's a woman?" He turned to Dr. Sugar. "Is she right, Doc? The vic a woman?"

"I won't know for sure until we get the bones back to the

lab," Dr. Sugar said. "But you're right about the duration. This person has been planted for some time. No soft tissue remains on the bones. No insect casings are apparent."

My stomach lurched. I covered my mouth to hold the retching noise in. I wasn't used to discussions of dead people, bones, and soft tissue. I glanced up to see Wayne staring at me, apparently considering his next move.

He rose and escorted me over to my truck. Opening the door, he maneuvered me into the driver's seat. His gaze softened. "Let's forget about the deal, babe. You're not cut out for police work. Your first instinct on this was right. Stick to your plants and pets."

His remarks infuriated me, especially since I needed this job. I was doing this. "The deal stands. One woman and two children are buried here. They used to live on this land."

He studied me. "Foul play?"

"It didn't feel that way. Just sad. Very sad."

"You're sure about this?"

He wanted to believe me. I concentrated on that and projected every bit of assurance into my answer. "Yes."

He nodded. "You want one of us to take you home?"

Alarm flared, tamped down. "I can drive." I gripped the steering wheel and stared through the bug-splattered windshield. The conversation had gone the way I'd hoped, but it felt unfinished. "Do I have a job?"

A muscle twitched in his cheek. "Can't take intuition to court or even write it up in my report. Let's see what Dr. Sugar learns, and I'll call the historical society. Someone knows the history out here. But there's good news."

"There is?" Anticipation jetted through me. News? Would there be a reward or something? A cash payout for closing a case? I held my breath.

His lingering gaze swept my seated length. "You and I will be spending a lot of time together."

"And?"

"And I know how to get to a woman. You'll be in my bed before the week is out."

My spine stiffened, my resolve strengthened. "That's a bet you don't wanna make. You're dead wrong. I don't date married men."

"I'll put my track record up against your *intuition* every time."

I allowed a ghost of a smile to cross my lips. Wayne had no idea what he was up against. "You will, will ya? In that case, bet's on."

CHAPTER 6

Tendrils of steam curled up from my mug. I inhaled deeply, warming my airways, restoring my sense of balance. How many times had I sat here in Mama's kitchen trying to pull myself together?

From the gold stovetop to the white oven door and rusted refrigerator, this kitchen resembled an appliance orphanage. Most of the green paint was long gone from the tabletop; the shine had worn off the linoleum countertops. Sagging tie-dyed curtains added to the dated look of the room.

If one judged this place by appearance, as I had once done, one would be sadly mistaken. My parents didn't cultivate the worn-out look; they were oblivious to it. They focused on intangibles.

Like the location of this house.

Daddy had hiked through a vast pine forest to select the perfect site for the house. My maternal grandmother said he was a kook because he could have built closer to the water, but he'd deemed this to be the spot. For many years she'd been outspoken about his folly, but in due time, she'd more than accepted his choice.

The pervading sense of calm and well-being in this house was a veritable chicken soup to the world weary. I'd benefited from this setting, and others had, too. For a kook, my father had darned good sense.

"Feeling better?" Thick, curly gray hair framed Mama's thin

face. Released from its braid, her gray locks roiled and sprang independently with each motion of her slender body. Concern radiated in her brown eyes. Wind chimes outside the kitchen window danced in the sunshine, a lilting discordant song heralding a strong onshore breeze.

I nodded. From the living room, the television blared on the weather station. I never knew why my parents insisted on the TV being turned on all the time, but that was an unwritten rule of the house. They'd long since tired of talk shows, soaps, and crime dramas. Now they exclusively tracked the weather.

"There's a bad storm in Chicago." Mama's voice trembled as she spoke.

I bit my swollen lip. Why was Mama so worried about distant weather when I'd been through one heck of a personal storm? Was she afraid of what had happened to me?

"California is having a heck of a time recovering from the fires this past fall," she continued. "Those people are in a world of hurt."

I didn't understand her conversational thread, nor did I want to. Even though I'd told the sheriff I had recovered, my nerves were still raw. The words rose in my throat and came out in a rush. "Virg shot me with a Taser gun."

"He did?" Puzzlement creased her features. "He was such a nice boy. What's gotten into him?"

I hoped she meant that as a rhetorical question. "The sheriff said he might hire me as a consultant if I help him close the case of the body I dug up. I tried a touch reading on the skull. I had regressed to the time when the bodies were buried when Virg zapped me with fifty-thousand volts of electricity."

Mama's knobby fingers worried over each other. "But you're all right now?"

I nodded. "Getting there, thanks to you."

"Your father sensed the disturbance."

I blinked in surprise. "He did?"

She stared into her cup as if it contained the secrets of the universe. "He was working in the garden. Said it knocked him to his knees. Took him two cups of tea to get his color back."

I drained my cup. "Then it looks like I've got another cup to go to catch up with him. Are you sure he didn't mind meeting Larissa's school bus?"

"He said he was fine, so he will be fine. But he needs to retire from the business. He can't hold out until Larissa is ready to take over."

My jaw clenched. "I can't talk about this now."

Daddy wanted me to step into his role as county dream-walker. A highly unprofitable volunteer effort with unpredictable hours. During my childhood, we'd had visitors at all hours of the day, from every walk of life, each wanting to communicate with their dead relatives. Daddy puttered around his herb garden during the day and dreamwalked for free at night.

I'd avoided this discussion with my father, and I didn't want to have it with my mother. "Daddy could change his schedule. He could put the word out that he dreamwalks only one night a week now. Maybe he could locate everyone's relatives in one dreamwalk, one-stop shopping, if you will."

The phone rang. Mama ignored it. I half rose from my seat. "Aren't you going to answer that?"

"Nope. It doesn't feel right."

I sank back down in my chair. "What if it's Daddy or Larissa?"

"It isn't. They would have called your phone first."

Hmm. She was right. If Larissa needed me, she'd phone or text me right away. Still it worried me that the house line kept ringing. What if they'd won the lottery or something? "Don't you want to know whose calling?"

"They will call back." She refilled our mugs from the tea kettle on the stove.

I wished I had her sense of complacency. When Roland left on his Army missions, I'd dreaded and longed for every phone call and email. Sure enough, the day came when the call I received was very bad news. Roland was missing, presumed dead. Months later, the Army declared him dead, but according to my father, Roland wasn't among the dead.

He still walked the earth.

I didn't know why he stayed away from us, but I finally understood why his Army benefits were fouled up. They could hardly pay out death benefits for a guy who was still alive, could they? Someone in the Army knew the real story behind Roland's disappearance. The only thing I could think of was that it was safer for all of us if Roland was officially dead. Which was a worrisome thought all on its own.

Mama handed me another cup of tea. I took it with a bone-deep sense of gratitude, savoring the warmth of the floral mug in my hands. "Thanks."

"Tell me about your dreamwalk."

"It wasn't exactly a dreamwalk."

"Oh?"

"I touched the remains, and time folded in on itself. Or at least that's how it seemed to me. The people wore old-timey clothing like it was many years ago."

"Did you hear anything?"

"Nope. Sound was dampened. I registered an overwhelming sense of sadness. I saw the man and woman burying a small child. The scene shifted, and I saw the man burying the woman with a baby in her arms."

Mama's eyes sparkled with interest. "Fascinating. And you experienced no spatial disorientation accessing the dream-scape?"

"There was some of that, but it wasn't bad going in. Not like it was that time in Uncle Emerald's chair. Or when I tried to find Roland two years ago. I got in, saw the events unfold, and I was headed out when I got tased."

It was my turn to look away. I studied my hands for a moment. "Thanks for coming to my rescue. I don't know how long I would have been trapped in the void otherwise. Thank you for knowing what to do."

"I didn't do much. You listened. That's a skill in itself."

"It could have been much worse. All those people could have touched me with my senses wide open. I could have been transported to the hospital and trapped with all those heightened emotions. You saved me, and I'm grateful."

"Hush up. You're making me turn all red. I did what any mother would do."

She'd done more than that, but she would never admit it. If they'd started pouring drugs into me, I could've ended up as crazy as Uncle Emerald.

Best if I changed the subject. I fumbled in my pocket for my pendant. "The catch failed on my necklace."

Mama extended her hand, palm up. "I'll repair the catch, if you like. Leave it here."

I pocketed the moldavite stone. "I can't leave it behind. It means too much to me."

"We really need to talk about so many things," she said.

My breath hitched. I was at her mercy, but I needed a respite from the dreamwalker campaign. "I told you everything that happened. I need to get some rest so that I feel whole again. Then we can talk about the big picture."

A car door closed outside. I turned to the welcome sound. My daughter breezed through the open doorway, her honey-brown braid flying like a kite tail behind her. "Mom, Mom, you all right?"

Larissa dove into my arms. I hugged her close, needing the physical contact as much as she did. "Now I am."

"I felt it when something happened to you," my daughter said in a rush. "I was sitting in math class, and suddenly you weren't there."

My mouth dropped open. I stammered out an apology. "I'm . . . I'm . . . I'm sorry, love. I never meant for anything to happen to either of us."

Larissa's arms tightened around me. "I'm so glad to see you."

My father walked in behind Larissa. He ruffled my hair. "You all right?"

After Mama's warning about Daddy's health, I studied him. His color was off, and his gait was uneven. Had my trouble today done that to him? My skin prickled with guilt. "Fine, Dad."

His gentle eyes filled with emotion. "You gave us a scare today."

Guilt-laden thoughts clogged my head. My actions had put the whole family at risk and nearly cost me my life. My voice came out at half-volume. "I scared myself."

"Wait for me!" My plus-sized friend, reporter Charlotte Ambrose, careened through the door. Her lime-green slacks and green and white polka-dotted blouse added a whimsical zest to the kitchen. Light glinted off her narrow glasses. She'd overdone her makeup again, with her drawn-on eyebrow arches giving her a surprised expression.

Charlotte's reporter bag dangled in one hand; keys and a smart-looking purse occupied her other hand. "Don't start without me!"

"Char, how'd you find me?" I asked as she hurried to the nearest chair.

She huffed a few minutes, catching her breath. "You're kidding, right? The only place you'd go when you're in trouble is this kitchen. Hell, half the county comes here to heal up when bad things happen. I could fill the newspaper pages with a log of the people who visit this house."

My heart sank. White spots danced before my eyes. This was *my* family, *my* sanctuary. We weren't newspaper fodder.

What would govern Charlotte's actions?

Our years of friendship?

Or her new ambition to be a big-time reporter?

CHAPTER 7

"But you wouldn't." I caught her gaze and held it. The bolt of unease accompanying her words had shaken me. Of all the people in the world I trusted most, Charlotte ranked right up there with my parents. But her loyalty had never been tested like this. I couldn't predict what she would do, and that uncertainty tied knots in my stomach. "You wouldn't abuse your welcome here and betray those people, would you?"

Charlotte waved dismissively. The big frog face on her chunky watch flashed before my eyes. "Oh, you never know what I might do. I'm a woman of mystery and adventure, and I'm dying to hear about your bit of fun this afternoon." She frowned at me. "Why didn't you call me?"

"Hey, Charlotte," Mama said. "Want some tea?"

"Love some." My friend shot Mama a bright smile. "There's nothing like a cup of your tea. You put some secret ingredient in it, right? I've never had anything like it anywhere else."

"I blend it myself." Mama's mouth tightened.

Did it finally occur to Mama that Charlotte might bring the wrong sort of attention to her cottage in the woods? For years I'd wondered about my parents' source of income. They'd evaded any questions I asked point-blank, fueling my concerns that something not-quite-legal was going on here.

"You could make a fortune if you marketed this brew." Charlotte eased into a wooden chair. It creaked under her bulk but held. She turned to me. "Now, you got some 'splaining to do,

Miz Baxley. Why are you holding out on your best friend? Bernard would have scooped me if I hadn't been glued to my new police scanner. He and the sheriff are like this." She crossed her fingers to demonstrate the intimate connection.

The mental image of virile Wayne spooning with crusty Bernard tickled me. I laughed from deep within my belly, shooting a spurt of tea out my nose, barely missing Larissa, who still occupied my lap. I clamped my hand over my face and caught Charlotte's eye. She threw her head back and let out a peal of laughter, which infected all of us.

When we pulled ourselves together again, Mama nodded encouragingly. "It's like old times to hear you girls laughing like that. We need more laughter in this house."

I hugged my daughter and realized Mama was right. Laughing took the knots right out of my stomach. The weight on my chest lifted as well, and I felt human again.

"So? You gonna tell me what happened or am I supposed to connect the invisible dots?" Charlotte asked.

I made an empty-handed gesture. "Nothing to tell. I was finishing up a landscaping job at the north end and dug up a human skull."

"Sounds like something to me." My friend slapped a narrow notepad on the table. "Tell me more."

My newfound lightness of heart subsided. "I want you to be successful, Charlotte, but I have to look out for myself. My client, Carolina Byrd, is very low profile. She doesn't like to be in the news. She will be upset enough as it is."

"Have you told her yet?"

"No. And I'm not saying another word until you put that pad of paper away. Get the official incident report from the sheriff."

Charlotte's lower lip jutted out. I could imagine the wheels of pros and cons whirling in her brain. She wanted the story, but I was her best friend. Friendship won out, and she stuffed the notepad back in her purse. Only the mugs of tea remained on the worn table.

Charlotte leaned forward, expectation pulsing from her in waves. "Reporter mode is turned off. Dish."

"Promise this won't go in the paper."

"Do you see me writing anything down?"

"What's the capital of Montana?"

"Helena. What's that got to do with anything?"

"Everything. You remember stuff. Unless you promise, my lips are sealed."

"Come on, Aunt Charlotte, promise," Larissa urged. "I want to hear what happened."

"All right already. I surrender." Charlotte's hands stabbed the air. "Y'all are relentless. Come visit me in the poorhouse because Bernard will crush me under his scrawny heel."

"You can handle Bernard," I said with confidence. "But never turn your back on Virg Burkhead. He tased me today."

I heard my father's sharp intake of breath from across the room, felt Larissa stiffen in my lap. Since both of them had enhanced perceptions, they knew that short-circuiting someone with heightened senses would be awful. Every nerve ending, normal and paranormal, would short out, leaving the recipient blind, deaf, dumb, and mute. Mama had mentioned Daddy knew something had happened, so maybe he had an inkling of the distress I felt.

My fingers sought the smooth stone in my pocket.

"Get out!" Charlotte exclaimed. "We've got a trigger-happy deputy and I can't write about it? No fair."

"I'm fine, thanks." I shot my friend a sharp look. It crossed my mind that she might not be strong enough to refrain from betraying my confidence. I could have stopped right there. But I told them about my deal with the sheriff to become a consultant. "If you write about this, it could mess things up for me. I need this extra income. Larissa needs braces, and my house needs a new well pump."

"Dang." Charlotte guzzled her tea. "How soon will you know if you got the job? I can write about it then, right?"

"My arrangement with the sheriff is private. I don't want to call attention to myself. I need to earn my own way."

"We can help." Mama and Daddy linked arms over by the sink, faded tie-dyed curtains framing their gray heads.

Temptation reared its head. I could become my parents' daughter again. I could move in here with them, as they wanted, and let them help me raise Larissa. It would be much easier with someone sharing the load. But they'd be calling the shots. This was their home, not mine. My resolve to obtain financial independence solidified. "I appreciate your help, I do, but I need to stand on my own two feet."

"Wayne will try to weasel out of the deal," Charlotte said. "How do we know he won't suppress the findings?"

"I'm not going to snoop around Dr. Sugar's morgue, and you shouldn't either. There's something about that man that makes my skin slide."

My friend shuddered. "He makes everyone's skin slide. What about the other angle? The historical angle."

"What about it?" I shrugged. "Wayne's gonna contact the hysterical committee."

"And the hysX will check their archive." My friend's face lit with amusement. "But we can beat them at their research game."

"We can?" My stomach tightened again, and my fingers closed around the moldavite stone in my pocket. I felt a flash of the old Charlotte coming on.

"Yep. Your grandmother had a more extensive archival collection than the historical society. All we need to do is comb through your living room bookshelf."

"Huh." There was merit in her idea. I'd inherited Grandmother's house. Ever since I'd moved in, I'd been meaning to offer her collection of reference books to the historical society, but I hadn't gotten around to it. "Why didn't I think of that?"

"Because I'm the brains of this operation." Charlotte stood. "Come on, let's go. We can find this information before they start looking."

Never get between a determined Charlotte and her goal had been my motto for most of my youth. People wrongly assumed Charlotte was mentally slow because her girth restricted her momentum. All the hair raising and trouble we'd ever gotten into as kids had been her idea. I'd been her trusty sidekick in our capers. In the last ten years, though, she'd taken the criticism to heart, withdrawn socially, and gradually acceded to people's perceptions of her.

Recently, the tables had turned. I'd helped her move up in stature at the paper by giving her first access to the Maisie Ryals story. The change in status had invigorated my friend. Now she had an idea that would secure the consulting job I wanted. I didn't have to think long about jumping on the Charlotte train. "Great idea to do our own research."

Larissa scrambled from my lap and tugged me to my feet. I glanced over at my parents. "Y'all wanna come?"

"We belong here, Baxley," Daddy said. "But you and I need to talk."

"I know, I know. We will. Just not today."

"Don't leave it too long."

Winging at the wistful note in his voice, I drew in a guilty breath. "Soon."

"Don't rush off," Mama said. "I've got a pot of soup in the fridge. Stay for dinner?"

I hugged her. "Next time. I promise."

A pulse of something dark flashed through me at the touch. I glanced up and saw wariness in my mother's sad eyes. Something else was bothering her. Something they'd been hiding from me.

"We'll come for dinner tomorrow," I conceded.

Larissa chattered about a new boy at school all the way home, but I couldn't stop thinking about the dark flash. What could be so terrible that my parents weren't telling me? I knew my father wanted me to take over the dreamwalking business, but it seemed something else was afoot. Something dark and twisted. Something they were fighting on their own.

Something they couldn't mention in front of Charlotte and Larissa.

CHAPTER 8

A sneeze ripped through my body, followed by two more in rapid succession. I set aside the dog-eared journal of a rice plantation owner and grabbed a tissue. Dusk was falling outside my windows, and my empty stomach expected dinner. Mama's soup sounded awfully good right about now. I shouldn't have let my pride stop me from bringing some home. "Searching through these records could take a very long time. We don't even know what we're looking for."

Charlotte wrinkled her freckled nose. "It would help if we knew more about that parcel of land. Did Mrs. Byrd tell you anything about the property's history?"

"No. It didn't come up during our conversations. She only spoke to me to indicate which plants she wanted where. She even specified the height of her foundation plantings. It cost her more to start out with larger plants, but she wanted the plantings to look finished when she moved in."

My friend tsked. "Sounds like a hard person to work with."

"Truthfully, it was a relief to work with someone who didn't keep changing her mind. I admire Carolina for her accomplishments. She runs that factory in Macon, takes care of her special-needs kid, and manages to stay trim and attractive."

Charlotte tapped her pencil against the tome she was perusing. "Is she old money or new?"

Inwardly, I groaned. Nothing good could come of this avenue of conversation. I busied myself returning the journal to the shelf and making another selection. "I don't gossip about my clients. Particularly ones that owe me money. The world is too small."

"Don't hold out on me. What's her deal?"

I was afraid of this. Charlotte wouldn't let the matter drop. If I didn't give her something, she'd drive me crazy with questions. "The deal is she's new here, and people shouldn't prejudge her."

She rose and stretched, dazzling me with her rippling polka-dotted top. "Dang. I hate it when you take the high road. I'd much rather gossip about the fascinating people you get to meet."

"You've met more people as a reporter than I ever will as a pet and plants gal."

"Yeah, but you're meeting the new people. Do you know how many stories I've written about the giant vegetables from Mc-Murphy's farm? Way too many. Besides, I figure it's best to get a heads-up on the competition for your friendship."

I quit flipping through the book on Georgia's early settlers. "You'll always be my friend. Carolina Byrd sees me as the help. We're business associates, not friends."

She turned away, but not before I saw moisture brimming in her eyes. I wanted to give her a reassuring hug, but this was Charlotte we were talking about. She didn't like anyone to touch her, not even her best friend.

"Sounds like new money to me." My friend opened up a map tube from the upper shelf, her needy moment apparently forgotten. Not wanting to make her uncomfortable, I peered with interest at *The Land Survey of 1855*. Unfortunately, there were no owners' names on the plats of land. "It would help to narrow down the time frame. Didn't you learn anything concrete when you touched the skull?"

"Sure. I got a little bit before Virg hit me with the Taser." I glanced up and caught her intent expression. Something inside me tightened. My friend was on an emotional roller coaster these days, and I doubted her judgment when it came to out-scooping the competition. I would never sell her out, and I hated being concerned about her intentions. I'd never been a poker player before, but I was learning to keep my cards close to my chest. If Charlotte succumbed to editorial pressure, she might leak information.

To put it bluntly, saving her job could cost me mine.

My fingers sought the green pendant at my neck. "I sensed three people buried there and that they had been there a long time. Then Virg shot me, and I blacked out."

Char took my explanation in stride. "Could you go to the morgue and try the mind-meld thing with the skull again? If you had more time, you might be able to see more."

"If you only knew what it took to touch that skull the first time." Chills fluttered down my spine. I covered the tremors by rolling my neck and stretching my arms. "Plus I'd have an audience for sure. If I showed any outward indication that I was in trouble, Wayne wouldn't allow me to consult for him. No telling what Dr. Sugar would do to me while I was out of it. I'd be too vulnerable."

Charlotte made an icky face. "I see your point."

My stomach rumbled again, reminding me of our lack of dinner. Inspiration struck. "We don't have to finish this today. Besides, I've got to start on dinner. We're having canned soup and tuna sandwiches. Wanna stay?"

"Thanks anyway." She glanced at her frog watch and gathered her stuff. "I'm heading back to town. Let me know what you find out, okay?"

Larissa clung to me as I tucked her in that evening. Stud Muffin, the little Shih-poo we were pet-sitting for a friend of a friend, nestled into her other side. "Be careful, Mom. I know we need money and all that, but you're the only mom I've got."

I patted her shoulder. "Don't worry. Virg won't shoot me again." Larissa's expression clouded. I had to do better. I sat beside her on the bed. "I'm sorry if today's events frightened you. Do you want to talk about it?"

Her lower lip trembled. "I was scared. I was helping the new kid in math class, and your situation hijacked my thoughts, like a switch went off in my head."

Her fear grabbed me like a crab pincher. The scene she suggested played out in my head. My heart hurt at her visible distress. Like me, she had no one to confide in. No one but me. I stroked her hand. "How so?"

"You know how you're in a room of people and someone leaves. You don't see them slip out, but the room feels emptier? That's what happened. I couldn't sense you. The place where you normally are in my head was vacant."

Air whistled through my teeth. I'd never thought of it like that, but I understood what she was saying. If anything bad happened to her, I'd know immediately. "I'm sorry. I was frightened, too. So much of this is new to me. I really need to spend some time with my father."

"Pap will help you. He helps everyone."

"I never meant for any of this to affect you. I'd hoped that you'd grow up without having the problems I had fitting in."

Larissa nodded solemnly. "I don't worry about that. I am who I am."

"You sure sound grown-up for ten."

Larissa grinned. "Mama Lacey says I have an old soul." Her expression sobered. "Are you going to take over Pap's dream-walking job?"

My back teeth clamped tight. I didn't want to, but my options stank. "I don't know."

"Because you'd be good at it."

And if I did it, Larissa wouldn't have to. That thought weighed heavily on my mind. "This isn't a simple yes-or-no question. There are a lot of considerations. Our lives would become more complicated and unpredictable."

Larissa snuggled deeper in the sheets. "I can do complicated and unpredictable."

She probably could, but it wasn't what I'd wanted for her, or for myself. With a last kiss goodnight, I puttered around the house, loading the dishwasher, flipping the laundry into the dryer, watering my houseplants, and gearing down for the night.

I curled up in bed with the early settlers' book again. For some reason, my eyes kept going back to a certain name. Robert Munro, age thirty-two, seemed about the right age, as did his wife, Selena, and toddler son, Hugh. They'd arrived in coastal Georgia between seventeen thirty-six and seventeen forty-one. They easily could've had another baby after they got here. The only thing I wasn't sure of was where they settled in the region. For that I'd need to visit the library.

The phone shrilled, jarring the silence of the house. A sense of doom flitted through me. Late-night calls never brought good news. Air whistled in through my teeth as I braced myself for bad tidings.

Pure venom blasted in my ear.

"Who the hell do you think you are, Baxley Powell?" A sense of foreboding flickered through me as Carolina Byrd breathed dragon fire into my ear. "I gave you strict instructions to keep Mallow low profile, and you go and call the cops on me?"

CHAPTER 9

Her anger revved my heartbeat. Blood and adrenaline careened through my bloodstream. My mental barriers thinned to a worrisome level. I shored up my barricades, but I got the sense that it was too late. I was too late.

"Take it easy." I'd overheard my client light into one of her corporate employees on the phone when she was out at Mallow, but she'd never directed the full force of her wrath at me. Until now. I didn't much like being in her crosshairs.

The urge to crawl under my four-poster bed and hide tempted me. My fingers sought the green stone. Thank goodness I'd had another chain to replace the broken one. Relief swept through me as I held the stone in my hand.

If only I could send that semblance of calm through the phone line to my upset client.

"How can I take it easy when the cops are calling me because there's a problem on my property?" Carolina's commanding voice rose an octave. "I demand a full explanation."

Calm. I could do calm. But only if she quit shouting at me. "I was planting your weeping cherry where you want it, and I uncovered a human skull."

"A body? You found a body out at Mallow? I've already dealt with a manufacturing problem on the assembly line today and defused a potential labor strike. I don't need this. Make it go away."

I would if I had a magic wand. Or a time machine. "I'd love

to make this whole day vanish. I can update you on the progress of the investigation. The coroner is examining the bones. The bodies were down pretty deep and under thick roots. They aren't recent, if that's any consolation."

"Bodies?" she screeched. "I thought you found one skull."

My gut tightened as if she'd punched me. So much for Carolina being my ideal of a businesswoman. The demands of her career were tearing her apart. "I did, but there may be three people in the immediate vicinity."

"What is going on down there in Sinclair County? I buy a perfectly good piece of waterfront property in the county with the lowest crime rate in the state, spend a fortune to build a decent-sized house, and now I've got bodies? This can't be happening."

I closed my eyes for a moment. Even though I worked for this woman, her self-centeredness was a bitter pill to swallow. "I'm sorry you've been inconvenienced. It was a pretty bad day for me, too. I've never seen a skull before." I'd never touched one either, or gotten tased.

"Yeah, yeah. We all got problems. What will this do to our timeline?"

Not a drop of sympathy in that woman. Her coldness sharpened my voice. "I can't finish the installation until they clear the restricted area. The sheriff and his deputies are very territorial about protecting the scene."

"The *scene*? Is this a criminal investigation?"

I hugged the covers closer, centered myself in the warm glow of the lamp to help ward off her chilling words. "I don't think so. Like I said, the coroner is examining the bones. I'll relay his findings once they are available."

"What does that man know about bones?"

"I don't know, ma'am. The situation is out of my hands."

"I won't allow some country bumpkin to tell me what I can

or cannot do on my property. The state archaeologist is one of my sorority sisters. I'm calling Gail in to expedite matters."

A train wreck was in the making. Locals hated for the state people to start telling them what to do. Should I tell her she was making a mistake? Or should I keep my mouth shut?

I wanted to help her, I did, but it cost me time and money every time I did. Until her weeping cherry was installed, she wouldn't pay me the last thousand she owed me. I didn't have the luxury of stating anything contrary to her wishes. "If you think that's necessary."

"Of course it's necessary. Gail Bergeron is exactly the person for this situation. She'll cut right to the chase and expedite an immediate solution."

Silence snaked through the line, coiling tightly around my pride and self-respect. Larissa. I had to think of her. Of the braces she needed.

"I expect you to maintain those beds around the house until this is wrapped up," Carolina continued. "I can't move down there in the midst of turmoil. The house has to be a serene environment for my son. I expect the landscaping to be picture perfect. Until I pay you the final installment, those plants are still your responsibility. Do I make myself clear?"

The force of her stern command resonated in my ear. It was all I could do not to snap to attention and holler, "Sir, yes, sir," like a trained soldier. Instead, I summoned a crisp professional voice and assured her of my competency.

She ended the call. With relief, I closed my phone. My hands were trembling. Who was this woman that she could order state officials around? And why couldn't she move into the house on her precious timeline? The crime scene tape around the entryway bed would hardly block the driveway; plus, it should be gone in a day or two.

Once this case was closed, I'd plant the cherry tree and get

paid. Carolina Byrd would no longer be my problem. The tightness in my gut eased, but it didn't go away.

My emergency chocolate bar came to mind. Comfort food.
Absolutely a good idea. I needed a treat after all I'd been
through today.

But eating rich food this late at night might prompt a
nightmare. I'd be better off taking my last sleeping pill. The
prospect of indulgence beckoned as seductively as the glitz of
Las Vegas and then receded under the harsh glare of reality.

If I took the sleeping pill, I would not be coherent enough to
answer the phone.

Better not take the pill. But chocolate had caffeine in it. That
would keep me awake. What to do?

I padded over to the dresser, snatched the candy bar from its
hiding place inside my wool socks, and tore into it. I meant to
savor each bite, but it was gone before I knew it. I enjoyed the
rich chocolate taste in my mouth, wishing I had an endless supply.

It wasn't fair that chocolate came with calories.

That night I dreamt of a lonely woman sitting amidst rumpled
bedding. In the faint starlight, she wept, tears streaking her
angular cheeks. A cloud of dark hair cascaded over creamy
shoulders, spilling down across her rounded breasts.

Her despair trickled through the misty veil separating us, a
mournful pathos that pierced my soul. Whatever had happened,
this woman had suffered a heart-wrenching loss.

Who was she?

Not anyone I knew.

What did this dreamwalk mean?

I tried speaking with her. "Miss? Is there anything I can do?"
She didn't appear to hear me. I spoke louder. I shouted. In
mid-sob she stiffened as if she'd been mortally wounded. She

turned in my direction, and I was struck by her ghostly violet-hued eyes.

I didn't know when or where this was happening, but I felt an intangible connection with this woman. With the thread of connection came clearer sensing.

Sheets rustled as if they were on my bed.

The musk of passion filled my lungs.

She spoke, "Help me."

CHAPTER 10

After putting Larissa on the school bus, I drove to the Rankin place to care for their Irish wolfhound. Though Hobo's owners were officially retired, Charles, a former federal agent, still guest lectured about terrorism threats. He and his wife were on a multi-city tour right now.

Hobo liked to lope along, and I needed to run away from my thoughts, so we were good companions on this blustery morning. Swags of Spanish moss swayed in the oak canopy throughout Deerplace, a new development on the outskirts of Marion. My sneaker-clad feet pounded the pavement, my arms swung rhythmically at my sides. Hobo's tongue lolled as he smiled his way down the road.

Two survivors, slogging down the highway of life. We had food, shelter, and people who cared for us, but we'd come to this place broken. Hobo seemed worry free, but I couldn't put my past behind me so easily.

I'd married young, swept off my feet by a high school charmer with emerald green eyes. Roland Powell spirited me around the country as his Army postings changed. Two and a half years ago he'd gone missing on an assignment. Six months later, the Army declared him dead, but they'd stonewalled me on his death benefits.

My daughter and I returned to coastal Georgia, back to the house I'd inherited from my grandmother, back to the town where Daddy's psychic ability was valued.

Back to the place where people knew I had the same ability.

For most of my adult life, I'd run from that extrasensory heritage, but it had saved my life a few months ago. Now I wanted to use it for profit. Only I hadn't had the requisite training. Last night's dream had been unsettling. That was the trouble with opening doors—once you walked through them, you were in a different place, with different rules, where the line between danger and safety blurred.

"You doing all right, Hobo?" I asked the dog between strides. Hobo's head bobbed encouragingly.

We lapped the neighborhood twice. On the second pass, I was more aware of the brown lawns, the brick house that needed my landscaping services, the thin clouds overhead, and the ocean fresh breeze.

A bead of sweat trickled down the channel of my spine; more gathered at my hairline under my ball cap. I was blessed with an athletic build and a good metabolism, and so far I'd been healthy as a horse. Larissa, too, except for her needing braces. Crooked teeth being a defect in the Powell lineage. No one in the Nesbitt family had needed braces before.

I snorted. How could I blame the Powells for faulty genetic material when my ten-year-old daughter had inherited the Nesbitt psychic ability? That sobering thought put matters in perspective.

Back at the Rankin house, I unclipped Hobo's leash. He sniffed around his fenced yard, played fetch for a bit, and licked my hand. "Good dog." I rubbed beneath his ears until his eyes closed in bliss. Then he rolled over so that I could rub his tummy.

The rhythmic stroking calmed my thoughts. Setting aside the dream of the crying woman, I wondered about the bones I'd found. Did those people have a great dog like Hobo? Had they enjoyed living by the sea?

What had their lives been like?

They'd been formally dressed, with hats. The man wore a waistcoat and breeches, the woman a long flowing gown. Their antiquated clothing reminded me of a museum.

A museum! I could approximate the era through the clothing styles. Wait a minute. I'd seen clothing like this before. Roland and I had strolled through a re-creation of Colonial Williamsburg when Larissa was an infant. The people in my vision were dressed similarly.

Euphoria swept through me, and I clapped my hands. "Colonists, Hobo!" The dog squirmed enthusiastically on the ground, his paw knocking into my ball cap. I fixed my hat and went back to rubbing the dog's tummy.

If my graves were of colonists, the Munro family could be the people I was looking for. Scottish Highlanders had settled the Georgia frontier. Only the family at Mallow hadn't thrived.

"Wasn't such a good start, was it, boy?" Hobo cocked his head at my grimace. "I saw them burying their son. Then I saw the man burying his wife and a baby. That was a huge price to pay for a fresh start."

I could search online historical databases at the library. That's what I'd do. I'd prove to the sheriff that I was an asset to his staff.

"I'll be back this evening." I herded Hobo inside his house. I had this pet gig through the weekend.

My truck came into view, and I noted a long stick on the driveway behind it. Best move that out of the way. The sun shone brightly on the gray stick. Odd. It looked too straight to be an oak branch. My breath caught in recognition. It wasn't a stick.

"Sss-snake," I stammered.

Terror struck lightning-bolt fast, molding my sneakers to the concrete driveway. Adrenaline poured into my veins, and I considered leaping on top of my truck. In the blink of an eye, I was five years old again, staring down the throat of a venomous cottonmouth.

Move, my brain urged. Run. Get far away from here.

My feet refused, but my heart raced. I tried to think. This snake didn't have bright coloration. There were no telltale diamonds on his unremarkable skin. No triangular head. No rattles, either.

A good snake. A rat snake, most likely.

Not a life or death situation.

I stomped my feet to make noise. "Go on from here." I hoped the snake would slither off on its own.

It didn't move.

With the Rankins' garage in front of me and the snake behind, I couldn't back out without running over the snake. Though I didn't like snakes, I wouldn't intentionally hurt any living creature. I grabbed a hoe to encourage the snake along. Finally, the reptile edged under the sago palm fronds.

Whew. Crisis averted. My heart rate slowed.

I tossed the hoe in my truck and realized the sheriff still had my shovels. I needed those tools. Bad enough I had to replace my trowel a few weeks ago. What if I got a call today for a landscaping job and the sheriff had my tools?

The jail wasn't far from the library. I'd pick up my shovels first and hit the library second.

Easy-peasy.

I should've known that anything involving the sheriff wouldn't be easy.

CHAPTER 11

"Come on in." Sheriff Wayne Thompson gestured toward my tools over in the corner. "You paint those orange paw prints on the handles?"

I perched on an upright chair. It was one thing to decide to consult for the sheriff. But sitting here in his office under his watchful cop gaze while being bombarded by the emotions trapped in this building was something else indeed. Success in this potential career meant putting myself in harm's way. It meant dwelling in an unstable energy field.

Nothing a determined woman couldn't surmount.

Now that I might be working here, I had more curiosity about this office space. I tried out my version of cop eyes, assessing, weighing, deciding. Not much had changed since I was here a few months back. No curtains to soften the glare from the high transom window. No knickknacks to smooth the sharp angles of the serviceable desk, chairs, and filing cabinets. No rug for the tile floor.

All hard edges, like the man opposite me.

Athletics had saved Wayne from his neglectful and abusive parents. Sports had given him the confidence to become a cop and had saved him from being on the other side of the jail cell.

I realized the silence had stretched too long. The sheriff was no doubt wondering if I'd lost my mind. I hastened to answer his question about my tool handles.

"My daughter drew those paw prints. She customized my

tools, said it would help me keep track of them." I paused for a moment, wondering how to proceed. "Did you find more bodies?"

He tapped his fingertips together. "One more skull. Not two more, as you said."

My nerves flared. I waited a beat to respond. "I'm sure there were three. One of them was a baby. Do you know who they are?"

"No. Do you?"

Was he up to something? If he learned of my research intentions, would he claim my ideas as his own? "What do you mean?"

"Did they tell you their names?"

His unblinking stare got to me. My voice rose a bit. "They might have if your trigger-happy deputy hadn't lit me up with his Taser. As it was, I only saw them being buried."

"That is some weird stuff you got going on up in your head."

He didn't know the half of it, and I wasn't gonna tell him. "What did the coroner find out?"

"Not much since your client"—he grimaced as he spoke, adding extra syllables to the final word—"since your Mrs. Got Rocks client ordered the state archaeologist down here. Bo's hands are tied eight ways to Sunday."

"Is she here already?"

He nodded. "Gail Bergeron arrived this morning. About gave Bo a heart attack. They have a history, those two."

"She'll prove I'm right." I held his gaze. "Then you'll hire me as a consultant."

"The deal was that I had to close the case." He folded his hands behind his head, leaning back in his chair. "There's no way this moldy-oldie will close."

He expected me to fail? My competitive instincts kicked in. "Wait and see. When can my client get her yard back?"

He shrugged one shoulder, as if it wasn't worth a two-shoulder effort. "It's up to that Bergeron woman. When she completes her inquiry, it will be released."

"I hope she works fast."

Wayne leaned forward, his palms flattening on top of his uncluttered desk. His sensual eyebrows waggled suggestively. "She doesn't work nearly as fast as I do. How about I take you out for lunch today?"

I rose to get away from his musky cologne. "Not happening. I wish you'd get over yourself." Wayne had been the high school quarterback, the man who walked on water all four years of school, the man who had slept his way through almost the entire female alphabet. But not me. It irked him that I'd said no.

That I still said no.

He clutched his heart in mock agony. "You're killing me, babe."

It looked like the only luck I'd have at the library would be bad luck. Our courthouse had burned twice in its history, and Colonial land records had literally gone up in smoke. Also the first three United States Censuses of 1790, 1800, and 1810 were missing for Georgia. In 1820, there were only breakdowns to the county level, which meant no individual listings by heads of households. No help there.

I caught a break in the library's Special Collections section. A book of photocopied journal entries from Annabel Broadfield McCrae, something I picked up randomly, listed the deaths of her grandfather's first family, the Munros. The four-year-old boy drowned, while the mother and infant daughter succumbed to a marsh fever. They'd been buried on family land.

Excitement pulsed through me. This was fabulous. I read on, but the only other relevant observation was that Robert Munro seemed sad the rest of his life. In my mind, he mourned the loss of his first love, Selena.

I couldn't prove this family lived at Mallow, but it felt like I was closing in on the truth, which is what I wanted.

I felt drained after leaving the library. On a whim, I drove out to my parents' house to recharge. I didn't expect to see anyone, but Daddy was expecting me. He sat on a shaded bench in their front yard.

Though he wore his standard garb of faded jeans, long-sleeve T-shirt, and flip-flops, a sense of weariness pervaded his space. His frame bent forward; even his ponytail drooped. When had Daddy gotten old? Seemed like yesterday when he introduced me to the world as his daughter.

"Hey, sunshine," Daddy said as I sat beside him on the rough planks. "You here to talk to me?"

"I am." I swallowed around the lump in my throat. "I haven't been avoiding you, just avoiding this topic." I noticed how quiet the house was. "Where's Mama?"

Daddy studied the mockingbird and cardinal playing king of the bird feeder. "She's visiting a friend. It's the two of us."

"Great." But I didn't mean great-great. I meant great in the what-have-I-gotten-myself-into mode. If Mama was around, I could bail out for a soothing cup of hot tea when the discussion got uncomfortable.

He turned his steady gaze to me. "Don't be afraid. I'm your father, same as I've always been."

The petulant child in me rebelled. I didn't want the responsibility he wanted to yield. "You're more than that, and you know it. You're the county dreamwalker. Maybe even the region's dreamwalker. Folks come to you for help, and you help them."

"I can't help everyone. But I try." He nodded his head in the affirmative. "I try." He interlaced his fingers in his lap, the picture of patience. However, the air around him snapped with current. "But this isn't about me. This is about you, my beautiful daughter, who is coming to terms with her many talents."

My cheeks stung under his compliment. "About that. I apologize for being such a snot-nosed kid about dreamwalking before. In my quest to be normal, I said hateful things. I'm sorry for that."

His face relaxed a bit, the grayness lessened. "No need to apologize for being a teenager. Your mother and I rebelled against our parents, too."

I'd never known my Nesbitt grandparents, but Mama's family had been straitlaced to a fault. Janie and Norton Daughtry were pillars of the community. Grandmother Janie founded the historical society and the garden club.

"I kind of figured that, what with Mama being so different from Gran." A grin warmed my face. "What about your folks? How come I don't know much about them? Were they dreamwalkers too?"

"My father was struck by lightning when I was three. I don't recall much about him. My mother dreamwalked. The family trait is strongest in the female line."

"Oh." The ramifications of his comment sunk in. "You mean, I have as much ability as you do?"

"Probably more, but we'll figure that out in time. The important thing is not to feel pressured."

"Too late. I am worried sick. I can't do what you do."

"Chances are you can do it better. Tell me about your abilities."

My jaw clenched at his request. I was sitting on a bench, talking about my abnormal abilities. How surreal was that? Who sat around talking about psychic talents?

Freaks?

Settle, I told myself. I'm not abnormal. I'm normal for me.

Who better to explain my abilities than the person who shared a similar profile and had had years of experience?

"The thing is, I'm not sure, myself." I began slowly. "My gifts seem linked together. Hearing is the strongest, but that's accentuated through touch. I can hear more and see more if I touch an object that someone with highly charged emotions handled. Other sensations come through distorted. And I have odd dreams on occasion, like last night."

"Both Larissa and I picked up your distress call from Sparrow's Point a few months back. How long have you been aware of your telepathic ability?"

"What's that old saying? Necessity is the mother of invention? I hit upon the ability to broadcast my thoughts in that moment of desperation."

"Did you pick up a return signal from either of us?"

I shook my head, my ponytail waggling across my upper back. "I was too busy staying alive to listen."

"There are techniques I can teach you to sharpen your reception skills, but let's leave that for another day when you're not so anxious. Tell me about your most recent dream."

I described the crying woman. "I don't recognize her. Do you have stranger dreams like that?"

"Sometimes I'll get a stranger vibe in a dreamwalk. But my dreams at night are my own."

"Oh."

I must have looked disappointed. He leaned toward me. "Does it bother you?"

"The whole thing bothers me, but there isn't much I can do about it." I clapped my hand over my mouth. "Oops. I didn't mean to be negative. It slipped out."

Laughter danced in his eyes. "It's all right. I didn't come into this gracefully, either."

"How did you get started?"

"Mama Mary trained me from the git-go. Her brother's tuning ability was unstable, and she was determined that my mind would be fit enough to accept the calling. My mind had other ideas."

Daddy's uncle. That would be—"Uncle Emerald?"

He nodded.

I let out the breath I'd been holding. During Uncle Emerald's funeral reception, I'd become trapped in his psychic delusions. That experience soured my outlook on extrasensory experiences.

"That's when I knew I'd messed up." Sadness permeated Daddy's facial features. "I resented that Mama Mary trained me to do a job that I had poor aptitude for. I wanted you to have a choice, so I waited for you to come to me about your abilities. If I'd trained you from the cradle, you would have shielded yourself at the funeral. I failed you, and I'm sorry for that."

Daddy's apology caught me by surprise. I hadn't known he carried guilt and shame for all these years. I'd been so busy focusing on *my* perceptions, I'd forgotten to be attuned to his.

"Don't beat yourself up about it. I know how hard it is to be a parent. You believed in what you were doing. Never once have I blamed you for that event. No one is to blame. Stuff happens. We deal with it."

The lines on his face relaxed. His color brightened. "Thanks for saying that. You've no idea how much better I feel."

I lowered my shields and enjoyed his relief. "Actually, I do."

We both laughed, and an oppressive weight lifted from my chest.

"How about your shielding?" Daddy asked. "That still working for you?"

"Thank you for teaching me how to do that. I wouldn't have survived without that skill." I pulled out the stone Roland had given me. "And this. Roland gave it to me."

"Moldavite. Good choice. I carry crystals in my pocket during dreamwalks. Lacey covers me in them afterward."

Made sense. Mama was a healer. My husband was not. The disconnect jarred me. "How did Roland know?"

Daddy shrugged. "How does anyone know anything? They look and learn." He hesitated before patting my shoulder. "Be careful. Trouble is in the air."

I drove out to Mallow to be alone with my thoughts. The talk with Daddy helped ease my mind, and I felt better until he issued that odd warning. My repeated questions on the matter fell on deaf ears. The only thing I was certain of was that the cosmic clock was ticking. Sometime in the near future, trouble would strike.

Well, it wouldn't strike here because I was alone at Mallow. Just me and the birds out here right now. But I couldn't hide out here for long. I wanted to be home before the school bus came by. If I didn't get the Mallow people identified today, that matter would keep until tomorrow or the next day. Much better to lie low and let trouble find someone else.

Since the irrigation system wasn't working, I watered everything that a length of hose would reach and made a mental note to call the repairman. A *Podocarpus* on the left side of the house angled forward. I walked closer to inspect the gangly shrub, swatting at the profusion of small flies in the area.

That was odd. The side stakes were loose. The one closest to the house had worked itself out of the ground. Carolina Byrd would have my hide if anything happened to her precious landscaping, and this plant was a perfect-size match to one on the right of the mansion. I hammered the stake with my fisted hand, but the shaft wouldn't penetrate the ground.

What rotten luck. I'd dug this hole myself. Nothing was down there but root ball, sand, and peat moss. Why wouldn't the darned stake go in?

Dropping to my knees, I folded back the black fabric I'd installed to deter weeds and scooped the soil out of the way with my hands. I used the edge of the stake to loosen the soil as I dug. A putrid smell rose from the ground, gagging me.

I coughed the odor from my lungs and summoned a barrier to block the noxious scent. The fine hairs on the back of my neck stood at attention, putting me on high alert.

I grabbed another handful of dirt and saw a curved object. *What's that?* It seemed familiar, and yet I couldn't make it out in this context. Curious, I brushed more dirt away and the object came into view.

A hand.

A woman's hand.

CHAPTER 12

I wanted to bolt, but I couldn't move. Time slowed to a crawl, thrusting my thoughts into overdrive. Hands didn't spontaneously occur. They were attached to arms. Which were on bodies. This one was on a dead person.

Dread mounted. I'd found another body.

Only this one wasn't two-hundred some-odd years old. This person hadn't been in the ground long. I'd planted this *Podocarpus* ten days ago.

The body wasn't here then.

I'd have noticed.

My temperature soared and plummeted. Blood ripped through my system as if chased by the denizens of the deep. Pressure built in my lungs until I forced in a breath of air.

I fell backward in a clumsy tangle of limbs, swatting at a thicker cloud of white flies, gagging on the smell of decay. I vomited. Moisture trickled behind my ears. My breath came in pants.

I crawled away on hands and knees, drained of energy, with the single-minded purpose of getting far away from that person. Leaning against the nearest palm tree, the irony stuck me hard. This was what psychic consultants did. They found bodies. How could I do this on a regular basis?

No answers came to mind.

Instead, dread whispered through my pores, inoculating me with a near lethal dose of fear. I couldn't worry about all the

what-ifs in the world of police work. My here and now was hor-
rific enough.

With trembling hands, I dialed the emergency number and
summoned help. I tried to pull myself together. Not an easy
task, when the dead woman commanded my attention. The
thought of uncovering more of her or taking another look
prompted another bout of retching. I was definitely not a natural
fit for this type of work.

A brisk sea breeze swept the scent of my vomit and her decay
away. Overhead, dark clouds thickened, and in the distance,
thunder rolled. A storm was coming. Mama had been right with
her weather prediction. Only, was the storm a meteorological
event or a portent of something more sinister on the horizon?

I'd discounted the divination of signs and symbols along with
my extrasensory talents, but in hindsight, I realized I'd made
another mistake. There were intangible connections to things
seen and unseen. My enhanced senses were proof of that. Even
so, the new and improved Baxley Powell didn't know much of
anything.

Lightning flashed. Thunder rolled. Rain splatted. I let it wash
over me.

"I thought you had sense enough to come in out of the rain,"
Sheriff Wayne Thompson growled.

He'd plunked me in the front seat of his SUV upon arriving.
That was positive. He could have cuffed me and tossed me in
the back of Virg's patrol car. Or allowed Virg to tase me again.
Instead, he showed me mercy and ordered his uniformed deputies to erect a tent over the hand.

Though my teeth wouldn't stop chattering, I welcomed the
cozy fleece blanket around my shoulders. Wayne's woodsy after-
shave permeated the space, but instead of my usual revulsion,
his familiar scent lent comfort. I wasn't interested in the sheriff,

not in the way he wanted me to be, but I trusted him to sort this mess out.

I shivered. "Sorry. After I found the body, I kind of lost it."

"I see that." He stared at me. Wipers squeaked across the windshield. Hot air blasted from the heater. "You want a Coke or somethin'?"

I grimaced at the thought of putting anything in my queasy stomach. "No, thanks." Water dripped from my ball cap brim onto the navy blue blanket. I was probably soaking through the blanket and drenching his seat, too.

"I have to question you," he said. "Why were you here?"

"Carolina Byrd said she wouldn't pay me until I got that cherry tree planted near Misery Road. She made it clear that the landscaping was my responsibility until the job is completed. The irrigation system isn't working, so I watered with the hose. The rear stake from the *Podocarpus* was out, and the tree leaned at an odd angle. Carolina is so exacting, I knew I'd better fix it. Only the stake wouldn't go in. Something was in the way.

"It should have gone in. I dug that hole myself. Nothing but sand and peat moss down there." I paused for a breath. "So I dug down to find the obstruction. That's when I found the woman's hand."

"The victim is a woman?"

"Yes."

"How do you know that?"

I shrugged. "I just do."

He stilled, the intensity in the vehicle amping up a few notches. "What else do you know?"

"Nothing. I couldn't bring myself to go over there again. I believe she's our age. She's someone's daughter. Or wife or sister."

He glanced over at the sagging tent. "We have no missing women reported in our county."

"She came from somewhere."

"Can't you tap into the woo-woo stuff and tell me who she is?"

"Not today. Besides, if I consult for you, I expect to get paid for my work."

He covered my trembling hands with his capable ones. "You don't have the stomach for this work, babe."

My heart agreed with him. My pocketbook did not. I chose my words with care. "This was a nasty surprise. It rattled me. I admit it. But I didn't run screaming from the scene. I called you and waited here. I'll bet even your seasoned officers would hurl if they'd dug up a rotting corpse."

I glanced over my shoulder at the tented area. Near the dogwood, Ronnie held a cloth handkerchief to his mouth. When I turned back, I saw Wayne had noted his deputy's distress.

"You may be right," he admitted.

"I know I'm right. Cut a rookie a little slack."

He turned down the heat and was quiet for a minute. Windshield wipers cleared the droplets off the glass. "You see the paper today?"

"Not yet."

"Charlotte wrote a front-page feature about the mystery people you dug up out here. She came right out and said we'd dug up old bones dating from another era."

"So?"

"So, Running Wolf and Gentle Dove have been marching outside the funeral home all morning. They claim the bones belong to their Native American ancestors and demand they be given the honor and respect they deserve. They've mobilized the regional tribes to mount a major protest. We've already had calls from network news in Savannah."

I swore under my breath. This notoriety would anger Carolina Byrd. "We have to shut that down."

"I agree, but the damage is done. The state archaeologist and I have an interview with a television reporter late this afternoon."

My empty stomach lurched. I fought a battle with nausea and won. "My client won't like this."

"Neither do I."

CHAPTER 13

An hour later, the rain stopped, but judging by the leaden sky, more was on the way. Thanks to the sheriff, I'd mostly dried out, and my hands had stopped trembling. My hair was still a sodden mess. I tugged off my ball cap and undid the ponytail, combing through my wet hair with my fingers.

Outside the sheriff's SUV, where I'd been told to sit, Mallow bustled with activity. Virg and Ronnie dug up the body and stood around with their hands in their pockets trying to look busy. Wayne snapped pictures of the dead woman. The show began when the coroner and the state archaeologist arrived. I rolled down the window to listen.

"I'm taking over this case, *Dr.* Seavey." The state archaeologist gave extra emphasis to our coroner's title. Gail Bergeron's tone was as crisp as the pressed pleats in her immaculate seafoam green coveralls. "The board will sanction you for your inappropriate conduct. This time you won't wheedle your way out of it. This time the charges will stick."

For a slight woman, Gail sure packed a lot of heat into her words. What had our skeletal and oversexed coroner done to earn her scorn? Had he made a pass at his blond superior? Had he screwed up a case? He'd been the county coroner forever. If he'd mishandled cases, Sinclair County could be forced to revisit every death in the last thirty or so years.

"Gail, dear, there's no need to get hot and bothered." Bo Seavey trailed her around the shallow grave. "I'm grateful for your assistance on the other case. Your in-depth training in old bones will help us to narrow down the possibilities in an expedient manner."

She shook her pen at him. "If you keep talking down to me, old man, I will file another written complaint with the disciplinary board. They will yank your medical license."

The coroner fiddled with his bow tie and shot her a roguish smile. "I call every woman dear. Don't take it personally."

Dr. Bergeron looked up from her notepad, pen poised like a deadly dart. Her pale blond bob softened the line of her angular jaw. But there was no softness in her anger. "That doesn't excuse your lecherous behavior. In this day and age, your actions constitute sexual harassment."

They continued to trade barbs, Dr. Bergeron asserting her authority, Dr. Sugar, as we called our oversexed coroner, tried to placate her and made the situation worse. Meanwhile, the body was exhumed, bagged, and loaded for transport. Dr. Bergeron collected big clumps of earth as well.

Once they were through, I exited the SUV, grabbed another shovel, and hurried over to the gaping hole. "I can replant the tree, right?"

She looked down her aristocratic nose at me. Not an easy feat for someone four inches shorter than me. "And you are?"

Dr. Bergeron's acid tone made me wish I'd stayed put in Wayne's Jeep. "I'm the one who found the body, Baxley Powell. These plants are my responsibility."

"Miss Powell, this location is off-limits to civilians until we release it."

Her scolding voice angered me. I pointed to where the *Podocarpus* lay on its side. "I have three-hundred dollars invested in this tree. It is a perfect-size match to the one on the south end of the house. If I lose this one, I have to replace them both. I can't afford a six-hundred-dollar loss on this job. Surely you can allow some flexibility."

She flashed me a tight smile. "I appreciate you have a job to do. So do I. But the scene is off-limits."

"What about the tree?" My voice squeaked. I winced. "Is it off-limits, too?"

She marched over and inspected the root ball. She poked and prodded for a bit, then she stood. "You can store the tree off-site temporarily."

If looks could fry, I'd have cooked her goose permanently. Worse, I hated being indebted to this woman. Her demeanor did not inspire teamwork. I didn't have a wheelbarrow with me. I couldn't drive my truck across the newly installed sod. All I could do was drag the large tree back to my truck and take it home with me. I latched onto the trunk of the tree and pulled. It budged slightly.

Gritting my teeth, I tugged harder. My eyes filled with tears. I mentally called Gail Bergeron every name in the book. Anger fueled my steps. Then the sheriff and Bo Seavey helped me drag it and load it into my truck. Chivalry wasn't dead. Not by a long shot.

"That woman could use a lesson in diplomacy," I muttered after we finished loading the plant.

Bo Seavey patted my shoulder, light glinting off his horn-rimmed glasses. "I call her the Ice Queen, dear. She spews out frost everywhere she goes."

"Play nice, Bo. Gail's got you in her sights," the sheriff warned.

"What did you ever do to her?" I asked.

"Oh, it's nothing." He shambled off.

I was thunderstruck by the force of his lie. He was hiding something from me, and possibly from the sheriff. What had he done to the state archaeologist? What would we do for a coroner if she got him fired?

I turned to the sheriff. "I can go now, right?"

He nodded. "Don't leave town. And, babe?"

"What?" Unbidden sympathy welled up for the Ice Queen. I was dog-tired of being called babe as well. How many times had I corrected Wayne?

His dark brown eyes heated. "Wear your hair down more often. I like it this way." His voice roughened. "You look sexy."

"Get a life!" I stomped to the cab of my truck and roared out of there.

CHAPTER 14

When I left Mallow, soaking in the bathtub until Larissa's school bus came sounded like a grand idea, but having downtime right now might backfire. I didn't want to think about the dead woman at Carolina Byrd's estate or about the questionable wisdom of subjecting myself to Wayne's company.

I shuddered. I'd be better off staying busy.

Lucky for me there was a dynamite diversion taking place in town right now. A protest rally. A big-city stunt, the likes of which had never been seen in conservative Sinclair County. People would be talking about this for years. I wanted to see it, too.

Miles ticked by on the twenty-minute drive across the county. Chances were high there'd be a crowd gathered. I'd have to be careful to keep my senses buffered.

I could do careful. Heck after the day I'd had, I could do anything.

Cars and people dotted the streets of Marion as if it was parade day and everyone wanted a front-row seat. Folks hurried down the narrow sidewalks. Anticipation sparkled and shimmered in the air.

I parked on Drake's Way, which ran perpendicular to Main Street, and hoofed it to the rally. As I neared the two-story courthouse, I noticed the American flag hanging limply against the side of the flagpole. Too damp to fly. I sympathized.

Charlotte stood at the ready, camera around her neck, notepad in her hand. I stopped beside her on the narrow sidewalk. "Come to watch the fun?"

"Yeah."

An older woman I didn't know sat on the concrete bench pounding on a small drum. My parents' friend and car mechanic, Bob Brown, also known as Running Wolf, chanted foreign-sounding words as he paced, placard in hand. His sign read "Equal rights for Native Americans." Running Wolf's fringed trousers and feathered breastplate left no doubt as to his ancestral heritage. His wife, Earlene, who was known as Gentle Dove, limped a few paces behind him. Beads, shells, and feathers adorned her soft leather shift. Her sign read "Honor our dead." Another aging warrior carried two signs: "Stop the Madness" and "We were here first."

I glanced down the street at the casually garbed onlookers. There must be close to a hundred people out here along with both of the city's police officers. A giant crowd by Sinclair County standards. More than one of them held their cell phones out and appeared to be photographing the event.

I whispered into Charlotte's ear. "What have you done?"

"Cracked open the second biggest story of my career, that's what." Her short brown hair puffed out around her moon-shaped face, cemented in place with what had to be a whole can of hair spray.

Tears sprang to my eyes at the too-sweet scent. The constant beating of the drum pulsed into my thoughts. "I dunno, Char, this doesn't feel good."

Her plump hands fluttered through the air, the glare off her chunky watch crystal nearly blinding me. "Don't go all sensitive on me. WAGN is coming any minute now to interview me, the woman who broke the story on the historical remains. They're going to love the protest rally." She shot me a hundred-watt smile. "I'm going to be famous."

She'd dressed for fame in a chartreuse pantsuit and a shimmery yellow top. A triple row of coordinating polished stones adorned the neckline of her plus-sized frame. She'd drawn in cheekbones and eyebrows with a deft hand, concealing most of her freckles. Even her narrow glasses sparkled.

"I hope you get what you want." My nerves jittered as if another nasty storm was approaching. Charlotte's career was on the rise, but the more features she wrote, the more dramatic her writing style became.

Had I contributed to today's lunacy by withholding details of my vision from her? I believed the bones weren't American Indian. My vision had shown people wearing Colonial garb. I couldn't very well tell Charlotte that fact without breaking my promise to Wayne that I'd keep my mouth shut.

Worries ricocheted through my head. This protest could blow up in everyone's faces. Would Charlotte's career crash and burn when the remains were positively identified? Would my parents' friends get hurt or jailed by overzealous law enforcement officers?

Gentle Dove caught my eye and waved. I waved back, realizing she limped more than usual today. She and her husband had foresworn moccasins for thick-soled athletic footwear, while their companions sported native footwear. Good for Gentle Dove and Running Wolf. For standing and walking, cushy sneakers were the only way to go.

This morning I'd dressed in my standard outfit of jeans, faded tie-dyed tee, and ball cap. Instead of my still damp work boots, I'd changed into my running shoes. My brown hair was tucked up in its usual ponytail. I'd skipped the makeup step, not that I fooled with that much anyway. Next to Charlotte's peacock plumage, I was a plain sparrow. Which was just how I liked it. Charlotte craved the spotlight. Not me. I'd rather be invisible, a chameleon.

A white TV van pulled up. Two cameramen spilled out, panning the protesters, the cops, and the onlookers. My friend shot forward to intercept the sleek and beautiful talking head, Barbie something-or-other. "Yoo-hoo! I'm Charlotte Ambrose, the reporter who broke this fascinating story."

The slender beauty offered Charlotte a limp handshake and quickly withdrew her hand. "Babs Lawrence." The cameramen circled like grinning piranhas. One of them nodded toward the granite courthouse sign. "Over there, Babs."

Babs obediently trotted across the browned lawn, a mean feat in her spiky heels and the heel-sucking sand of coastal Georgia. Bright lights illuminated her face, and the camera rolled. Babs gave a succinct account of Charlotte's newspaper article. When she stopped speaking, the cameras panned over to the protestors, who chanted all the louder.

Charlotte elbowed me in the side. "Isn't this grand? Who'd'a thunk we'd get TV cameras here in Marion?"

"Who'd'a thunk." The sense of dread was growing in my gut. Electricity snapped in the air. Protestors chanted and marched. Cameras rolled. More people stopped to watch. My skin tingled. Dread skittered across my nerves. It was only a matter of time until lightning arced out of the primordial stew.

Don't let it hit me. Or Charlotte.

Babs waved Charlotte over. "Miss Ambrose, what can you add to the story?"

Charlotte's head jerked back slightly, as if she weren't prepared for questions. She covered her lapse with a thoughtful glance to her notepad. "It is believed the bones are from several individuals. Preliminary reports from the coroner indicate one body was an adult female, and at least one other was a child."

Babs nodded encouragingly. Charlotte continued, "The state archaeologist is here examining the remains. She should issue a statement very soon about her official findings."

Babs stifled a yawn, as if this news was dull as a mud puddle. Without warning, Charlotte pointed me out. "My friend Baxley Powell found the bones."

The cameras panned over to where I stood under the shade of the Highlander oak, the oldest tree in the county. Babs scurried to my side, a story hound fast on the scent. "What can you tell you us about the remains?"

I wanted to make the sign of a cross to ward her away. I shot Charlotte a lethal look. No way was I telling this Teflon bimbo anything. "No comment."

"Were you alone when you made the chilling discovery?" Babs asked.

"No comment."

"How many bodies did you dig up?"

"No comment."

"Do you have any idea who the dead are?"

I must have hesitated before I spoke again. "No comment."

Babs made the cut sign to her camera guy. She whispered to me, her breath a tepid confection of breath mints. "Look, I can't air this if you don't give me something."

As if I cared about my television debut. I shrugged. "Air the clip with Charlotte."

A bald-headed guy with dark glasses darted from the TV van, hurried to Babs' side, and spoke to her in confidence. Babs motioned the camera on again, and bright lights blinded me. The urge to hide was overwhelming. I angled my face down so that my ball cap shielded my eyes from the glare.

"Sources close to this investigation tell us you unearthed another body hours ago." Babs licked her chops. "What can you tell us about this amazing coincidence? Do you have a divining rod for the dead?"

Charlotte gasped from behind the cameras. I couldn't worry

about her feelings right now. I had a bona fide crisis on my hands.

Seconds ticked off my life clock. Babs' spur-of-the-moment question hit very close to home. I had to be careful here or these bright lights would bedevil me for a long time. I didn't want that.

Instinct took over. I tensed in an athletic crouch, ready to take on a fight, ready to run like hell. Either option would invite more scrutiny. My brain churned like my stomach.

What could I do?

I could accommodate the reporter, hoping my extrasensory abilities would encourage her to dismiss me as the flake of the day. I could say nothing and invite more speculation. Or I could remember that I hoped to be paid for my police consulting work.

I leaned close to her mike. "No comment."

CHAPTER 15

Larissa trotted off the school bus and ran straight into my arms. "You okay? Something felt different about today."

I ruffled her hair, hugging her close. She pulsed with youthful vitality and concern. More than anything, I wanted to have a quiet evening at home with my daughter. She shouldn't be subjected to the things I'd seen and done. "I'm fine. There was a little hiccup at my work today, and I took care of it. But I'm sure it wasn't as fun as fourth grade. Tell me about your day?"

Larissa beamed and grabbed my hand as we walked up the grassy drive. "The new boy ate lunch with me. Both of us like to draw and build tree forts. Can I invite him over to play on Saturday?"

I inhaled a satisfied breath. This was more wholesome than talking about dead bodies. "As long as it's okay with his parents. You have their number?"

Her face fell. "Do you have to call them? Can't he just come over? He said it was okay, that he could ride his bike over."

Alarms sounded in my head. I didn't want anyone's kid riding their bike on the highway. People drove too fast on that road. It was too dangerous. "Yes, I have to do that. We could pick him up right after I take care of Hobo on Saturday."

"He can stay all day?" At my nod, she whooped and skipped ahead. "I'll ask him for the phone number at school tomorrow. He's gonna love Muffin."

While macaroni and cheese baked in the oven, I helped

Larissa with her homework. All in all, just another quiet evening at home. Until Charlotte arrived still brightly decked out in fluorescent green and yellow.

My bubble of normality burst. I could divert the intrusion of current events by hustling my best friend out, but that would alert Larissa. She'd hear about the body tomorrow anyway. If there was one thing you could be certain of in Sinclair County, it was the viral transmission of news like this. Every kid on the bus would be infected with the story.

At least we'd had a few hours of normality.

"Hey, hey, hey!" Charlotte bustled in the back door and saw us sitting at the kitchen table. "How's my favorite kid?"

"I hate social studies, Aunt Charlotte." Larissa glanced up from her essay. Stud Muffin lifted his furry Shih-poo head from Larissa's lap, saw it was Charlotte, and settled back down for another snooze.

"Join the club, my dear. Social studies is not our friend." Char dropped into a padded chrome chair and nodded toward the tiny TV on the kitchen counter. "You don't have it on?"

I held her gaze. "No. I don't."

"We have to watch the news." Charlotte's chin jutted out. She sniffed the air. "Is that mac and cheese I smell?"

"Yep," Larissa said. "Want some?"

"Of course. When have I ever passed up mac and cheese? But I insist we watch the news."

"Why's that?" Larissa chewed on her pencil.

"Because your mom and I were interviewed by the WAGN news crew today."

Larissa's jaw dropped. "Mom?"

For a split second, I had the thought of being a supercharged Kudzu vine and engulfing Charlotte, covering her colorful garments, and silencing her inquisitive mind with my dense foliage. I gave one last try to divert the tide of news. "It was nothing."

"It wasn't nothing. And I've got a bone to pick with you." Charlotte blushed. "Sorry for the pun. Unintentional. But you didn't tell me about the new body. You told skanky Babs."

I stilled. "Not true. She told the world. I didn't tell anyone except the sheriff."

"Wait." Larissa tossed her pencil on the table. "What's this about a new body? You found another dead person?"

The incredulous note in her voice made me wince. I rose and busied myself with pouring tea for my friend. "I was in the wrong place at the wrong time. Anyone could have found that body. It just happened to be me."

"Spill." Charlotte grabbed my shirttail as I placed a glass of sweet tea in front of her. Charlotte and Larissa leaned forward in their seats.

Nothing to do but tell them the bare minimum. "I was watering the plants out at Mallow. One plant didn't look right, so I tried to fix it. There was a body underneath."

"And you didn't pick up the phone and call me?" Charlotte asked.

"You didn't transmit the news to me?" Larissa scowled, accusations swimming in her emerald green eyes, her father's eyes. "You didn't even mention it until Aunt Charlotte brought it up."

I crossed my arms in front of my chest. I wouldn't let them hang a guilt trip on me. "I planned to tell you later this evening, but I wanted to forget about it for a few hours. Other than the initial shock, it was no big deal. I handled it. I am a big girl."

"Sounds like a big deal to me," Charlotte said.

"Me too." Larissa's brows bunched. "I didn't even sense a hint of trouble. How'd ya do that?"

I didn't want to smile. It really wasn't appropriate when we were talking about a dead person, but a wisp of a smile snuck out all the same. "I haven't been entirely idle these last weeks. I figured out how to shield my thoughts better. Like I said, I handled it."

An urgent knock sounded at the front door. Muffin barked and ran toward the door. Relieved by the distraction, I hurried to answer the summons. I peered through the peephole before opening the door. Muriel Jamison's exotic features came into view.

Though we both had brown eyes and dark hair, I could never achieve that degree of smoldering with my eyes, that degree of poutiness with my lips, that degree of seductive vixen with my tousled locks. Muriel was a former landscaping client, and now that I thought about it, a friend of Carolina Byrd.

I swallowed around the lump in my throat and opened the door. "Muriel, what can I do for you?"

"You can start by answering my questions." Muriel breezed past me, her silver bracelets jingling, her lilac-colored gauzy skirt billowing in her wake. She successfully navigated around the yipping dog, over the sliding rug in the hallway, and halted in the center of my living room, her jeweled fingers clenched in tight fists.

Her voice blared trumpet loud, "Why are they calling you the Deadly Landscaper on TV?"

CHAPTER 16

Chairs scraped across the kitchen floor. Larissa and Charlotte peered around the corner, curiosity stamped on their faces. I had the sense that my world was coming unglued. Not good. This was so not good.

"None of this is my fault." Given the circumstances, I thought I sounded very reasonable. "I don't know why there are people buried out at Mallow. I didn't put them there. I'm the unlucky sapsucker who found them."

Muriel paced the living room in fits and starts. Muffin dove under the sofa to avoid getting trampled. I'd hide, too, if that would help. Waves of anger rolled off Muriel, polluting my house with an excess of negative emotion.

"This is unacceptable. Completely unacceptable." Muriel's haughty tone rubbed me like sandpaper. "Carolina's very protective of her son's condition. She won't tolerate any publicity."

"I understand, believe me, but I didn't do anything wrong. Carolina insisted the plants were my responsibility until the job was completed. I was out there, at my own expense, watering her foundation plants. Some joker hid a body under my tree. I didn't do it."

Electricity snapped around Muriel. "Carolina isn't a patient woman. She expected this situation out at Mallow to be resolved by now. Instead, you've turned her private retreat into a three-ring circus. Mark my words, if those Native Americans step foot on Mallow soil, she will have them arrested for trespassing."

My emotions spiked. "Those Native Americans are exercising their constitutional rights of free speech. Even Carolina has to abide by our federal, local, and state laws."

"Carolina is low profile."

Did this woman think I was stupid? Breath huffed out of my nostrils. I fought for control of my temper. "I got that. I'm low profile, too. I didn't seek out the television interview. I didn't say anything about Mallow. I said nothing of any interest to anyone. Carolina's friend, Dr. Bergeron, is working both cases. Once she finishes the forensic work, the sheriff will ID the killer, and this will all fade away. Carolina has nothing to worry about."

Muriel stopped in front of me. Emotions writhed in her sphere. Her beautiful face tightened into a snarl. "Stay away from Mallow. She doesn't want you out there. Not until this is settled."

My blood ran hot and cold. Everything about this job was messed up. I wished I'd never signed a contract with Carolina Byrd. "What? Who will water the plants? I can't afford to replace them."

"The plants will be fine for a few days. They're under warranty, right?"

A muscle in my cheek spasmed. She was right about the warranty; even so, if I had to replace the plants, I'd be out my labor and transportation costs. Or I could make a fool of myself and risk being arrested for trespassing. Putting things in perspective cooled my temper a bit. "If that's what she wants, fine."

Muriel left, narrowly avoiding the sheriff's dark SUV as she sped off. I sagged against the doorframe, Charlotte and Larissa crowding in close. We watched through the screen door.

I blew out a deep breath. "Great. This day couldn't get any worse. My client has barred me from her property, and now the sheriff has come to call."

Wayne slammed the door on his Jeep and strode our way. His gold badge caught a late afternoon sunbeam, nearly blinding me.

"He looks pissed," Charlotte observed.

With each step he took, dread clotted in my veins. My hand went to my chest. "I've got a very bad feeling about this."

Charlotte and Larissa stepped back when I opened the screen door for Wayne. "Yes? Has there been a breakthrough in the case?"

A second police car pulled into my grassy driveway. Adrenaline rushed though me. Whispers arose from my subconscious. *Run. Run while you've still got the chance.*

I struggled for composure. My hand strayed to my green pendant. My shields bolstered, warmth flowed into my icy veins.

Wayne nodded tersely toward Larissa. "Send the kid into the kitchen."

His command brought a fresh chill to my bones. Everything was turning to crap today. But in this house, I was in charge. Things went the way I wanted them to go. It was time I asserted my authority. "The *kid* has a name. Larissa stays. What is this about?"

He stood too close, his strong cologne choking the breath from me. "Step outside, Baxley."

My heart raced as I obeyed the curt command. On the shaded porch, I met Wayne's dark gaze. "I don't understand."

Virg huffed up the steps with a crisply folded paper bag in one beefy hand. Wayne reached inside the sack. He pulled out a trowel. One decorated with bright paw prints. "Does this belong to you?"

Recognition flamed my cheeks. "Where'd you find it? I've been missing that trowel for a few weeks."

"Two weeks?"

"Could be. I didn't notice it was gone until I went to use it to plant some late pansies in my backyard. I couldn't find it anywhere. Did I leave it at your house?"

His gaze shuttered. "You'll have to come to the station with me."

I groped behind me for the screen-door handle, stepping back until my fingers latched onto the cool metal surface. "I can't leave. Dinner is in the oven. I have a kid."

Wayne clamped a beefy palm on my shoulder. "Charlotte can stay with your kid. If you don't want her to babysit, I'll call your parents."

His anger channeled into me, overloading my senses. I tried to block him, but with the bridge of his hand on me, I couldn't stop the transmission of emotion. His anger burned white hot.

This conversation had a surreal feel to it. I had the sense of observing and experiencing events simultaneously. Fear thickened like day-old gravy in my gut.

I glanced over at my best friend, not knowing how to ask. "I can stay," Charlotte said. "We'll be fine."

"Thanks." My voice sounded husky, like it belonged to someone else.

Wayne propelled me toward his Jeep. Outwardly, I complied. Inwardly, my thoughts tumbled like laundry. Something was very wrong here. My head felt so heavy I was amazed it didn't fall off my shoulders. Moisture dampened my hairline, spine, and palms.

I found my voice. "What does my trowel have to do with anything?"

"The dead woman's blood is on it," he said.

My pulse stalled. I forced a sip of air in my lungs. "Blood?"

"It also contains fingerprints."

Time froze. "Prints? Whose prints?"

"Yours."

Chapter 17

Trembling, I hunched forward in my seat, hugging my middle. My heart raced, and I could barely make sense of anything. One thing I knew for sure. This sucked. I didn't kill anyone. I was innocent. But Wayne hadn't looked at me like I was innocent. He'd looked at me like I was the crud stuck in the crook of the sink drain.

"Am I under arrest?" I asked.

"You should be. Right now you're considered a person of interest." Wayne sped onto the highway, the rapid acceleration pressing me back into the cloth seat. His stinky cologne overpowered the small space. I tried to breathe around it.

"I've got blood and your fingerprints on an item that was found with the murder victim," he said.

"Murder?" The word came out as a whisper. My fingers fisted, the blunt edges of my short fingernails biting into my palms. I'd never felt more alone in my life. There was no white knight to sweep in and save the day. Roland was gone. I was supposed to be taking care of things, but I wasn't even taking care of myself.

I could go to jail for this. That's what someone wanted. Why else would my trowel be in the dirt with a dead woman? I was supposed to take the fall.

I wouldn't have to worry about making ends meet in jail. Someone would take care of me there. Shivers raced up and down my spine. They'd tell me when to eat, where to sleep.

They'd cover my room and board. All I'd have to do is go along with the program and stay mentally shielded the rest of my life.

And forget I had a brain or a responsibility to my daughter. And my parents. I couldn't let them down, either. I had to pull myself together. First I worked on a steady supply of air coming in. Then I tried to figure out what Wayne knew and got nothing but anger. Wouldn't it be handy if I could read his mind instead of the pissed-off emotions he was broadcasting?

"That woman was murdered?" I asked. "With my trowel? How is that even possible?"

"Hold up. We can't have this discussion in the car. Wait until we get back to the office."

The office.

He meant the jail. I'd spent too much time at the jail already. It was not a place I liked to visit. "You know I didn't do this. It doesn't make any sense. Why would I kill anyone? I'm a single parent, for goodness sake. I don't even know who this person is. Why would I go around killing people I don't know? It doesn't make any sense."

He floored the accelerator. "People under stress don't act like themselves."

Was he trying to kill us? "I've been living here a year and a half. I've been under the same amount of stress the entire time. You've seen me at my worst already."

"You saying you don't think you're capable of killing anyone?"

"Yes!" Relief surged through me like a fire hose. Finally. He understood. I was not a murderer. I was a mom.

He shook his head. "You're wrong. Given the right motivation, every person on this planet would kill. You'd kill to protect your kid."

"Leave Larissa out of this." My insides iced. I waved my hand dismissively. "This is ridiculous."

"This is reality. Law enforcement officers put their butts on the line every day. Some days we get bit on the butt. Some days we bite back."

Miles slid past in a blur. Tears rolled unchecked down my face. Where the hell was my husband? Why couldn't he come home and take care of this mess? Why did all the crap fall on me? When would it be his turn to take care of our family? When?

I was sick and tired of being the responsible one.

But what choice did I have? Someone had gone to a lot of trouble to mix me up in the middle of this. I wasn't going down without a fight.

They'd learn not to mess with Baxley Powell. I'd figure this out, and I'd kick killer butt all the way to the Atlantic Ocean. They might think I was a defenseless female, but I had my talents, my family, and my pendant.

I'd beat them at their own game.

CHAPTER 18

"I didn't kill anyone. Why don't you people understand that?" I smacked my palms on the metal tabletop for emphasis. It was getting harder and harder to breathe in this small room. What I wouldn't give for a baggie of potting soil to sniff right now.

Wayne reached down for the paper sack he'd placed on the floor. "We have evidence that puts you at the scene."

My gaze went to the bag, which held my trowel. My bloody trowel. How the hell had that happened? This was not going well. Wayne's face was inscrutable, and Gail Bergeron's pale features were frozen into a scowl. In her ice-blue slacks suit and frosted hair, she very much looked like an Ice Queen.

I couldn't afford a lawyer, but I was starting to feel like a lawyer was a good idea.

I drew my hands back toward my body. "I never denied being there. I installed every foundation plant at Mallow. There's probably *evidence* of me at each installation."

"You have an unlimited supply of trowels, Mrs. Powell?" Gail asked.

"I own exactly two trowels, one of which has been missing for a couple of weeks. I don't know when I lost it. I thought it would turn up somewhere."

"It did turn up somewhere." Wayne spoke through clenched teeth. "At a murder scene."

Gail tapped her glossy fingernails against the tabletop. "Why didn't you report it missing?"

"You're kidding, right? The trowel cost less than five bucks. It's nothing that would require a police incident report. I've lost two pairs of sunglasses this past year. Should I have reported them, too? Don't you people have better things to do than harass hardworking citizens?"

"Your tool at the scene puts you there," Wayne said. "That's opportunity. Tell me about your guns. What kind of guns do you own?"

I didn't like the way his voice roughened. I shivered and gripped my hands tightly together. I could barely breathe, let alone speak. "Two pistols and a shotgun."

"Tell me about the pistols."

I couldn't contain my trembling. I shuddered outright in fear. I had to make them see I was innocent. I had to do more than cower in this chair. I could turn this interrogation around. It wasn't too late. It couldn't be.

"Wait. I'm confused. Are you telling me that this wasn't death by trowel? Was the woman shot? With a gun?"

He leaned in close. "I'm asking the questions."

Every sense I owned was screaming at me to run. My leg muscles twitched, my gut churned. So far no one had lied to me. I clung to that truth.

"You already know the answer." I tried to sound confident, to keep him from knowing I was scared out of my gourd. "I've got Roland's Glock and a little Beretta."

"You sound very familiar with weapons. Who's to say you don't have another gun tucked away somewhere?" Gail turned to the sheriff. "Get a warrant to search her property."

Her nastiness made my blood boil. I leaned forward in my chair. "My husband made sure that I was trained in self-defense. Plus, guns are a staple down here. Everyone owns guns."

"She's right about the guns," Wayne said. "And if she had a

murder weapon, she wouldn't keep it at her house. Too obvious."

"I want a list of every place she's been in the last three weeks."

Wayne straightened. "I'm running this investigation. Just because you managed to sideline Bo, don't think you can walk all over me, too."

Two powerful opponents, now at odds with each other, one loaded with testosterone and a badge, the other laden with feminine arrogance and political connections.

I glanced from Gail's stony face to Wayne's stormy one. "What happened to Bo?"

Gail looked down her nose at me. "Dr. Seavey has been relieved of duty pending an investigation into his unprofessional conduct."

Dr. Sugar was a jerk. A letch, too. But he was our jerk. I didn't like an outsider coming in here and making waves. "Bo can't help how he is. You have to get past his personality. He gets the job done, and he's the only coroner we've got."

"Right now, you've got me. I've been temporarily reassigned here during this investigation."

Great. A ball-busting, upwardly mobile do-gooder muscling in on poor old Dr. Sugar. Even though I didn't care for the man, I respected that he was different. Hell, I understood different better than anyone.

Could I use my difference to buy extra time to snoop around? I stared at Gail. "What about the first remains I found? Did you find all three bodies?"

Gail exchanged a look with Wayne. He nodded. She cleared her throat. "We only found two skulls. However, there are a few bones intermingled with the adult female's that might belong to another individual. At this point, I can't tell definitively. Why do you think there are three bodies?"

I glanced at Wayne, hoping he'd jump in and explain. No

such luck. I was on my own. My choices were few: clear the air or go to jail. "I have a strong sense of intuition. Oftentimes I know things about a person by touching an object. When I touched the skull, I got a strong sense of three people."

"Three Native Americans?" Gail's voice shrilled.

"Definitely not. Three settlers of Caucasian descent. A woman, a young boy, and an infant. Possibly two hundred years old. And quite possibly the family of colonist Robert Munro."

Gail's jaw dropped. She glanced over at the sheriff. "You didn't tell me this."

He shrugged. "I didn't know."

"We can't operate as a team if you withhold information," Gail said.

Wayne's dark eyes glittered with menace. I had the feeling he didn't want to be on Gail's team. Me neither. I wanted my life back. I wanted Gail to go away. I wanted to pretend none of this had ever happened.

I stood. "Unless you're charging me, I'm going home."

"Don't leave town," Wayne said.

I reached for the doorknob, thought about it, and turned back around. "Why do you think I killed anyone? Any of the workers out there could have taken my trowel and planted it with the woman."

Gail arched an eyebrow. "Is this another of your intuitive perceptions?"

"No. It's common sense. The realtor, the builder, the owner, and the subcontractors have been alone at Mallow recently. I'm not the only one with opportunity and means. But why would I kill a stranger? I don't know the first thing about the victim, except for you telling me she was shot."

"Your intuition didn't kick in when you touched her?" Gail asked.

"It doesn't work like that. And I wasn't trying to read her.

103

Once I dug up the hand, I stopped digging and moved away. I can't tell you the first thing about her. Well, she wasn't African American. Her skin tone was too light for that. Don't you know who she is?"

"Our investigation is ongoing," Wayne said.

Great. Standard double-speak. "I guess if I'm a suspect I won't be a consultant on this case."

"You are a person of interest in this case," Gail said. "You will not be allowed access to any information we uncover."

Her words didn't ring the same as her previous statements.

She was lying.

Why?

What reason would the state archaeologist have to lie to me?

CHAPTER 19

Charlotte scrambled to her feet in a flurry of green and yellow as I entered the jailhouse lobby. Without thinking, I hugged her. Miracle of miracles, she let me.

"I thought you were home with Larissa."

My friend stiffened and backed away. Ever since we were accused of being dykes in high school, she was sensitive to any touching in public. "I called your parents. They insisted on staying with Larissa and sent me here. I'd've come back there too, except Hitler"—she stopped to point at Tamika behind the bulletproof glass—"Hitler wouldn't let me in."

Noise from the protest outside filtered through the front door. I nodded toward the thronged parking lot. "Let's get out of here. This place is a zoo."

"Your wish is my command." Charlotte opened the door, and we started down the sidewalk. The television crews were gone. Stark overhead lights illuminated the area between the courthouse and the jail. Two uniformed deputies stood at the ready on the jail side of the demonstration. Four Native Americans chanted on the street side. A crowd of onlookers watched.

"We demand justice," Running Wolf shouted hoarsely. "We are oppressed. Our people have been dishonored. The land is angry. The Great Spirit is deeply troubled."

I had half a mind to tell him the bodies weren't Native American, but I had enough problems with the sheriff right now. Gentle Dove looked like she was ready to drop. She flashed me a sad smile and trudged on with her placard.

Off to one side of the demonstration, realtor Buster Glass-man stood beside my well-intentioned brother-in-law, Bubba Powell. They moved forward to intercept us. Great. Just great.

"You okay?" Bubba Powell strained at his shirt buttons. I hoped he wouldn't ask to borrow money again.

"Fine." I kept moving toward Charlotte's trusty Jetta. Getting drawn into an extended conversation with Buster wouldn't be good. I would never help him with online betting. "I'm overwhelmed by all the commotion though. I'm ready for peace and quiet."

Bubba shoved his hands in his jean pockets. "I hate that you're tangled up in another murder case."

"Me, too." He matched me stride for stride. Buster Glassman trailed behind with Charlotte. Tall and thin next to short and round. Reminded me of the fairy-tale characters Jack Sprat and his wife. Out of the corner of my eye, I saw Charlotte and Buster exchange business cards. What was that about?

Charlotte clicked her key fob, and the electronic door locks released. Bubba held the passenger door for me. "Let me know if there's anything I can do for you."

I nodded, thinking how our situations had reversed. I usually rescued Bubba, not the other way around. Charlotte hefted herself into the driver's seat as Bubba closed my door. I looked over his shoulder, and Buster caught my eye. He put his hand up to his ear as if it were a phone. "Call me," he mouthed.

I groaned. "Let's go home."

"Roger that." The engine roared to life, and Charlotte zipped us out of the lot.

My head pounded with unasked questions. I couldn't keep them in. "What was that with you and Buster?"

"Saw that, did ya?" Charlotte's freckles danced on her nose. "I want to interview him about the Mallow property. He's gonna meet me for lunch tomorrow." She giggled. "Imagine that. Me having lunch with a real-live stud muffin."

My hands clenched reflexively. Air whistled in through my teeth. I'd hate myself if I didn't warn Charlotte. "Be careful. He's not what you think."

She arched a plucked eyebrow. "You know something about him?"

"He's a heavy gambler. But if that fact gets back to him or in the paper, I'll deny I said it. This is strictly off the record."

Charlotte banged her hand on the steering wheel. "I hate off the record. It's like knowing the answer in school and the teacher never calling on you. Wait. How do you know that? Did you peep inside his head?"

I shuddered. "Gross. No. Yuck. I can't think of anything more disgusting. I'm no mind reader. And even if I could read minds, why would I want to? People think ugly thoughts. I don't want to know what people think." I sighed. "Buster asked me to partner with him in some online gambling scheme. Naturally, I said no."

"Is he in financial trouble?"

"Who the hell cares? He's a big boy. He can take care of himself."

CHAPTER 20

Hobo and I went for a run first thing the next morning. It felt good to feel the wind on my face, to outdistance my thoughts. My arms swung with each stride. We ran until my chest burned, then we strolled back to the dog's house.

Last night, I'd quieted Larissa's concerns about my near arrest. Today, I owed my parents an explanation, so I headed there when I finished with the dog. I parked my truck in the side yard and stared at the multicolored cottage.

My aging hippy parents loved everyone and welcomed everyone and everything into their home. I'd grown up here in this concrete block cottage deep in the woods. There were no signs marking our front and back entrances, no mailbox, no house number. There was no need. Everyone knew where the Nesbitts lived.

Mama appeared in the open doorway in a faded denim jumper and waved me in. I managed a smile and obeyed. My pulse raced oddly. This conversation would change things. I knew it as well as I knew my name.

"I've got a pot of tea steeping," Mama said. "Soup pot's on for lunch, too."

"Thanks." From long habit, I sat in my chair at the kitchen table. "Where's Daddy?"

Mama joined me, her white braid slipping over her shoulder. "Fooling around with his herbs. Once he knew you were headed this way, he ducked out for a bit to give us a few minutes alone."

"How'd he know I was coming?"

Mama looked like the early bird who'd swallowed the worm. "He said you told him."

"I came over right after I finished with my pet-sitting client."

"That's what he said. You must have been broadcasting your thoughts."

"Guess I'll have to watch that. I'm not used to communicating this way."

"Relax. Let it happen. Your father used to know his mother's schedule, too. You'll be much happier if you don't fight your nature."

"Well, I'm not completely freaked out about it. That's a start."

"More than that, dear." She reached into her jumper pocket. When she opened her palm on the table, a fistful of gems were in her hand. She scattered them on the table between us. "Since you only have the one crystal, I thought you might like to have backups."

My eyes were drawn to the stones, in particular a stone that was somewhere between pink and purple. It called to me.

"Go ahead. Touch them. Pick them up. You can have as many of them as you like."

I touched the various stones, picking them up, looking through them, but the only stone that felt right was the pinkish one. I stroked the polished surface. It felt sweet, made me feel as if I was encased in a bubble of light.

"You like the amethyst?" Mama beamed as if I'd just aced an exam.

"I've never thought much about stones before, but I really like this one. May I have it?"

"Absolutely. With my blessing. You've made an excellent choice."

"It chose me."

"Even better."

"Hey, hey, hey, look who's here." Daddy carried a basket full of fresh herbs, their pungent fragrances dueling with Mama's soup for precedence. In the other room, the weather-station meteorologist forecast a snowstorm in the northeast.

"Mama already spilled the beans. She said you read my thoughts and knew I was coming."

"That I did." He grinned, bright color flagging his pale cheeks. "I'm proud of you."

"I haven't done anything noteworthy, and I was nearly arrested."

"But you weren't arrested. You're going to show Wayne Thompson you can still think circles around him."

"If you say so." I hadn't actually come to that realization until he said it, but after hearing the words, I knew they were true.

He tapped the side of his head. "You said so."

I sighed. "I don't understand nearly enough about all of this. I know I need to ease your dreamwalker burden, only I don't have any idea how to proceed. I will do whatever you need me to do." I gestured toward the heavens. "But I need it not to interfere with my work or care of Larissa."

"You're willing to be the dreamwalker now?"

"Yeah, I'm willing. I don't want anything to happen to you."

"It's going to be all right." He clapped a hand on my shoulder. Energy filled me. "You're going to do just fine."

"How does this work? How will people know to come to me for dreamwalking?"

"We'll have a gradual transition. I'll walk you through the first couple of times. Once word gets around, people will seek you out."

"Couldn't they just come here?" I wasn't so keen on strangers showing up at my house at all hours of the day and night. "Couldn't you give me a call when a client arrives, and I could come over?"

"We could do it that way, but the source of your power is your home. Your home isn't here. Mine is. To maximize your success, you must utilize every aid possible."

Mama served mugs of steaming tea all around. I pocketed the amethyst. Grateful for the distraction, I sipped my tea. The idea of strangers in my home wasn't to my liking, but Mama and Daddy never had a problem. Neither had I as a kid in their home. We talked a bit more about how we'd work through the transition, and I agreed I wouldn't dreamwalk without my father until I was ready.

"Let's do a practice dreamwalk now," he said.

The idea staggered me. I was theoretically ready, but I wasn't ready-ready. "We don't have any particular information we're searching for. There's no person here requesting we contact their ancestor or loved one."

"What about your case? Why don't we contact your homicide victim from Mallow?"

"I don't know anything about her."

"You know where she was buried."

What did I have to lose? "All right. Let's give it a shot."

I followed Daddy's lead, altering my breathing, slipping through the psychic gateway. We met on the spiritual plane. Shady shapes surrounded us. I ignored them. "Now what?"

"Think about the woman out at Mallow."

All I had was a hand and a location. I tried. And tried some more. "I got nothing."

"That happens sometimes. What else is on your mind?"

We weren't actually conversing out loud, but it felt like a conversation with his thoughts seeming to ring in my ears. Not any weirder or less believable than the rest of the dreamwalker world, when I stopped and thought about it. I concentrated until something occurred to me. "There was this dream a few nights ago. I saw a woman crying."

"Bring the image to your mind. Show it to me."

The dream unfolded as before. The violet-eyed woman sobbed amidst rumpled bedding. Her straight hair was so black it was almost blue. Her pain resonated throughout the airy bedroom, piercing the gauzy bed canopy, bouncing back off the pale walls. Light streamed in the sheers covering the windows, but the woman wasn't aware of the light. She was in a very dark place.

I glanced over at my father. He nodded perceptively, so he saw her, too. "Who are you?" I asked. "Where are you?"

The woman startled visibly, drawing the mossy green linens up to her chin. She wiped tears from her high cheekbones with the back of her slender hands and stared in our direction.

"Ma'am, I want to help. Tell me your name."

She fought for her voice. It came out in a thready whisper. "He called me Angel."

My heart leapt. I had a name. "What's wrong, Angel?"

Big gulping sobs erupted from Angel. "He's gone."

I drifted farther into the room. My hand glided over her silky hair. "I'm sorry."

"I can't live without him. He was everything to me. Everything. Now he's gone." She folded her head down on her knees and wailed.

I exchanged a glance with my father, hoping he would step in and give me a few pointers. His lips pressed close. I was on my own.

"Losing a love is difficult. I know what you're going through. My husband isn't with me anymore. It hit me really hard."

"I don't want to live. I want to die. I would, too, if it weren't for . . ." Her voice trailed off into another sob. "Why is life so complicated? Why can't people live how they want to?"

I didn't have an answer. Daddy nodded toward the ceiling

where we'd entered. I got the message. "You'll be all right, Angel. I know it doesn't feel that way now, but time will ease the pain. We have to go."

We floated through the ceiling, back to the shadowy plain. I glanced over at my father. His face was gray, too gray. "Let's go home," I said.

We awoke to the sounds of dishes rattling in the kitchen, Mama's bean soup, and bright sunshine. Daddy's color was still off.

Energy flowed back into my numb limbs, warming me. Mama guided Daddy to the sofa in the living room. He leaned heavily on her. When he reclined, she lifted his T-shirt and placed crystals on his abdomen. She placed a dark stone on his forehead. Then she cupped his head between her hands and chanted in a near whisper.

Before my eyes, Daddy's color came back. It was as if I were watching time-lapse photography. As his breathing deepened, Mama and I slipped into the kitchen.

"How'd you do that? What did you do?" I asked.

Mama avoided my gaze, busying herself with setting the table. "Your father's chakras are weakened by going through the veil. Dreamwalking always takes a lot from him, but lately the effects have been much worse."

"No wonder he wants me to take over the family business. I had no idea he had such an aftereffect." I hugged my arms tightly around my middle. "Will that happen to me? Will dream-walking take me to the verge of death?"

Mama's smile didn't reach her eyes. "Each dreamwalk is a mini-death, but each dreamwalker responds differently. Your grandmother used to clean her house from top to bottom after she dreamed for someone. Dreamwalking energized her."

"I don't want Daddy risking his life anymore. This has to stop. He can't survive many more of those rugged transitions."

"He will do as he does, dear."

"We'll see about that."

Chapter 21

Back at my kitchen table I thumbed through a stack of bills. The money I'd get for watching Hobo wouldn't cover everything. I'd thought I was in good shape with the Mallow job, but I didn't know when I could get back out there to finish that job. The Mallow timing was out of my hands.

I could make up those business cards to give Buster Glassman, but I'd have to obtain the card templates from a store or online first. Was it even worth the effort? Since I wouldn't help Buster with his gambling scheme, chances were good he wouldn't help me.

A sigh slipped out. Man, I was chasing my tail here. I had enough groceries to see us through for now. But the utility bills, my home equity loan, and the property tax bill. How would I pay them?

Assets. They were always talking about assets on financial shows. I had my truck and this house. That was it. And I'd already taken out a loan on the house to get this far.

I paced the house, wishing for a secret wall safe full of valuables or a chunk of real gold saved for a rainy day. No such luck. Just me, Muffin, and Grandmother Janie's old furniture.

Wait. The furniture. I could sell some furniture. Antiques held up their value. The marble-topped pieces throughout the house were in mint condition. With that thought, I dialed Prudence at the Antique Palace. Prudence's aunt and my grandmother had been friends for sixty years.

"Baxley, how lovely to hear from you." Prudence had a tremor in her voice. "What can I do for you?"

"I'm hoping there's a market for some of the furniture here in the house."

"Your grandmother's antiques? Oh my goodness, I'd kill to have them in my shop." Prudence's thin voice gushed and trilled. "But you can't. Those pieces are heirloom quality. You should hang onto them."

"This wasn't an easy decision. The pet and plant business is slow this time of year. I don't have other employment options."

"Even if I took a few of them, it would be on a consignment basis. There's no way I can pay you what they are worth."

"Why don't you come out here and tell me which items are more sales worthy? That would be a start."

"I don't want to do this, but I will. Janie would skin us alive if she knew we were breaking up her collection."

"She's been dead for five years. She won't care."

Prudence snorted. "Shows what you know. She'll care. But I'm curious as to what all's in that house. I'll be there tomorrow morning."

After I hung up, I felt oddly drained. I hadn't brought any of Roland's and my furniture home with us. It cost too much to ship it across the country. If I sold furniture from the house, there'd be gaps. I stood in the living room and tried to imagine the room without the three marble-topped pieces. It would be empty. And wrong.

This wouldn't be easy.

But I had to generate income. Otherwise, I'd lose the house altogether, which would be the ammunition Roland's parents needed to prove they could provide a better home for their granddaughter than I could. I couldn't let it come to that.

The idea of calling Buster Glassman glimmered in my head. I could try his get-rich-quick scheme. If we won, I'd have some breathing space. But I knew it was a dumb idea. Plus, I didn't want to hang around Buster. For all his handsome looks, he was a user.

A crisp rap sounded at my front door. Muffin jumped down from the sofa and barked his way to the door. I glanced through the sidelight. Duke Quigley. In clean jeans and a pressed shirt. His broad forehead was furrowed, his eyes and mouth drawn severely down. Why was he so troubled? Why was he here?

I scooped up the squirming dog and opened the door. "Yes?"

"You're a fool for messing with me." He stormed past me into my house in a haze of alcohol, slipping a bit on my small braided rug in the foyer, and halting in front of the carved mantel. His invasion made me downright uneasy. Anger rolled off him in churning waves, filling the room with ugly emotion. I left the front door wide open and reached for the amethyst in my pocket.

"I don't know what you're talking about." I bolstered my shields, protecting myself with a bubble of light. His voice rang true, but his anger concerned me. He was taller than me, outweighed me by at least fifty pounds, but that paunch on his middle wasn't all fat. He'd hefted that axe out at Mallow like a champion weight lifter.

Options for protection raced through my head. My Beretta was in my bedside table. Roland's Glock rested on the top shelf of the pantry. Grandmother's shotgun was in the hall closet. That was the closest weapon. But I couldn't retrieve it, load it, and aim it before Duke overpowered me.

That meant I had to rely on my wits and self-defense skills Roland had taught me. I steadied my breathing, assuming a "ready" athletic stance. He wouldn't be expecting resistance. Guys like Duke thought women were helpless. That was my ace in the hole.

"You screwed everything up," he said. "Why'd you have to

find all those dead people at Mallow?"

My fingers spasmed and accidentally gripped the dog too tight. Muffin yipped. I placed the small dog on the sofa where he paced anxiously. "I didn't do it on purpose."

"Liar. You had to plant that woman near the house. There was nothing but fill dirt there when I had my dozer on-site. That Byrd woman owes me a hundred grand, and she won't pay me a thin dime until she can move in. The cops won't let me near the house to finish my punch list. I need that money. This is all your fault."

I allowed myself a half breath. "Carolina withheld my money, too. I need that final payment. I'm selling this furniture to feed my family."

"It sucks to be you." He crossed the room to snarl in my face. A vein in his forehead pulsed. "What are you going to do about my problem?"

I retreated toward the hall closet. He was so junked up on adrenaline and booze, a little self-defense maneuver wouldn't stop him. If he came after me, it would take a shotgun blast to stop him. "There's nothing I can do. I'm caught in the same bind you are."

"You got ties with the sheriff. Screw his brains out, and he'll make this go away."

My jaw dropped, and I saw red. I marched at Duke, steaming with righteous anger. "Get out of my house. You have no right to barge in here or say such filthy things."

He seemed surprised that I'd backed him all the way to the doorway. He gripped both sides of the door jamb. "I know all about your murdering ways, woman. You can't hide what you did."

Cold fury settled on me. "Get out. Right now."

"Rumor down at the Fiddler's Hole is you killed Roland. Now you're back home to lure another hapless fool into your lair. It won't work with me. You mess in my business, and I mess right back."

I reeled as if he'd punched me. People thought I'd killed my husband? "Who said that?"

"Dr. Sugar. He's spilling his guts at the watering hole. He got fired cuz of you. Well you ain't getting me fired. I know all about you, and you aren't getting away with one more thing. Hell, I bet you set up poor old Maisie Ryals. That woman never did anyone any harm before you came to town."

My blood iced. This fool believed every word he spoke. There was no reasoning with a drunk. "I don't know what you had for lunch besides booze, but you're trespassing. Get off my property, or I'll call the sheriff."

His crooked teeth flashed in my face. "I'm leaving, but mark my words, I'll get even. I know your weakness."

My heart stalled. "You touch a hair on my daughter, and I will hunt you down like a mangy dog."

"The kid's not part of this." He raised his right hand up, curling his fingers into a tight ball. Without warning, the coiled fingers darted toward my face, stopping just short of impact.

The hissing sound Duke made froze my lungs. God, no. He knew I hated snakes. A shudder rippled through me.

He nodded in satisfaction, pivoted on his booted heel, and hurried away. I locked the door behind him and raced to the closet for the shotgun. Tears fell unchecked as I patrolled my house, gun in hand, tiny Muffin trotting at my heels.

Once the premises were secured, I sank down to the heart pine floor with the shotgun.

Damn him.

Double damn him.

CHAPTER 22

By the time the bus came, I'd calmed down enough to put the gun back in the closet. Duke Quigley wasn't a nice man. He definitely had it in for me. But I couldn't let him get to me. Staying vigilant was the key. Avoidance was good, too.

Larissa dragged her heels down the grassy driveway. Guilt assailed me. I'd been so busy worrying about our financial future, I hadn't paid enough attention to my daughter. Had the trauma from my day spilled into her head again? We sat at the kitchen table drinking apple juice and eating peanut butter on crackers. She pushed the crackers around on the plate without eating them.

The silence weighed heavily on me. "What's wrong?"

"Nothing."

I tried again, peering under the curtain of her long hair. "It doesn't feel like nothing. It feels like something."

Her shoulders sagged. She shook her head.

The ache in my heart intensified. My kid was hurting, and I needed to make it stop. "I'm so sorry about today. I thought I'd shielded my thoughts so you wouldn't be bothered. I apologize if they spilled over into your head."

She kept her gaze on the plate. "They didn't."

Well, that was progress. I was learning how to cope with my extrasensory abilities. What else could be wrong? "Did I forget an appointment at school?"

She shook her head again.

I found it harder and harder to breathe. What was troubling her? What could be so awful that she couldn't even talk about it? "Is it about the food stamps? Are the kids at school giving you a hard time about us being poor?"

Dead silence.

I reached for her hand. "Whatever this is, we can get through it. Please, let me in. I want to help. If I've embarrassed you, I apologize."

She swiped her cheek with the back of her other hand. "It isn't about you. Everything isn't about you. I have problems too."

I gently squeezed her hand. "Let me help."

Slowly her head came up. Tears spilled out of her sad eyes. Anger churned in my gut. I'd fix this all right. Whoever had hurt my daughter would answer to me. And by God, they'd better not ever cross either of us again.

I couldn't stand the distance between us. I opened my arms, and she scooted onto my lap, dumping poor Muffin on the floor. She sobbed in my arms. I stroked her hair. "It's okay. Whatever it is, we can fix it."

Her tears subsided in time, but she still clung tightly to me. "Tell me about it," I prompted.

"It's Marcus," she whispered.

"Marcus?" I didn't recognize the name.

"The new boy."

Larissa had been jabbering about her new friend for days. I waited in agony.

"He doesn't like me anymore."

Compassion drowned my fear. I knew what it was like to be excluded. Kids at school had shunned me because I was different. That aspect of human nature hadn't changed in twenty years. I stroked my daughter's silky hair and down her back. "I'm so sorry."

"I thought he really liked me, Mom."

"Did he hurt you?"

She nodded against my chest.

"How?"

"He didn't sit by me at lunch. And he gave Rozella the drawing he made. It was a sea monster. The sea monster I asked him to draw for me. He gave it to her."

"Oh, dear."

She sat up straighter. Her emerald eyes met mine. "I thought he liked me, but he wouldn't even talk to me today."

"Why? What changed?"

"That's just it. I don't know. I thought we were best friends. But now he's best friends with Rozella. She's pretty. All the boys like her."

The tightness in my chest eased. This wasn't about the bodies I'd found at Mallow. This was fourth-grade drama. "She won't be content with one boy for long. I had a Rozella in my class, too."

"You did? The same exact name?"

"Different name, but a pretty girl. Every boy in our class was crazy about Juanita. If she dropped her pencil, boys fell on the floor to pick it up."

Larissa snorted. "Silly boys."

"Boys and girls like each other for different reasons. If you and Marcus are meant to be friends, he'll make it up to you. Give him time. Meanwhile, just be yourself. Don't be spiteful or mean. That always backfires."

"I wanted him to come over tomorrow."

"I know you're disappointed. Marcus will realize he's made a mistake soon enough. And if he doesn't, he isn't the kind of friend you want."

"Like Charlotte?"

I nodded. "Charlotte and I went through a lot together. We'll always be friends. We stayed friends even though I didn't live here anymore. That's how you can tell who your friends are. They want to stay connected to you. If Marcus doesn't want that, it's best to find out now."

"What about Dad?"

My sense of calm evaporated. "What about him?"

"Did you know he was the one for you the first time you saw him?"

I exhaled in relief. "Nope. I didn't know. He'd never noticed me before my junior year. We'd been in the same school forever, but we'd never spoken to each other outside of class. Then he filled up the empty space in my life. I didn't trust him in the beginning. Boys shied away from me and Charlotte. But Roland won me over, and I'm glad he did because I have you."

Larissa reached for a cracker. "I'm glad, too."

The sound of weeping penetrated my slumber. It was the woman again. Angel. Back in the rumpled bedding, crying her heart out again. I called her name. She glanced up, recognized me, and collected herself.

"You! How are you here?" she asked.

The shadows in the room lightened. I sat on the canopied bed with Angel. She smelled of exotic spices. "We meet in my dreams."

"How is that possible?"

"I don't understand it either. But here we are. Did your love return?"

She shook her head sadly. "He's gone, and I have to leave this place. Our place. My heart is breaking all over again."

"Tell him your feelings. You can patch things up."

Violet eyes drooped. "I can't. He died."

The pieces of this puzzle fell into place. Somehow my psyche had picked up on her distress across the miles. I was supposed to do a dreamwalk for her to contact her loved one. But could I do it without my father? I wanted to help her.

"Sometimes I'm able to speak with the dead," I began hesitantly. "But it doesn't always work, so I can't promise success. Describe your lover for me."

"I don't understand, but I need help." Angel's tight grip on the cover released, revealing a lacy spaghetti-strap negligee, the likes of which I'd never owned. The tasteful beige color flattered her creamy complexion and contrasted with her long dark hair.

"Tell me about him."

"He's handsome, sexy, generous, tender. Everything I ever wanted in a man."

"What's his name?"

Her eyes rounded. "I can't say his name. I can't. He made me promise never to say it. I call him Jay. I miss him so much. I'm sick to my stomach with grief."

"Why the secrecy?"

Angel smiled sadly, her image fading into the ether. "I have Jay's heart, but another woman owns his soul."

CHAPTER 23

Prudence from the Antique Palace called first thing Saturday morning. "Baxley, I need to cancel."

I'd dashed around dusting and vacuuming my furnishings for nothing? My hope of financial rescue dimmed, and a faint pounding in my head intensified. I threaded my fingers through my ponytail. "I'm so sorry to hear that. Is everything okay?"

She chuckled. "As okay as it ever gets. Something has come up, though, something I left a little too late. I know you wanted to do this, but I'm not available today or anytime soon."

The force of her lie nearly blinded me. I staggered over to the sofa and sat. "I see."

"Do you? Well, then, it's all for the best. Give my love to that beautiful daughter of yours and to your parents."

She clicked off, and I was left holding the warm phone against my ear. I snapped the phone closed, listening to the familiar sighs and creaks of this old place. I'd always loved this house and every stick of furniture in it. Deep down it felt right not to be selling the furniture.

Along with that satisfaction was a burning curiosity. Why did Prudence lie? Was she in trouble?

Muffin trotted down the stairs, his tiny paws ticking on the bare wood risers. He gazed at me expectantly as he did his morning pee-pee dance. Though Prudence's lie rankled, I was pragmatic enough to realize I couldn't do anything about it right now. I could, however, make one small dog very happy by letting him outside.

We charged out the back door, and there on the steps was a basket of fresh vegetables. I picked up one of the jumbo turnips and savored the earthy fragrance. The onions were baseball-sized globes, the mustard greens leafy. A still warm loaf of cornbread and a bag of hulled pecans completed the content list.

I glanced around. Who had done this? Birds chirped. The sun shone. Nothing seemed out of place. Nothing felt wrong. Hmm. Daddy used to explain away the bundles of food that appeared at our door as karma. Was this food basket karma? Had karma somehow found its way to my house?

Muffin looked up at me expectantly. I sniffed the mouthwatering fresh cornbread again, unshielding my senses to search for the face of my benefactor in the nearby woods. Nothing. Well not nothing exactly. White light. Lovely, embracing white light. I hugged it close and powered down my search. Joy flooded through me.

"Thanks!" I shouted. I could get used to karma.

My voice echoed through the thick pines bordering my property. I carried the basket in and set it by the sink. I'd have a tomato sandwich for lunch, and I'd cook up the rest for dinner. Stewed tomatoes and onions sounded great alongside a mess of collards.

On the way back outside, I caught a glimpse of myself in the microwave door. I'd pulled my hair back in its customary ponytail this morning, but I'd skipped the ball cap because I'd had a low-grade headache all morning. I hadn't wanted a hatband to intensify the headache.

Wait. I looked twice at my reflection. My widow's peak area seemed lighter in color. Significantly lighter than my dark brown hair. What the heck?

I hurried to the bathroom under the stairs to get a better look, Muffin at my heels. Sure enough, my hair looked different. Removing the hair tie, I pulled the ends of my hair forward, threading my fingers through various dark strands, examining them in the incandescent light. I dug another mirror out of the vanity drawer and checked the back of my head.

Nothing different there.

Only the one pale spot in the front.

Pale was putting it mildly.

In an area the diameter of a quarter, the roots and about half an inch of my shoulder-length hair was devoid of color. It had bypassed gray and gone straight to snowy white. The texture didn't feel any different, but it felt heavier to my fingers.

Out of the blue, a memory popped into my head. One of my father teaching me how to fish. Back then, he'd had a streak of white hair in the front, too. I hadn't thought about that in a long time. Daddy's thick mane of hair had gone white all over not long after that.

Would that happen to me? Was this the downside of karma?

I wasn't vain about my appearance, but at twenty-eight, I wasn't ready to look like a senior citizen. Something had to be done. Charlotte would know how to fix this. She'd fooled around with hair color in high school.

I heard the patter of steps overhead, the creaking of old wood as Larissa clumped down the stairs. I didn't keep secrets from Larissa, but this hair thing was too new, too upsetting to think about. I needed to come to terms with it first. I grabbed my hair up in a ponytail and stuffed it under a ball cap.

"Morning!" I thought I sounded pretty cheery for a woman with a headache.

Larissa yawned. "You've been busy, Mom. Vacuuming. Talking on the phone. Shouting outside. What's going on?"

"Someone was planning to stop by this morning, but they cancelled. Then when I let Muffin out, there was a basket of food outside."

"Like at Mama Lacey and Pap's?"

"Yeah. Like that."

She nodded, unfazed by this unexplained development. "Cool."

"Very cool," I echoed. "Let me fix you some breakfast before I go take care of Hobo."

Larissa bounced a bit. "Can I come, too?"

"Sure."

We ran Hobo around his neighborhood, gave him lots of hugs and attention, then headed over to my parents' house. Larissa seemed to have put Marcus out of her mind, and I was glad to have my sunny daughter back. We spent the morning there, painting and visiting with Mama and Daddy. I helped Larissa paint a sea monster on the west side of the cottage.

My headache persisted, and I ended up leaving Larissa there to paint in the rest of the sea. On the way home, Charles Rankin called. His wife had become ill on their trip, and they'd cut their trip short. Bottom line, my gig with Hobo was up. Worse, my check would be smaller due to the reduction of service.

I parked in my driveway and walked back out to the road to collect the mail.

Maybe karma would send money my way today. With a light step, I hurried to the street-side box and pulled out the mail.

I sorted through the pile quickly. Junk. Junk. Bill. Catalogue. And a letter from Carolina Byrd. Hard to miss that embossed stationery and the shiny white envelope.

My fingers tightened around the slick paper. If the check was in here, I had a financial reprieve. I tucked the other mail under my arm and ripped into the expensive envelope, making it as far as the front porch steps before I pulled out the embossed note card.

No check fluttered out.

The words leapt off the page, sticking in my throat, knifing through my gut. My services were no longer required. She was dissatisfied with the service I'd provided, and since the job was incomplete, no final payment was due.

I sank down on the steps. The sunny warmth faded, and a chill permeated my bones. Fired. I'd never been fired from a job before. My gut twisted. Moisture dotted my palms.

There had to be a mistake. I must have misread the note. Drawing in a shaky breath, I read it aloud, one word at a time. At the sound of my voice, Muffin finished his sniffing patrol of the front yard and hurried my way.

I was right. I had been fired. And not just fired. She would have me arrested if I trespassed on her land.

Air huffed out of my lungs. How was this possible? I had her *Podocarpus* here, and it was a twin to the one installed on the other side of Mallow. She'd want that tall shrub and her weeping cherry.

But not as much as I wanted that last thousand dollars I was due.

What was I going to do?

I rubbed my eyes. My income opportunities had dried up faster than a July mud puddle. I had no pet clients, other than Muffin, who we were watching for free, no contracted landscaping jobs, no chance at being a psychic consultant for the sheriff. On the flip side, I'd agreed to take on the dreamwalking business from my dad, but that didn't pay an income.

The Army still stonewalled me about my widow's benefits, and with good reason. They couldn't admit Roland was alive. The small government stipend we received for Larissa and food stamps wouldn't get us through. I'd counted on this job from Carolina Byrd paying in full and generating referrals. With this letter, that opportunity faded into a dust mote.

I'd call her. Reason with her. Beg if I had to.

Carolina Byrd didn't answer my call. The phone rang and rang.

Her voice mail did not pick up.

Dread gathered in my heart.

Something was very wrong here.

CHAPTER 24

The summons to the sheriff's office wasn't entirely unexpected. But I was surprised they didn't send a squad car to haul me to jail. I'd been torn about what I should do with Larissa. Should I take her back over to my parents or should she hang out with Charlotte? A glance in the mirror reminded me I needed to talk with my best friend about hair color, so I headed there with Larissa first.

"Playing hooky from church this morning?" I asked after she'd invited us in. My daughter and I eased around Charlotte's waist-high stacks of magazines, newspapers, and electronics that had been retired in place. We followed my friend's magenta-clad body through the dark and dust. I was thankful for Charlotte's Day-Glo wardrobe. If we made a wrong turn in this maze, we could still find her.

At one time the furniture in her parlor had been visible, but it had succumbed to the encroaching tide of Charlotte's possessions. Like me, my friend had inherited her grandmother's furniture, but she'd wanted light-colored wood in sleek contemporary lines instead of dark claw-footed monstrosities that gathered dust in every ornate nook and cranny.

Instead of protecting her inheritance, Charlotte had treated it like shelving.

"The choir can make it without me once in a blue moon. What's up?"

I didn't normally drop in on her, but I hadn't called ahead

131

because I didn't want Charlotte to over-think my problems. I waited until we were seated on the rattan furniture on her sun porch. "I have a hair emergency."

Speculation filled her intelligent eyes. "What did you do?"

"Nothing." I yanked off my ball cap and tugged the ponytail holder out. The pressure that had been building inside my head eased; my headache tamped down to a moderate pounding. Charlotte and Larissa sucked in their breaths at the patch of white hair on my head. Overnight, the color had faded from even more of that forelock.

"Man, Mom. That's so radical." Larissa circled around my chair, a goofy grin on her face. She waggled one of her blond braids at me. "Can we add a white streak to my hair, too? I'd be the coolest kid in town."

I blinked. "You want to look like a science fiction reject?"

She punched me lightly on the shoulder. "I want to look like you. That's such a rad look. All the kids in school would be jealous."

"What happened?" Charlotte asked. "Were you bleaching your hair? Was it lemon juice?"

My lips pressed together. "I didn't do anything. It changed overnight. Well, in two nights. At first the white part was the size of a quarter and now look. It's a hank of hair. Right in the center of my head. I could be the only Gray Panther under the age of thirty. We have to fix this."

"You sure about altering this new look?" Sunlight sparkled off Charlotte's narrow glasses. "Larissa's right. This is a serious kick-ass look. No one would mess with a woman who looks like she can perform superhuman feats."

I rubbed my eyes. "God. I am a mutant. Roland's parents get a whiff of this, and they'll say I'm an unfit parent. They'll petition the courts again to take Larissa."

"I'm not going anywhere. The Colonel and Elizabeth can

petition all they want. We belong together."

"If only it were so black and white. They've got power and money. I've got neither."

"You've got me," Larissa said.

"Me, too," Charlotte chimed in. "And if you want to dye your hair, we'll do it today. I'll just need to slip over to the drugstore to find the right color for you."

I gathered my shoulder-length hair in a ponytail and donned the cap. The pounding in my head intensified. "This is the strangest thing. Every time I put this hat on, I get a screaming headache."

"Hmm." My friend reached over to a straw hat covering the bucket of brand-new gardening tools I'd bought her for her last birthday. "Try this one."

I switched hats, though big and floppy wasn't my style. The hat fit loosely, but the headache intensified to the point of nausea. I took it off and felt better. Charlotte and Larissa gazed at me expectantly.

"This is weird. My headache is a killer when I wear a hat."

My daughter flashed a radiant smile. "The universe wants you to show off your new look. It's like fate or something."

Fate.

Or karma.

Either way, I didn't want it. "I have to wear a hat in my line of work. The bugs won't leave me alone otherwise. And my eyes. I need to protect them."

"You wear sunglasses," my friend pointed out helpfully.

"This is nuts. I want my old life back."

"Not me," Charlotte said. "I'm happy with my new life. Two of my articles have been picked up by the Associated Press, and I've been interviewed on television. That's pretty darned good for a reporter in Podunk, USA, pardon my French, Larissa. I shouldn't be cussin' in front of you."

"That's okay. I know you're a good person."

I cleared my throat. "Touching as this tender moment is, I've got another favor to ask. Would you take Larissa with you to get the hair dye? I'll pay for it, but I have to run another errand."

Charlotte's narrow glasses rose on her freckled nose. She cocked her head to one side. "Oh?"

I took a deep breath. "The sheriff wants to see me."

"Is this about the bodies you found?" She leaned forward, the rattan underneath her squeaking. "Is there a story for the paper here?"

"Honestly, I don't know. But I'll make the required appearance, then I'll come back here. Deal?"

"Only if you promise to tell all."

My eyes watered at the strong ammonia smell. "How long does this stuff have to cook on my head?"

"Not long." Charlotte capped the bottle and took the gloves off her hands. "I held up my end of the bargain. Spill, sister."

Larissa munched on animal crackers. "Yeah, Mom. Spill."

"It was fairly amazing, actually. The state archaeologist was there. She confirmed that there were three bodies in the first exhumation."

"Wait." Charlotte dashed over to her tote for a notepad. She huffed back to the kitchen table. "Okay. Continue."

"That's just it. There wasn't much more. That's how I was able to beat you back here. They told me the news, and then I walked out."

"They must have said something else," Charlotte prodded.

"They are issuing a press release midweek on their findings."

Charlotte beamed. "A press release. That's more like it. I wonder if I can catch them before they leave today."

"Not a chance. They left when I did. But there was something I noticed."

"What?"

"Gail Bergeron looked at me differently."

"How?" my friend asked.

"Like I was a bug under a microscope. Good thing she didn't know about my mutant hair. I don't think I can take much more of this hair dye. It's burning my scalp."

"Yikes. Let's wash it out," Charlotte said.

Dutifully I hung my head over the kitchen sink and let her rinse me with the sprayer nozzle. Using an old towel, she dried my hair. At the set expression of her jaw, I knew something was wrong. My stomach rolled. "What?"

"Not only are you resistant to hair dye, that entire length of hair is now snowy white."

I hurried over to the microwave to get a glimpse of my hair. Sure enough, even though it was dripping wet, that entire forelock was completely devoid of color.

I was a bona fide freak of nature.

CHAPTER 25

Could my life get any more fouled up? I had a missing husband, rising debt, striped hair, and no immediate employment prospects. Plus I was a murder suspect. In the history of crappy Mondays, this one took the prize.

I couldn't remember the last time I'd stood in the pantry sneaking a spoonful of peanut butter. Technically, the jar and the pantry were mine, so I wasn't sneaking anything, but I relished the illicit sensation anyway. Roland used to sneak peanut butter, too. I smiled at the memory of what his tongue could do to a spoon.

Opening the jar, I scooped out a mound of the gooey stuff, savoring the rich scent. I half-nibbled, half-licked the thick spread until my spoon was clean. My eyes closed in heavenly bliss. I waited for inspiration to strike.

Nothing.

Not even a half-baked idea

Chocolate. I needed chocolate—brain food. I munched on a handful of semisweet chips, followed by a crisp apple. No brilliant ideas on how to better my situation emerged. And if I kept eating at this rate, I wouldn't fit into my clothes.

I yawned, thinking how easy it would be to climb back in bed and sleep for a few years. Not a good thought at ten in the morning.

I should be out in the world, working, only I had no work. Muffin padded into the kitchen, quivering with excitement from fluffy head to fluffy tail. He must have smelled the peanut butter. I loaded up a doggie chew toy with the stuff for him. The Shih-poo darted out of the kitchen with his treasure clamped between his teeth.

My victory with the state archaeologist over the number of dead in that first gravesite hadn't landed me a job with the sheriff's department. Now they were checking historical records to see if my "hunch" about the Robert Munro family was correct. Being a potential suspect in the Mallow woman's killing had dashed those consulting hopes. But the puzzle of the woman's murder called to me. If I solved the case, chances were good I'd be reconsidered for that consultant job. Only I had no leads, and no access to the property.

An idea flickered to life. I could sneak into the morgue. If I touched the victim again, really touched her with my senses wide open, I might learn who she was.

Or I could try to find her in a dreamwalk. But I had no context. No way to draw her to me through the mist of the spirit world. That was not wise, to blindly stumble around out there without a focus.

But if I went to the morgue, I would literally be walking among the dead, picking up the energy of all who'd passed through the funeral home, the grief and despair of their family members. Not fun. But it was the best idea I had.

So it was off to the morgue then.

Resolved, I gathered myself for the trip into town. No way was I heading out without a weapon. Buster and Duke were out there somewhere. Glock or Beretta? I went with the smaller gun, slipping it under the waistband of my jeans and covering the grip with my T-shirt. I tucked the amethyst in my front pocket and made sure the moldavite pendant was secure around my neck. I carefully wove the hank of white hair into the middle of my ponytail, then clapped a ball cap on top of the glowing forelock. God willing, no one would find out about my hair anomaly for a long time to come.

My phone rang when I was halfway into town.

"You thought about my offer?" Buster Glassman's polished voice ruffled my nerve endings in a bad way. My fingers spasmed on the phone. I gripped it tighter.

Dotted lines on the highway sped by. "I'm going to pass on that opportunity."

"You know you need the money. This is win-win for both of us. Real estate is slow right now, and I'll bet your business is slow, too."

I caught up with a log truck. Bits of bark swirled past my windshield. "So?"

"Joining together in a new venture would save both of us. I'll even cut you in on some of my winnings."

I worked my back teeth apart. "No. I don't gamble. I don't have money or time to waste."

"Sweet thing, you gamble every time you get into a car, every time you get behind a log truck on the highway. You gamble that someone won't hit you or your kid."

The fine hairs on my neck snapped to attention. I glanced in my rearview mirror and surveyed the deserted road, sure that Buster's monster truck was bearing down on my bumper. No one was behind me, but that didn't stop my heart from racing. "You threatening me?"

"Why would I do a thing like that?" he oiled into my ear. "You're my ticket to the big show. I want us to work together."

He mumbled something else. Something dark. His sinister tone took my breath away. "What was that? I didn't quite catch what you said."

"I said, if you don't help me, you'll regret it."

The sun still shone, but the color drained from my sight. I shivered. "That sounds like a threat."

"Why would I threaten you when I can ruin you with a few carefully placed words here and there? I don't need threats, not when I've got the ear of homeowners across the county. You want new landscaping business? You better play ball with me."

The connection ended. My hands shook so much that I pulled over and dug out the amethyst crystal. I ran my fingers over the smooth stone until a sense of calm returned. Buster Glassman was not a nice man. He'd threatened me all right. He'd threatened to ruin my business and suggested that a traffic accident was in my future.

Was it possible that Buster, a man from one of the "better" families, had strayed across the line between right and wrong? I believed it. But how far into the garden of good and evil had he strayed?

Had I just conversed with a killer?

CHAPTER 26

He couldn't threaten me and get away with it. I changed my destination from the morgue to the jail. Leaving my gun in the truck, I blustered my way past Tamika back into Sheriff Wayne Thompson's lair.

He hung up the phone as I entered. Tamika must have warned him I was here. A thick stack of folders occupied the center of his desk. He yanked off his reading glasses and rose. Tension radiated from his athletic body. His eyes narrowed in speculation.

I sailed on in as if I had an engraved invitation. "I thought you should know Buster Glassman just threatened me."

Wayne gestured to the empty chair. He continued to regard me with his cop eyes. "Sit." We sat.

"He said he would ruin me," I stated.

"You want to file an incident report?"

"Nope. I'm here to tell you this man is a worm."

"Already knew that."

"An evil worm. He hinted that Larissa and I would get into a nasty traffic accident."

"We should write up a report."

"I don't want a report. I want him to behave."

He leaned forward with a boyish grin. "You want me to rough him up for ya?"

A squeak came out of my throat. "I want to go about my business without having to worry about Buster Glassman breathing down my neck."

"What does he want?"

"He thinks I can help him. You know, use my psychic powers and make him rich."

"Can you do that?"

I shot him a look of exasperation. "If I could do that, would I be worrying so much about my unpaid bills?"

Wayne shrugged. "I can't arrest him for being a jerk or he'd'a been rotting in jail for years. He's got a mean streak when it comes to women."

Buster had a mean streak, and we had a dead woman. That information ping-ponged through my head. "He does?"

"Roughed up a couple of escort women a few years back."

"Escorts? He can't get a date?" I blinked. "We have escorts in Sinclair County?"

"Nah. He got tangled up with a pair of Savannah women four years ago. Their pimp beat the crap out of him. Knocked out both his front teeth. That perfect smile? Fake, just like him."

"Is he a suspect in the Mallow woman's murder?"

"Absolutely."

"Am I still a suspect?"

"Absolutely. I am not close to solving that case. Can't ID the chick."

"I have a favor to ask." I swallowed around a lump in my throat. "I want to see the woman. The dead woman. I want to see if there's anything I can learn from her."

"You're not working the case. You're a suspect."

"I understand, but if I learned anything that leads you to hard evidence, that would help us both. Win-win." I echoed Buster's words to me.

"I don't know. It sounds irregular."

"Of course it's irregular. But since when have you played one-hundred percent by the rules? You could have a deputy there to make sure I didn't destroy evidence."

"The autopsy is complete. There is no evidence to destroy. All we have is a woman who was shot."

Shot. I had suspected that but hadn't known that for sure until now. Hmm. Maybe I wouldn't suck at investigation. "What else do you know?"

He waved dismissively. "It's all in Gail's autopsy report. A young female of mixed race. Mid-twenties. Physically fit and pretty." He paused as if remembering her features. "She had a nice rack, all natural. I verified them myself."

I rolled my eyes. "Nobody reported this woman missing?"

"She doesn't match any missing person report in the state."

"May I see her?"

He studied me. Was he weighing the pros and cons?

I amped up my campaign. "I have seen a dead body before, and I didn't pass out. Plus, I helped you flesh out Buster Glassman as a murder suspect. He had opportunity with his easy access to the property. Now we know he had the means as well. All you need is a motive, and you've got your man."

"Or woman," he added sternly.

"I want to clear my name. I need this job consulting for the sheriff's department. Please let me try with the dead woman. It won't cost you anything."

"I know that. I'm hesitating for your sake. Right now you're a civilian. If you clear your name and consult for us, you will be forever stuck with images of dead people in your head. Is that what you really want?"

"I want to keep a roof over my head. I want to pay my bills in full. I want a chance to make it on my own. If my best shot at self-sufficiency is through helping you, so be it. I've got dead people in my past and in my future. Daddy handed off his dreamwalker job to me, though that isn't a paying job either."

Wayne tapped his fingers together, his expression thoughtful.

"What the hell. Let's give it a shot."

The morgue occupied the back of the Marion Funeral Home. We didn't have a hospital in the county. Marion Funeral Home was the only game in town for dead people.

Billy Ray Jordan, funeral director, greeted us in the spacious but rundown foyer, once the parlor of the former home. Billy Ray could have given Dr. Sugar lessons in being a walking cadaver. His threadbare suit hung on his narrow frame, but his dark brown eyes glinted with intelligence.

"Got a new lead on the victim's ID," Wayne said. "We need to take another look at the body."

Billy Ray's eyes rounded. "You talk to Dr. Bergeron about that?"

"Dr. Bergeron isn't running the murder investigation. She's the acting coroner right now. That's the extent of her authority." Wayne pointed to the shiny gold badge on his waist. "This says I'm in charge. You got a problem with me looking at my murder victim?"

Billy Ray's hands shot up in defeat. "No problem, sir. Right this way."

We walked down a narrow hallway, dimly lit by an overhead globe. Billy Ray opened the door at the end of the hall and traces of the former residence vanished. This room was all stainless steel, chilled air, and a wall of people-sized vaults.

My nerves flared up, past the cautionary range of yellow alert, all the way to orange, one step away from a full-fledged panic attack at red alert. I reached for my moldavite pendant. I needed the momentary calm before I plunged into the abyss.

"Change your mind?" Wayne asked.

In that moment I knew he'd expected me to fail, knew he thought I was too much of a wimp to do this. My competitive instinct rose to the challenge. "Yeah, I'm ready."

Wayne glanced toward the door Billy Ray had just exited through. "Get going. We've probably got five, maybe ten minutes before Gail gets here."

I listened to the sounds of the house, extending my senses through the walls. Sure enough, I heard the funeral director talking on the phone. I nodded. "He's calling her right now."

"Figured as much." He slid out a metal shelf complete with a body bag. "Her face is messed up from the bullet. You can do the woo-woo thing with her shoulder or arm or something, right?"

My gaze fixed on the zippered bag as he opened the black bag, sliding the zipper past the bandaged head, exposing a pale shoulder and an arm. The chill of the room infiltrated my defenses. I caught the rancid odor of meat gone bad, and my gut clenched. I gripped the edge of the metal table for support.

"Baxley?" Concern etched the grim brackets around Wayne's mouth.

"I'm okay." I removed my pendant and handed it to him. Icy cold air socked me hard, the antiseptic scent of the room no match for the decay processes in this woman's body.

I zoomed past red alert as my head filled with whispers of those who'd passed through this room. I swallowed hard. I could do this. I would not go insane. I wouldn't become a whack job like my Uncle Emerald.

With iron resolve, I touched her pale shoulder. Her flesh was cold to my touch, cold and hard. Time stretched and folded and spun. I tumbled through the vortex of time and space, anchored to the dead woman. Snatches of conversations blasted past at alarming speeds. My head whipped this way and that, until I remembered my early training.

"Don't fight it," my father had said all those years ago. "Think of it as a roller-coaster ride through a fun house. You'll be where you're going in a heartbeat. All the rest is blurred scenery along the route."

I visualized sitting in a small, open car with the woman, and the whirling tumbling freefall lessened. We coasted to a stop in a wooded area. I stepped from the car into the moonlight.

A hooded figure waited alone. Another person approached wearing a fedora, the wide brimmed hat shading the person's facial features. Both people in the dreamscape were of average height and weight; both radiated high levels of tension.

"Hello?" the hooded figure asked. "Who's there?"

It was a woman's voice, thin and trembling with emotion.

"He isn't coming, you fool. Did you think I wouldn't find out, *Lisa*? Did you think I didn't know about your weekends at Warm Springs? You will never see him again."

Hat person's voice was low and dangerous, a barely controlled rage. I couldn't tell if it was a man or a woman. I shuddered in dread at what was to come.

"I don't understand," Lisa continued. Fear tinged her voice. She edged back toward the ring of trees.

I silently urged her to run, but this dreamscape from the dead woman's mind wouldn't allow me to interfere. I could only watch events unfold like a movie reel, knowing that it would turn out bad. *Focus.* What can I take back to the real world to help us solve the case?

Both participants wore dark clothing, and I saw neither face. I didn't need to see the dead woman's face, but I keenly wanted to view her interrogator's face. The shadows deepened.

"Your boyfriend missed your last little appointment, didn't he? You sent him an email to his private account. It's over, whore. You can't have him."

Ah, the aggressor felt betrayed. The pieces fell into place. Lisa was in a love triangle.

"We never meant to hurt you," Lisa said.

"A little late for apologies, don't you think? I could have forgiven him for another slight indiscretion, but you've been going at it like bunnies for three years. Three years."

Lisa kept stepping backward. Her killer matched her step for step. Fear radiated from Lisa's body. "Run," I screamed. I ran to her side, shouted in her ear. "This person's going to kill you." My words fell on deaf ears. I was the ghost here. I couldn't change the past. A sob ripped from my throat.

"He loves me," Lisa insisted. "We are building a life together."

The killer slowly pointed a gun at Lisa. "He will never leave me, you fool. The money is mine, and he is a slave to my fortune. You're roadkill on the highway of his life."

Lisa's hands went up, shielding her face and torso. "No! I don't believe you."

The killer's gun leveled out shoulder high. "Believe this."

My gaze riveted on the pistol in the killer's hand. It looked like Roland's Glock, maybe smaller. The killer was right-handed. A filigreed silver ring glinted in the moonlight. The gun roared. Lisa fell backwards on the ground, her face imploding into an unrecognizable mass of flesh and bone.

I tumbled back through time and space, drawn to my earthly form by a sense of urgency. Nothingness ebbed. I gradually became aware of a woodsy fragrance. Of strong arms wrapped around me, of comforting warmth.

Wayne's arms.

CHAPTER 27

Wayne's dark eyes drilled into mine. "Hey there."

The room stopped spinning, but I still felt boneless. "What happened?"

"You started to fall. I caught you." His gaze warmed.

Heat rose from my shirt collar. Starch returned to my spine. "Thanks. You can let me go now."

His face loomed closer. "Not just yet. I've a mind to take some compensation. You've put me to a lot of trouble recently."

Tucking my chin, I pushed against his very solid chest. His thickly muscled arms didn't yield. "Don't."

The door opened. Gail Bergeron swept in, her short blond bob shimmering with outrage. "What kind of sick people are you? Good God Almighty, Sheriff. Can't you conduct your tawdry affairs someplace other than the morgue? What the hell kind of town is this? Is every male jacked up on testosterone?"

Wayne pressed my necklace into my hand and stepped in front of me. Calm sped through me, easing the ragged transition from dream world to the present. I wasn't ready to conduct brain surgery, but I didn't have to. All I needed was to get Wayne away from Gail so that I could tell him what I'd learned about the victim. Then I'd be one step closer to being a psychic consultant for local law enforcement.

"Dr. Bergeron. What a surprise." Sarcasm edged his voice.

Gail hustled over to the pull-out shelf. With brisk efficiency, she zipped up the body bag and stuffed Lisa back into the

147

refrigeration unit. "What is the meaning of this? I'm in charge of this morgue."

Wayne had her by at least six inches, maybe more, but the state archaeologist's voice rang with authority, making her sound ten feet tall. Instinctively, I edged toward the door, hoping to avoid further confrontation.

"You may be in charge of the morgue, Doctor, but I'm running the murder investigation. We are investigating a lead."

She arched a pale eyebrow. "Is that what they call it down here?"

Gail's bulldog tenacity concerned me. If I left, she'd come after me, snapping and growling all the way. With Wayne's pit bull mentality, this dogfight wouldn't settle anytime soon, not without damage control.

With a sigh, I stepped around Wayne. "I can explain. The strong smell in here made me woozy. The sheriff caught me before I fell."

"I'll bet he did," Gail said. "I won't have it. I'm writing a report to my superiors about the irregular activity in Sinclair County. Bo Seavey won't be the only one out of a job."

Wayne inflated like a blowfish out of water. "Report all you like. I'm an elected official. Your state pals can't touch me."

I projected calm and peace, hoping to diffuse the situation. "The sheriff was doing his job. I asked to view the victim, to see if I knew her. He said y'all didn't have any leads on identifying the woman, and it wouldn't hurt. But it was harder than I thought."

Wayne took the hint and nodded to the door. "Yeah. I should get you home."

"Wait." Gail stepped into our path. "Did you learn something?"

I sent Wayne a questioning glance. Unless he indicated otherwise, my latest dreamwalk would remain a private matter.

Gail couldn't get me fired because I wasn't officially hired.

"Gail's a hard-ass," he said out loud. "But I trust her."

I met her level glance and gazed away. Part of me wanted to bump her back with my psychic insight; the other part shrieked caution. Given my ongoing battle with Army disbursements, I knew a thing or two about hard-asses and bureaucrats. The trick was to reveal only the barest amount of information. "I didn't get much. I tapped into the victim's last five minutes of life."

Gail edged closer, speculation in her gray-green eyes. "You can do that?"

Once again I glanced at Wayne for direction on how to proceed. His nod was barely perceptible. "Sometimes. I don't choose what I see. It's what the dead want to show me that I have access to."

"Fascinating." Her forehead furrowed. "Go on."

I hesitated, running my thumb over the tips of my curled fingers. Authority figures like Gail had been my adversaries for so long, it felt reckless to speak freely. But this was what consultants did; they helped authorities. If I truly wanted a consulting job, I had to step it up, right now.

I cleared my throat gently. "The dead woman's name is Lisa. She had a three-year affair with her killer's lover, a man named Jay. I've been having visits from her for days as Angel. Anyway, Jay promised to leave his partner or wife but didn't because the killer controlled the money in their relationship."

"You got all that just now?" she asked.

"What about last names?" Wayne scribbled fast on a narrow notepad. "Where did the murder occur?"

As they edged closer, it took everything I had not to retreat. I didn't want any inadvertent physical contact while my senses were still jacked up. "They didn't reveal any last names. I don't know where she was killed. A clearing in the woods somewhere.

Something was said about weekends in Warm Springs."

Wayne glanced up from his note-taking. "Physical descriptions?"

I flipped back to a scene in my mind to double-check my answer before I spoke. "It was nighttime, and the killer wore a hat. Both killer and victim were the same height and weight." I shrugged. "That's all I got."

"What about age? Could you tell the killer's age from posture or voice?"

I nodded too fast. Pain lanced through my head, sliding from one side to the other. I reached up to cradle my temples. It took me a few deep breaths to beat back a twinge of nausea and disorientation. My head pounded. I made a mental note to start carrying ibuprofen for the aftermath of dreamwalking.

"You okay?" Wayne asked.

"Fine," I lied, though his concern was genuine. I was ready for this debriefing to be over. "Lisa's killer had a natural, prowling stride. The voice sounded low-pitched and gritty. I thought it was a man at first. And truthfully, I can't say it isn't a he. But the rage felt feminine."

The sheriff barred his arms. "To summarize, we can't narrow down the crime scene to more than a wooded area. The killer is a wealthy person of unknown race and gender, about five six and a hundred forty pounds, with a partner named Jay."

I was stunned he accepted my findings at face value. I'd expected him to challenge me every step of the way. "I know it isn't much, but it is a start, and more than you had before. It is possible I can contact the victim again in the future and learn more."

"Why wait?" Gail waved toward the stainless-steel wall of vaulted slots. "She's right here."

I tried to summon a smile, but I didn't have one in reserve. The bright overhead lights intensified, causing me to tug the brim of my ball cap lower to shield my eyes. "If she wanted me to see more right now, she'd have shown it to me. I've told you everything I know."

Almost everything. I hadn't described the silver ring I'd seen the killer wearing. It reminded me of a decorative pen I'd seen someone wearing recently.

Until I remembered who wore the pen, my lips were sealed about the ring.

CHAPTER 28

A storm was coming. The turbulent sensation throbbed in the marrow of my bones, down in the tiniest molecule in my red blood cells. Outside my house, not a clump of Spanish moss stirred in the centuries-old oak trees. The birds had gone quiet, too. My headache from yesterday was gone, replaced by a dull ache in my sinuses.

Mama had been our family's weather barometer for years. Now it seemed I'd acquired the forecasting skill as well. I wandered around my yard, tidying up the tools I'd left in the greenhouse, stacking discarded plant containers in the back of my truck along with downed limbs. I moved my hanging baskets into the shelter of the greenhouse with Muffin dogging my heels.

The Shih-poo acted like this activity was a big game, but a sense of urgency hurried me along. I tucked the ferns in next to the tomato plants I'd already started and raked up the oak leaves for my compost pile. It felt good to have something to do. I cautiously opened my senses to enjoy the buzz of nature. A flock of blackbirds winged past noisily, trying to outrun the storm.

As I expanded my listening boundaries, I hit a snag. A cone of no noise that was suspiciously human. My breath hitched at that anomaly. I'd encountered this void before, back during the Ryals investigation. I'd dubbed this person my watcher. Why was he here? What did he want with me?

I fiddled with the tarp cover of my truck bed, tying the corner grommets to eyebolts on my truck frame. I didn't feel threatened by his watching, and I wasn't sure it was a he. But having a gender made the watcher seem less abstract, more like a normal person. Since detecting him, I'd pinged my surroundings periodically and gotten nothing.

Until today.

Now he was back.

I thought about hollering that I knew he was out there, but that was dumb when my gun was in the kitchen. I could send Muffin after him, but who'd be scared of a twenty-pound ball of fluff? I needed a Rottweiler or a pit bull to send after him.

I listened intently, using my extrasensory perception. Nothing, not even the initial void. The person had vanished from my internal radar screen. Whoever this person was, he was very, very good about being invisible.

I hoped it was my missing and presumed dead husband, but I couldn't imagine Roland being so hands off or invisible. He'd want me to know it was him out there in the woods. Perhaps the watcher had to do with the current murder investigation, but I didn't think so.

If it weren't Roland out there, it was someone who wanted Roland, which was way worse. Whatever trouble my husband had found, it was still very much around.

A car pulled up in the driveway. I dampened my senses immediately. Louise Gilroy. With Precious, the high-energy, flat-coated Labrador that belonged to her missing daughter. The dog tugged the leash from her hand, bounded over to greet me, and sniffed Muffin.

I grabbed the leash and quieted Precious down. Once Louise saw I had the dog, she sagged back inside her car. I hurried over and tapped on her window. "Louise?"

She rolled down the window a few inches. Alcohol fumes wafted up to me. For a woman who prided herself on her conservative appearance, Louise Gilroy had taken a wrong turn this morning. She still wore her navy blue housecoat and hadn't bothered with a lick of makeup. Her matted salt and pepper bob had an inch of gray roots, giving her hair a two-toned appearance. With my recent hair woes, my heart went out to her. I tried again. "Louise?"

"I need a break." Her furtive gaze linked with mine briefly. I sensed a chasm of seething darkness. She turned her gaze to the steering wheel. "I'm going away for a few weeks. You said you'd watch Precious for me. Why don't you see if you can find her a better home?"

Her negative emotion doused me like a rogue wave. I mentally staggered under the load and set about clearing it from my person. A ball of white light soon surrounded me, and my thoughts were my own again.

This was a mistake, pure and simple. Once Louise processed her grief, she'd want her pet back. "I'll keep Precious while you're away. Why don't we hold off on a decision until afterwards?"

"I can't keep her. It hurts too much to remember." She flicked a button and her trunk popped open. "Her stuff's back there. Take it."

Louise needed help. Taking care of her dog temporarily wouldn't be a problem. "I will, but I'm doing this because I'm your friend."

It took me four trips to carry the food bowls, the fifty-pound sack of premium dog food, two fluffy dog beds, a heavy sack of doggie chew toys, and a thick accordion file of her veterinary records into my house. I closed the trunk and stepped back up to the driver's window. "All done."

Louise cracked the window again. "You're a lifesaver." Then she sped off.

Great. Now I had two dogs and no paying clients. Precious

was high energy, too. How would I keep her safe? She liked to roam. With the busy highway out front, I'd need a fenced backyard if she stayed here for any length of time. I'd figure it out somehow.

Back in the kitchen, I put together a ground turkey meatloaf for dinner. It was the last package of meat in my freezer. After that was gone, I wasn't sure what we'd eat. Hopes and promises most likely.

My phone shrilled. Charlotte. "Hey."

"Get your butt over here right now." My friend's words were packed with emotion. "You are never going to believe this."

Outside my window, tree branches danced in the wind. Bad weather was nearly here. "A storm's coming." How lame. I'd never been afraid of a storm before, but this one felt different.

"You're right. It's a media storm. A perfect storm. Gail Bergeron had Dr. Sugar arrested for stalking."

My jaw dropped. I glanced around my home to make sure I hadn't stepped in a rabbit hole. "You're kidding."

"Dead serious. The man's in jail. His reputation is in tatters. The Ice Queen is our new coroner."

"I had a run-in with the Ice Queen yesterday." Gail's icy fury and rabid curiosity surfaced in my thoughts. "I hoped she'd be headed back to Hot 'lanta soon."

"Our humble town must cramp her big-time style. But that doesn't stop her from throwing her weight around. She's making an example out of poor Bo Seavey. But that's not all. The television crews will be here any minute."

"What?" I couldn't process the news fast enough. Was this sleepy Sinclair County?

"Yep." Charlotte's ending "p" popped through the phone. "Carolina Byrd pressed charges against Running Wolf. He was arrested for trespassing on her property."

My heart beat wildly. Bo Seavey was lucky he hadn't been

brought up on harassment charges years ago. It was hard to feel sorry for a sleazy womanizer like him, but Running Wolf was a gentle soul. He would wither to nothing behind bars. "Running Wolf is in jail?"

"Yep. The tribal council is coming here to lodge an official protest."

I sagged against the kitchen counter, the dogs at my ankles. "This is all a big mistake. Those weren't even Native American remains out at Mallow."

"What can I say? At this point, the truth is irrelevant. Come help me sort this out. I need a human lie detector to tell who's fibbing."

"Where are you?"

"The jail."

Great. My sucky day just got worse.

CHAPTER 29

A tall, hawk-nosed man in buckskin garb read from a sheaf of papers into a bullhorn in the jail parking lot. From time to time he glanced up, his piercing brown eyes boring into every person in attendance.

"The sacred resting place of our ancestors has been disturbed. The spirits are angry. The land cries for justice. We must cleanse the land. The remains must be returned to their resting place. This abomination is a continuation of a centuries-long war against Native Americans—"

I tuned out the next three pages of rhetoric and half-listened to his call for ceremonial offerings with tobacco. I nudged Charlotte. "Who's that?"

"Jack Soaring Eagle. He's from the State Council on Native Americans. Supposedly someone from the Bureau of Indian Affairs is coming down here, too." My friend shivered with excitement. "Isn't this the coolest thing ever? We got a front-row seat to a full-fledged Indian protest."

A gust of strong wind ruffled papers, flapped poster boards, and buffeted my ball cap. I held my hat until the gust subsided. "These people will be seriously pissed when they find out the remains aren't Native American."

Charlotte snapped another picture. "Who cares? This protest rally is headline news for Sinclair County. We'll be on everyone's map."

"For the wrong reason. We don't want this kind of trouble.

When people feel passionately about injustice, things get out of hand. Think of poor Running Wolf sitting behind bars."

My friend's eyes sparkled. "Do you think they'd let me take his picture behind bars? That would sell a ton of papers."

"Snap out of it. This is his life we're talking about."

"I didn't tell him to protest or trespass. He put himself into this situation. I can help him by making sure his story gets out. Maybe I can overlay an image of bars over an archived photo of him."

She was right. I had to stop projecting myself into Running Wolf's situation. I'd hate being held in a steel cage. He must hate it, too, but it hadn't deterred him from standing up for his beliefs.

Movement over by the lobby doors caught my eye. Gentle Dove stepped out of the law enforcement center and scanned the crowd. She was dressed in a soft leather beaded shift with moccasins, her gray hair braided into two long plaits. I'd never seen her in her Sunday-best Indian garb. She looked one-hundred percent Native American, and in that moment she was.

Proud and noble. Sincere in her beliefs. I wished I had the same self-assurance.

I'd been a rebellious daughter and a compliant wife, and now I was a single mother adrift in the world. I didn't feel proud or noble. I was embarrassed this situation had escalated out of control, upset that a friend of my parents was in jail, mortified that I was here watching the show.

This situation was wrong on so many levels. Charlotte wanted to know who was lying. I was. Jack Soaring Eagle was. The sheriff's office was. The Ice Queen was. A better question might be who wasn't lying.

Gentle Dove touched my arm. "Come. He needs you."

Her words and her touch were infused with urgency, but I

resisted the call. Stepping forward would put me on a collision course with Carolina Byrd, who I hoped would come to her senses once this was over and pay me. Stepping forward would parade my extrasensory differences before the Ice Queen once again. She already thought I was a cross between a lab rat and a party trick.

The wind gusted again. Poster boards sailed through the air, and Gentle Dove caught one in the head. The poster flipped over, upended my hat, and flapped across the parking lot.

As suddenly as it started, the gust ceased. In the unnatural silence that followed, Gentle Dove reverently touched my brand-new shock of white hair. "It is as he foretold."

Charlotte snapped our picture. Too late, my hand shot up to block the shot. "If you print that, you are a dead woman."

"Lying," she said.

People stared at me. Their rapt fascination angered me. "Haven't you ever had a bad hair day?" I yelled.

The imports paid me no heed, but the locals nudged each other and murmured. I cringed and felt a queasy sense of déjà vu. This was my childhood all over again. Those murmurs reminded me of the voices always hovering at the edges of my mind, voices that never dialed in clearly.

"Will you come with me?" Gentle Dove asked.

Going into the jail was not high on my list of priorities, but getting away from all those stares held great appeal. I nodded, then glanced over at my friend.

"Don't mind me, y'all," Charlotte said. "I'm going to hang out here until the news cameras show up."

Gentle Dove linked arms with me, and we walked back up the sidewalk. Jack Soaring Eagle moved aside to let us pass. Questions burned in his eyes, but he didn't ask them. I didn't volunteer any answers.

The soda machine hummed, and the plastic chairs looked

deserted in the lobby. Tamika buzzed us in.

"Hey, Baxley," the dispatcher said. "Long time no see. Got a new doo going on?"

"Tamika." I managed a curt nod. I'd never been much to chat about my hair with anyone, but I sensed that something was needed. "Bad hair day."

Comprehension filled her eyes. "My cousin can take care of that for you. She's a dying fool and can match any hair color."

"Thanks." I smiled as if I'd never considered dying my hair before. "I might take her up on that."

Gentle Dove gave me an odd look, but before she said anything, the Ice Queen and the sheriff intercepted us.

"A word." The sheriff marched me into his office. After he closed the door, he touched my hair. "New look, babe?"

I brushed his hand away. "Why am I here?"

"Running Wolf asked for you." Wayne stopped and frowned. "Actually, he asked for the spiritwalker and sent his wife out to find whoever that was. What's the deal?"

"The deal is Gentle Dove asked me to come in here with her. I don't know why she singled me out."

Wayne studied me. His eyes kept going back to my white shock of hair. "You sure about that?"

"I'm here, aren't I?" Could this conversation get any more inane?

"Here's the thing. We haven't released the race of the first bodies you found. Gail wants to have the names and ethnicity of the people before we go public with that. I don't want you to mention race to Running Wolf."

"You could diffuse the mess outside if you went public with the information. Why the secrecy? It's too late to keep this secret. I already told Charlotte."

He got in my face. "Why the hell did you do that?"

"Because I didn't want her to write some big sappy piece in

the paper that would incite people to stand up and take notice. But I was too late to stop this circus. We should have come clean from the start."

"That was my call. Just as this one is. If you want to work as a consultant for me, you will do as I say."

Hope warred with my headache. "I still have a chance at a consultant's job? Does this mean I'm not a murder suspect?"

"If it turns out you didn't murder anyone, I'll use you." He stepped closer. "I'd love to use you."

The trouble with Wayne was that he couldn't dial back the testosterone. Working with him would be an ongoing struggle. "Knock it off."

His eyebrows waggled. "Can't blame a guy for trying."

"Yes, I can. As sheriff, you have a responsibility to uphold."

"As sheriff I get to make the rules."

"What century are you living in?"

His voice roughened. "You never should have left. Roland had no business spiriting you away from here."

I huffed out a breath of air. "I wouldn't change my past for anything. But I am hoping to improve my future economic outlook. Are you going to act like a grown-up or an oversexed teen?"

Wayne maintained silence for a few agonizing beats. In that time I was sure I'd stepped over the invisible line of power of his office.

"Message received," he said.

I allowed myself another lungful of air.

He nodded toward the door. "You can talk with Running Wolf in the interrogation room. We'll be listening."

Oh goodie.

CHAPTER 30

When I entered the interrogation room, Running Wolf, aka Bob Brown, started with recognition. Was he expecting my father? His gaze sharpened as he studied me, snagging on my white forelock. He rose, his hands cuffed before him.

My heart went out to this humble man. What was Wayne thinking to handcuff him? Running Wolf was probably embarrassed and humiliated. I walked to the side of the wooden table. "You sent for me?"

He reached up and awkwardly stroked the white stripe in my hair. "It is true? You are the spiritwalker now?"

I stepped back, motioned him back to his seat, and sat in the molded plastic chair across from him. "I'm *a* spiritwalker, and yes, I'm stepping into Daddy's shoes. I wouldn't say I am *the* spiritwalker. What can I do for you?"

"I need a voice in the spirit world," he said solemnly.

My heart skipped a beat. My first dreamwalker request. Adrenaline surged in my veins, as did a generous shot of unease. I folded my hands on the table. "Tell me more."

"There's a woman in my dreams. She comes to me each night, but I only see her face. I need a go-between to communicate with her."

Curious, I leaned forward. "Do you know her? What does she look like?"

"She is beautiful, but sad. She's one of my people, but she isn't."

"Huh?"

"Can you help me?"

"Now?" I shivered. Dread danced across my nerves at the thought of performing for an audience. I was barely okay with dreamwalking in private. What should I do?

"Yes, now," he said. "I need to ask her name; then we can help her find peace."

What would Daddy do? Would he ask his friend to wait until it was convenient? No way. Daddy would help Running Wolf as soon as he asked, to help ease the man's mind. Still. I wasn't as skilled as my father. What if I screwed up?

I glanced around the small room, trying not to look at Running Wolf. "I don't know if I can do it here. I haven't had much experience with unassisted dreamwalks."

He regarded me steadily, his dark eyes boring into my soul. "Not to worry. I can help you access the portal, but I can't hear the voices."

I shot another look at the mirror, knowing that the sheriff was there, wondering if Gail Bergeron was out there dissecting my behavior. The door didn't open. It looked like everyone expected me to dreamwalk. I drew in a deep, centering breath.

"Okay." I took off my moldavite necklace, removed the amethyst from my pocket. I placed them on the table off to the side.

Running Wolf covered my hand in his, the rough calluses of his work-thickened palms grazing my knuckles. I breathed in deeper, slower; I listened to the quiet of the room. When the moment presented itself, I crossed into the other world, Running Wolf at my side.

I shot him a happy grin, did a little pirouette on tiptoes. "That was great. I don't even feel disoriented. It's never been so smooth before."

His smile was bittersweet. "We all have our gifts. I'm able to enter the portal easily. I have assisted your father on many spiritwalks."

His voice sounded different. Older. Generations older. His Native American garb looked more rustic, less commercially perfect. His arms hung freely at his sides. I glanced down at my clothing. I had on a white cassock-like thing a priest might wear. A knotted rope snugged the outfit to my waist.

I held my hand in front of my face. It was both solid and an illusion. Interesting. Running Wolf took my arm and guided me down a narrow, dimly lit passageway. He paused before a closed door. We passed through the barrier as if it weren't there.

Inside was a nighttime scene, a blazing campfire, several teepees, and a sky chock full of twinkling stars. I spun in a circle feeling so free, so uninhibited. Running Wolf sat cross-legged by the fire and motioned me over.

I heard a haunting melody, a hummed tune that seemed age-less and familiar. A lullaby perhaps. A mother with an infant emerged from a teepee. The woman's long black hair was braided into two plaits, her cheekbones high and proud. With her gaze fixed on the baby, I couldn't see her eyes, but I assumed they were dark brown. The drowsy babe in her arms was tiny, no more than a few months old.

Could Running Wolf hear the music through me?

The answer came into my thoughts at once, "Yes."

I shot him another question. "Is this the woman you seek?"

"Yes. She is deeply troubled."

"How should we approach her?"

"We wait. She comes to us."

Sure enough the woman and baby circled the fire, the woman's hips gently swaying to her music, the child's eyes drift-ing shut. She looked younger than me. Something about her was familiar, but I couldn't place her.

Running Wolf spoke through me, "Daughter."

She faced Running Wolf. "Yes?"

"I brought the spiritwalker. How can we ease your mind?"

"My baby." She cradled the babe close to her chest. "She knows about the baby. My son isn't safe."

"Who knows?" I asked.

The woman peered into the licking flames of the fire. "The evil one."

I shivered at the hard edge to her voice. The evil one was not a nice person. "You want us to protect the baby? Where is it?"

"The child is with my mother. But they aren't safe."

"I don't understand," I said. "What are we supposed to do?"

"Save my baby. Don't let the evil one get her."

My companion stirred. "Daughter, your name?"

Her gaze connected with Running Wolf. "I am called Angel."

I blinked in recognition. "Wait. Angel? Are you the woman from my dreams?"

Before my eyes, the scene changed from campfire to mussed boudoir. Running Wolf stood at my side. Angel morphed from chaste Indian maiden to grieving sex kitten.

I recognized this scene from my dreams. Angel was the same woman who grieved for her lost lover. I searched my memory for details. "Is this about Jay? Is the babe Jay's child?"

She nodded, her gaze glassy, sobs in her throat. "He made me so happy. He was going to leave her. But his death changed everything. I lost my place and my job, and I almost lost the babe."

"But the baby is with your mother?" I asked.

The spirit woman wavered. "My son is in trouble. The evil one has found him."

"Where is your mother? What's her name?"

"Alabama. Mother lives in Alabama."

She started fading. "Wait!" I stepped toward the woman with the unusual violet eyes. "What's her name?"

"Dyani."

I shot a worried glance at Running Wolf as she faded. He shrugged. "She's gone, and we must return." With that, he guided me back through the portal.

Awareness of my body gradually returned, as did the musty smell of the jailhouse. Energy thrummed through me, and for once I didn't have an after-burn headache. I blinked against the bright fluorescent lights and stretched my arms. "That was wild. Your dream woman walks through my dreams, too."

He nodded. "It is often that way."

I jumped to my feet and paced the small room. "What now?"

"Now you find Little Deer."

I paused, holding onto the back of the plastic chair. "You lost me."

"The woman in Alabama, Dyani. Her name means Little Deer in our language."

"And she's important because— ?"

Running Wolf clasped his handcuffed hands together on the table. "Because Angel came to us in this place and time."

"Is she related to the graves at Mallow?"

"The wheels of fate continue to turn."

Puzzling. Enigmatic. Absolutely no help at all.

CHAPTER 31

The sheriff and the Ice Queen nabbed me as I stepped into the corridor. Somehow I'd known Gail wouldn't pass up an opportunity to see me in action. I didn't know what she planned to do about me, but her interest couldn't be good for my anonymity in the long run.

"Well?" Wayne stepped in front of me, blocking my way. "What did you learn? What was that part about Diane in Alabama?"

With my senses still jacked up, his woodsy cologne took my breath away. Gail's fake smile seemed twice as brittle as usual. I backed up so that I wouldn't inadvertently come in contact with either one of them in the tiled corridor. Fluorescent lights hummed loudly in the suspended ceiling overhead.

My fingers closed around the amethyst in my pocket. I took a deep breath. "We encountered a Native American woman, about my age. She wants us to contact her mother regarding her child."

"A young Native American woman?" Gail's voice carried a sharp edge.

Though I wasn't an aura reader, I could see them sometimes, like now. I glanced over at Gail's pulsing aura. The sheriff's aura remained constant, but Gail's vibrated with zest. My dreamwalk held meaning to her.

"That's right," I said softly.

"Was this the same person you encountered in the morgue?" Gail asked.

"No." I paused to reflect and changed my answer. "I don't know. Both women had long dark hair. Both were emotionally distraught. I didn't see the face of the victim in the morgue; both women were of similar body build, similar ages."

"We were unable to identify the woman from the information you previously obtained," Wayne said. "We need last names, hometowns, Social Security numbers."

I shrugged. "I don't control what the dead show me."

"How do we know Baxley isn't making this up?" Gail huffed out a breath of disgust. "Her psychobabble is muddying the waters of the homicide investigation."

Her aura drew in. Interesting tell. She had something to hide. Two could play at the accusation game. "Yeah? Explain to the sheriff why the Native American aspect is so important. Tell him how it connects to this case."

Her aura pulsed vibrantly. Satisfaction swelled within me. I smiled inwardly. Score another point for the backwoods psychic.

"That was a fluke." Gail waved dismissively. "With the Native American protest, it was a lucky guess on your part."

Her intonation sounded off. She was lying. I pressed my advantage. "The murder victim is Native American. Isn't that correct?"

Gail's face reddened. Her lips pursed tightly together. She turned to go, but Wayne caught her arm. "Is she right?"

She shook off his hand, eyes blazing. "Dead right. The victim has shovel-shaped incisors."

Wayne made a so-what gesture with his hands. Anticipation mounted as I waited. This revelation was important to the coroner. She didn't believe in my woo-woo powers, but now that her science had been confirmed by my dreamwalk, she couldn't dismiss me as a complete fraud.

"Native Americans have a distinctive incisor pattern. There is no doubt. The woman, Lisa you told us before, is of Native

American origin."

I thought of Running Wolf and Gentle Dove. Also Jack Soaring Eagle and his companions outside. All had dark brown eyes. If the woman named Lisa whom I'd encountered in the morgue was the Angel I'd just dreamed, then we had a serious problem. Angel had the most unusual, most non-brown eyes I'd ever seen.

"What color are the victim's eyes?" I asked.

Gail frowned. "How odd that you should ask about that."

"Not so odd from my perspective."

"They're a piece of the puzzle that doesn't fit." The coroner barred her arms across her chest, her silver necklace, a fancy set of her initials, caught the light. She gave me her bug-under-the-microscope stare.

I allowed myself a faint hope that I was a full-fledged dream detective. "How's that?"

"With the degradation of the corpse, along with the victim having been shot in the face, her eye color is undetermined. However, judging by the trace evidence at hand, I believe her eyes were not brown in color."

"What about violet? Do you think her eyes may have been violet?"

Gail's gaze turned speculative and cold again. "Could be."

"You know something else, Baxley?" Wayne asked.

I edged to the door and freedom. "Working on it."

"Jack Soaring Eagle posted bail for Running Wolf." Mama pulled down more mismatched mugs from the kitchen cabinet. In the background, the weather station warned about a flood in the Mississippi delta. "Gentle Dove took her husband home and said she isn't letting him out of her sight for a month of Sundays."

"I understand her concern," I said. The soup on the stove

made my mouth water. It never ceased to amaze me how my mother knew when she'd have extras for dinner. "He's not a young man, and dreamwalking is tiring. So is getting arrested."

"You don't seem tired." Charlotte sat in the chair next to me. In her raspberry slacks suit with white trim on the collar and sleeves, she reminded me of a yummy sherbet and ice cream confection. Once she realized she'd missed the action by not following me inside the jailhouse, she'd stuck like glue. Plus, the television cameras hadn't shown up for the protest. Sinclair County didn't rate prime-time news coverage tonight. "You seem fired up."

I stretched my arms high overhead and filled my lungs with the fragrant aroma of Mama's vegetable soup. "I feel recharged. It's as if, and I know this sounds corny, as if I was born to do this work. I'd have no qualms about this work if not for the crazy hair thing."

"Don't worry about that," Mama said.

"How can I not worry? A big chunk of my hair turned white almost overnight."

"Power does that to a person," Mama added.

"Power? What kind of power?" Charlotte reached for her notepad.

My palm smacked against the table. "If you write about my hair in the paper, you will no longer be my friend."

She grabbed her notebook anyway. "I need to write this down to understand it. It isn't for the paper, just for my own personal reference. Please continue."

"Nothing else to tell," Mama said. "When Baxley accepted who she was, her body responded. That's it, pure and simple."

Charlotte tapped her ink pen against her plump cheek. "She did this to herself?"

"It's a sign. A tangible and visible sign." Mama distributed mugs of steaming tea all around.

I touched my gleaming widow's peak. "It's a nuisance and an embarrassment."

"Nonsense. Nesbitts, for generations past, have had the white streak. All of the strong dreamwalkers, that is."

My jaw dropped. "I don't believe you."

"Ask your father to show you the old family photos."

Her words vibrated with the sure ring of truth. If this white streak was hereditary, would my daughter exhibit it next? I felt an urgent need to see her. "When will Daddy and Larissa get back from their walk?"

Mama nodded toward the open door. "Directly."

Great. Directly could mean now or anytime in the future.

"I want to know about the murder case," Mama said. "Dr. Bergeron's press release surprised me. You said the bodies were early settlers."

"It's confusing because I dug up two graves. The first batch of bones, out by Misery Road, is early settlers. That grave held a mom with her two kids. However, the female in the Mallow foundation plantings is a Native American."

"And you figured that out in a dreamwalk?"

I eyed Charlotte's swiftly moving pen with growing suspicion. Prudence tempered my tongue. "I saw it, but the coroner confirmed it scientifically. The woman's identity is still a mystery."

"It will come in time." Mama had a benign smile. "I'm so proud of you."

I sipped my tea. Warmth flowed down my throat and radiated from my core to my extremities. This was exactly what I needed and where I wanted to be. Funny how life worked out. "Thanks."

"I'm confused," Charlotte said. "Are you a murder suspect or a police consultant?"

I waggled my eyebrows like Groucho Marx. "Right now, I'm both."

"Who killed the woman at Mallow?" Charlotte persisted. "Is there a killer running wild in Sinclair County?"

I rubbed my temples, which had begun to throb. "There's a killer running wild somewhere, but we're closing in. I can feel it."

CHAPTER 32

I'd been surprised by two baskets full of fresh produce on the back steps when Larissa and I returned home at dusk. After walking Precious and Muffin, we enjoyed a low-key dinner of steamed vegetables and Mama's delicious soup. The relaxed sensation stayed with me all evening, through a dreamless night, and into the next day. I walked Larissa to the school bus with the dogs and then thought about my plan for the day as I ambled back up the driveway.

At the top of my list was identifying who killed Angel/Lisa. Was it someone I knew? In the beginning I'd thought the killer might be building foreman Duke Quigley, or realtor Buster Glassman, or even my client, Carolina Byrd. They each had unrestricted access to the property, but in truth Mallow wasn't secured.

Or it hadn't been until recently.

Anyone could have dumped a body there. Anyone was a pretty big subject pool. If I went by folks who had been in trouble with the law recently, then the suspect pool expanded to our ousted coroner, to Running Wolf, and to me. I had no way of narrowing the suspect pool, except for taking my name off the list. I hadn't killed anyone.

Even if my dreamwalks were the gospel truth, elements of them didn't track. Angel and Lisa weren't even close to the same names. And the killer's gender might be female. Angel had insisted that an evil woman knew her secrets. Any way you cut it, betrayal caused strong emotions. This Jay whom Angel/Lisa had been with was the third leg of the love triangle. The killer was the missing side. Which brought me back to Jay. According to Angel/Lisa he was dead. Where was he buried?

I didn't own a computer, but the library had some I could use. An online search for Jay and Angel/Lisa might yield some information. I'd like to visit Mallow again to see if I could sense more about the killer, but I didn't want to be arrested like Running Wolf. I'd have to figure out how to do that in stealth mode.

First up was that trip to the library and selecting a hat to wear with my green jeans and white T-shirt. I tried my favorite, my Life is Good ball cap. As soon as I got my ponytail pulled through the opening in the back and tugged the hat down over the offending white streak, my head started pounding.

I pulled the hat off, loosened the band, and tried again. No good. Even though the hat was non-constricting, it gave me a fierce headache. I tried a floppy, oversized gardening hat left over from my grandmother. Same deal.

Tossing the hats aside, I redid my ponytail, studying my reflection in the hat rack mirror. It seemed as if my hair didn't want to be covered, but hair didn't have feelings. I cared. I wished the whole world wouldn't see my freaky white hair, but I wouldn't wear a bag over my head. I had standards.

While I hung up my hats, Precious barked at the front door and Muffin joined in. I shushed the dogs and looked out the living room window. No cars in the driveway. No one standing on my front porch. Must have been an animal noise that spooked 'em.

I stuffed a notebook and some pens in my old bookbag and headed out. A flock of blackbirds settled in the treeline north of my property, chattering away in a loud cacophony. A flutter of something sinister ruffled the fine hairs of my neck once I stepped off the porch stairs. Instantly I stopped, my brain and senses at odds over my sudden need for caution in my backyard.

If the dogs heard an intruder on the property, I was vulnerable. With a killer on the loose, this was no time to take chances. My dog alarm had gone off, and my intuition was flagging something. I had a problem.

Weapons. I had a gun in the truck and one in the kitchen. The kitchen was closer. I pivoted on my heel and retrieved Roland's Glock. The dogs circled around me as if I'd been gone for hours. I thought about turning them loose outside to see what they'd find, but if they ran off, I'd have twice the trouble. Too risky.

I was on my own.

I tried extending my senses out to see if I located anyone nearby, but I was so nervous, I couldn't focus. Why would someone come after me? Had I actually turned up a useful clue in the murder investigation?

Or, was it the watcher? My heart raced as a third idea presented itself. Was Roland out there? Would I finally learn what kept him away?

Standing in my house wasn't solving anything. Time to get down to business. I could go out in a fighter's crouch, *Charlie's Angels'* style, or I could pretend I normally walked around with a pistol in my hand.

Strange as that sounded, I preferred the latter. With the gun in my right hand, I locked the kitchen door and started down the steps. The blackbirds had moved on, and the woods were silent. I expanded my senses again, but I didn't pick anyone up on my extrasensory radar.

This was crazy. I was in my backyard. There was no visible threat. But I couldn't calm my nerves. My terror seemed elemental, instinctive. A few more steps and I'd be safe inside my truck. Unlocking the door, I swung my backpack around to rest on the passenger seat. I climbed in holding the Glock. I didn't want to let go of it, but I couldn't drive holding the gun. I'd shoot myself for sure. I should put it somewhere—the glove box, under the seat, or in my backpack.

On my next inhalation, I became aware of an odd smell. A musky smell. Concurrently, I realized the passenger side window was rolled down because a strong cross breeze flowed through the truck since I hadn't closed my door. I hadn't left that window down. Someone had done that. Someone had been in my truck.

I should have come out in a tight crouch, shooting off random shots into the air. Out of the corner of my right eye, I saw movement. Bright patterns of color. Then I heard an ominous rattle. Automatically, I fired at the threat.

Snake guts exploded in the truck as the rattlesnake's triangular head came off. Bullets pierced the floorboard. I leapt out the driver's side door and listened for more rattles. Sure enough, I heard the dreaded sound. My stomach sank.

Inside my house, the dogs barked incessantly.

My legs trembled so badly I could hardly stand. Snakes. And not just any snakes. Rattlesnakes. Duke Quigley's scowling face popped into my head. I hadn't forgotten that threat he'd made in my house a few days back. He blamed me for Carolina's withholding his final payments.

"Not funny, Duke." I stepped away from the truck, circled it, listening all the while for Duke Quigley in my woods. "Come and get your snakes or I swear to God, I'll shoot every last one of them."

My front tire was flat. A bullet must have caught the tire after it passed through the floorboard. I stared at the deflated tire with disbelief. This day had gone from promising to majorly messed up in a matter of minutes.

How many snakes were in my truck? Did I even have a spare tire? Where the hell was it?

One thing at a time. I had to get the dead snake out of my truck. The live ones, too.

"Duke?" I hollered. "If you want these snakes, you'd better come get 'em. I don't want to kill them. But I will. I'll kill every last one of them if I have to. Come get 'em, and we'll call it good. No harm, no foul."

Duke didn't materialize. Figured. A man made this mess and now he'd run off to leave me in cleanup mode. When I opened the passenger side door, I was just in time to see the tail end of a snake edge out the other door.

The snakes didn't want to be in my truck. That was good news.

I scanned the woods one more time, stomping on the ground to make noise. "Last chance, Duke." A snake slithered out of the truck going God only knows where. "If you put more than two snakes in the truck, they are still in there, but they won't be for much longer."

Tucking the gun in my waistband, I grabbed up a shovel and picked up the dead snake. The head fell off the shovel onto the rubber floor mat. Gross. Nothing about this operation was going smoothly. I flung the dead snake into the woods, stomping my feet as I walked, thankful I had worn thick boots instead of sandals or sneakers. I didn't want to get rattlesnake bit, but from what I knew of snakes, they wanted to be left alone. If I made enough noise, they'd go the other way.

"You owe me a tire, Duke Quigley. Don't think I won't come after you." That was nerves talking. I had no intention of going after anyone, much less snake-loving Duke Quigley. I wanted to stay far away from anyone that handled snakes.

Grimacing, I shoveled the snake head from my floor mat and tossed it into the woods. With all my yelling and stomping, I must have scared any other snakes away. Even with a flashlight,

I couldn't find any more of them under the seat or behind the seat.

I closed up the truck, locked it, and went back inside my house. The dogs sniffed me like I was coated in peanut butter, but I shooed them away. I needed hot tea to settle my nerves and time to think. I placed the Glock on the counter as I made tea.

First of all, was it Duke Quigley who'd put the snakes in my truck? I could find out easily enough. I phoned Bubba Paxton, preacher of the church that used rattlesnakes in their worship service. Bubba answered on the first ring.

No point wasting time on small talk. "Your snakes missing?"

"Good morning to you, madam dreamwalker. I heard about your news already."

My blood iced. He knew about the snakes? "You know?"

"Sure I know. It's all over town that you bear the prophetic sign. I can't tell you how much I envy you. I wanted to be the one with the shock of white hair. Being the town's chief dream-walker would have put me on easy street."

I didn't consider my ghastly hair color to be good news, but everything was relative. "I didn't call about that. I just found two fat rattlesnakes in my truck. Besides the ones living in the wild, yours are the only captive rattlers I know about. Are your snakes missing?"

"I'm over at the church right now, but we don't keep the snakes here. I'll call you back in a few."

The call ended, and I sipped my hot tea. The steam curled up from the mug into my nostrils. My icy hands clung to the warmth, but the heated beverage was no match for the chill in my bones.

Bubba Paxton called back a few minutes later. "My snakes are gone. You still got them in your truck? I'll come right over and get 'em."

"Nope. I shot one, and I saw one escape. I don't know if there were others. My truck is now snake-free. How many are there?"

"Four. Did you see four snakes?"

"I only saw two. But that was enough. Bubba, you know what this means."

"Sure do. It means I've got no snakes for Sunday's service."

God, save me from obtuse men. I closed my eyes to keep the hot tears inside. "Wrong answer. Your snake handler tried to murder me."

CHAPTER 33

The sheriff was pissed I'd flung the evidence into the woods. His deputies located the snake head, but the rest of the body was gone. One of our eagle-eyed hawks must have feasted on the gourmet treat.

Wayne jotted down my summation of events. "Duke Quigley threatened you?"

I hugged my arms to my chest as Virg and Ronnie changed my tire. "He blames me for Carolina Byrd not paying us our final installments. The murder investigation stopped all activity on the lot."

"You sure you didn't piss him off some other way? That sounds kinda weak to me."

"I don't give a hoot what his motivation was. If one of those snakes had nailed me, you'd have another corpse on your hands."

"I'm sure Duke would've called EMS if he played this trick on you."

"Why are you so quick to defend him? He tried to kill me."

"You piss people off. He made a mistake. That's all."

"That was no mistake." Wayne thought this was my fault? My spine stiffened. "If you don't treat it seriously, I'll be forced to divulge other matters."

His expression tightened. "What other matters are you talking about?"

"Things I know."

"You threatening me?"

I didn't care for the menace in his voice, but I wasn't backing down. "I am. I've got a kid. If I'd driven her down to the bus stop this morning, she would have gotten rattlesnake bit. That first snake crawled out from under the passenger seat. This is a big deal."

"I'm eaten up with big deals right now. The state archaeologist thinks we're a hotbed of crime and rednecks. All this press and media attention confirms her suspicions. Looks like Bo Seavey will be lucky to ever work again. I've got Native Americans coming out the wazoo, and the remains of four people in our morgue. Now you're playing Annie Oakley in your truck."

"Just because there's no body here, you can't dismiss this incident. This was a pointed attack on me. This was personal. Duke Quigley came over here and threatened me with snakes. I'm telling you, he's the guy."

"You got any witnesses to back up these accusations?"

"No. But I swear they're true. Duke threatened me. Like this." I made a snake hand the way Duke had and lunged toward Wayne's face with a hissing noise. He batted my hand away.

"It's your word against his," he stated.

"My word is good, and you know it. Plus I've got that snake head to show intent. Putting rattlesnakes in someone's vehicle isn't a kid's prank. It's a lethal threat. That's not all. Bubba Paxton's church snakes are missing."

Wayne appeared to consider my words. "Dairy Queen lost his job over events that were out of his control. He had too much to drink, and he made a mistake."

He sounded so sure he had it all figured out, sure that one of his drinking buds had messed up a little bit. That really stuck in my craw. "How can you take his side so readily? Don't you believe me? I thought you liked me."

"I want to sleep with you. That doesn't mean my brain's stopped working."

"Depends on your point of view," I mumbled under my breath. "Are you going to arrest him?"

"I'm going to question him."

"That's not enough."

"You think you're the sheriff now?"

"I don't want your job. I want to know I won't be murdered for driving my truck. I want to know I don't have to check under my seats with a gun and a flashlight every time I drive somewhere."

"You've made your point."

"You're wrong, Sheriff. You've got a murderer right under your nose, and your good old boy self can't even see it. Gail is right. Sinclair County is a hotbed of murder and rednecks."

Angel came to me in my dreams that night in her tousled sex-kitten guise. I waited through her tears. Indeed, I understood the soul-deep wrenching loss that drove her to weep. I'd suffered great loss, too.

When she paused for breath, I interrupted. "Who did this to you?"

She shook her head in a fresh flurry of sobs.

"Please," I implored. "Tell me who caused your pain. I want to help you."

"I will lose everything."

I don't know if it was the snake episode or the sheriff's disbelief, but I'd had it with her deliberate evasions. "You already lost your life. Your baby, too. What else do you have to lose?"

"My baby," she wailed.

I mentally kicked myself to the marsh and back for mentioning her child. Larissa was my Achilles' heel, too. If something happened to her, I would be inconsolable. I would haunt the dreams of anyone I could reach, seeking justice for my family.

"Angel, where is your baby right now?"

She said a word, but it was unlike any word I'd ever heard. I had her spell it for me to make sure I had it right. Waking, I wrote the letters down and stared at the odd word.

Wetumpka.

Her baby was in Wetumpka.

Whatever the heck that was.

CHAPTER 34

After Larissa climbed aboard the school bus, I hurried home with my leashed dogs. I'd debated carrying the Glock to the bus stop but decided against it. No point in making my daughter afraid of her own shadow. I was scared enough for the both of us.

Back inside the house, I bolted the door and tidied up the kitchen. Another mild January day beckoned, but I was reluctant to face it. I brewed a pot of tea and was selecting a cup when someone beat on the back door.

My gaze went to the gun drawer as the dogs barked. The knob rattled, and the person pounded harder on the door. Precious and Muffin danced around the back door. My heart raced. Was Duke Quigley back with more rattlesnakes? Was a murderer at my door? I fumbled for the gun.

"Baxley? You in there?" Verbena Harris said.

Relief whooshed out of my lungs. I'd known this woman all my life. She was seven years older than me, and I'd always coveted her innate sense of style. I left the gun in the drawer. "Coming."

What did the owner of the Clip 'N Curl salon want with me? I wasn't one of her customers. Maybe she'd heard about my hair disaster. With that thought in mind, I shushed the dogs and opened the door. "Hey, Verbena. What brings you out my way this morning?"

"I've got a request for you. A dreamwalker request." Hope

brimmed in her warm brown eyes. But when Precious edged forward to sniff our visitor, Verbena retreated, her hand going to her heart. "Can you shut your dogs up? I'm scared of them."

A childhood memory surfaced of her baby brother getting mauled by a pit bull. I winced. "Sure. Give me a minute." I herded Precious and Muffin into the downstairs bathroom and hurried back to the door. "Come on in."

Even in her two-inch heels, the top of Verbena's forehead still hit me at eye level. Mounds of tiered curls of soft acorn brown framed her round face, bringing her total height close to mine. In her curve-hugging pistachio green blouse, walnut-hued slacks, and tasteful makeup, she looked every inch a fashion plate.

"Would you like a cup of tea?" I gestured toward the table, feeling underdressed in my jeans and pink sweatshirt. "I was in the process of pouring a cup when you knocked."

"Okay." She clutched at her small purse, her eyes scanning the old-fashioned cabinets, the dull linoleum floor. "Tea like your mama makes, right?"

I nodded, glad I'd tidied the breakfast dishes already. "Please, have a seat."

"This is some place you got here." Appreciation rang in Verbena's tone.

I carried the mugs over to the table. "I keep thinking I'll find the time and money to fix it up, but I haven't been able to swing it yet."

"Your granny done right by you, same as mine done by me. I wouldn't have my shop without Granny Lakeisa. You got yourself a nice house from your granny. Bought and paid for, too. And your roof don't leak. When I worked at Terrell's, the roof leaked right over my station. I hated working there."

Was this a dreamwalking request? My insides pinged with anticipation. "What can I do for you?"

"I got a message to send. Tell Granny Lakeisa that the shop is making money."

I nodded. "I'll get with Daddy, and we'll take the message to her."

"You don't need your Daddy for this." She waved her peach-colored nails in my direction. "Goodness sakes, you are a chip off the old block. That hank of white hair proves it."

My hand went self-consciously to my rogue hair. "Even so, I am brand new at this. I may not get the result you want."

Verbena wrinkled her broad nose. "Yeah, yeah. Can you do it now? I'd sure rest easier if my granny knew right away."

I chewed my bottom lip, considering. The smart thing to do would be to bank the request and attempt it later with Daddy. Except I wanted to accommodate Verbena, and dreamwalking had been a snap with Running Wolf.

I could do this. "I don't know how long it will take."

"I've got time. My customers can wait this morning. I can't do hair today unless Granny Lakeisa knows I've done my part."

The timing of her request suited my empty schedule. "I can't promise I can find her."

"Tab used to say stuff like that when I sent messages to her after she passed. You'll find her. You got the hair for the job."

"All right, then. I'll try it." I pushed my mug out of the way and interlaced my fingers. I closed my eyes, steadied my breathing, and entered the dreamscape. As with Running Wolf, the transition seemed so easy. I hugged the knowledge close, remembering this portal and set off through a sea of spirits.

One spirit intercepted me with a friendly smile. He walked with a swagger in expensive-looking black trousers, turquoise silk shirt, and matching turquoise fedora with a bright red band. "I haven't seen you around here before. My name's Joe."

The gold chain glistened around his neck, a bright contrast to his dark skin. I knew enough not to talk to strangers. I stepped around him and kept going.

"You looking for someone? I can help." Joe kept pace with me.

"No, thanks." I pushed on alone. For the first time, I grasped the enormity of the spirit world. It stretched farther than the eye could see. I could spend the rest of my life wandering around in here and never see it all.

I assumed that I would appear in the spirit world near Granny Lakeisa. But as I passed through entire assemblages of spirits, none of them looked familiar. Maybe I should wait for Daddy. I had no idea how long I'd been out here, but Verbena was waiting.

I thought of the location I'd entered and navigated back to that spot. Just before I departed, Joe approached me again. "Have any luck?" He had an expectant smile on his face.

On this second go-around, his face seemed welcome and familiar. I hated to admit defeat, but the words tumbled out. "Not this time. I'll be back."

"I know everybody." He snapped his fingers. "Why don't you leave a message with me?"

This situation had never come up before in my discussions with Daddy. But Joe's proposal seemed so logical. It would give me something positive to report. And, having an ally up here could be a big asset to my police consultant work. Besides, what could it hurt? I nodded my approval. "The message is for Lakeisa Upshaw. Her granddaughter's beauty shop is profitable."

Joe beamed. "I've zeroed in on it."

He faded from sight as my spirit returned home. Sunshine danced around me, warming me as I awoke. My mug of tea had grown cold. Verbena paced the floor, the room vibrating with her weighty steps. "Did you find granny? Did you tell her my news?"

I rolled my shoulders to ease the stiffness. It wasn't enough. I stood and stretched full out. "Sorry, I couldn't locate her. But I left word with a spirit. He'll pass your message along."

She grinned from ear to ear. "Granny's gonna bust a gut with pride."

"I'm glad I could help." Satisfaction hummed in my bones. I couldn't wait to tell Daddy of my success. Hard to believe I'd worried about dreamwalking for years.

"You was gone a really long time." Verbena pointed to a clean plate sitting in my dish drain. "I fixed myself a bologna sammich. Hope that was okay."

"No problem." Hmm. A bologna sandwich sounded yummy.

Verbena picked up her purse. "I've got folks waiting at the shop. Thanks for getting the word to my granny." With that, she left.

I felt so wonderful, so energized, I wanted to jog the five miles over to my parents' house, not my usual mode of operation. I should focus that energy burst on something productive. Like washing the snake guts out of my truck.

Did that.

Then I washed the outside of the truck and patched up the hole in the floorboard with duct tape. Washed both dogs. Took a shower. I twiddled my thumbs for a few minutes. No pet clients and no landscaping clients.

I decided to ride around town, to see if I could scare up some work. If that failed, I'd go over and catch Charlotte at the newspaper.

Oh, and the library. Mental head smack. How could I have forgotten that's where I wanted to go? The library it was.

I tucked the Glock in the glove compartment, in case I ran into trouble.

★ ★ ★ ★ ★

The Jeanie Mixon Public Library had two computers with access to the Internet. The clerk, Alpharetta Reid, a spinster with eighties hair and clothing, sat at the checkout counter and waved me over to the unattended computer. Seventy-year-old Edward Stafford had the other one.

Except for the occasional rustle of clothing and the muted fluorescent hum, the library was silent. I searched for the odd place name. Wetumpka. It sounded a bit like an Indian name. We had plenty of Indian place names in Georgia. Most of our rivers retained Native American names; several islands traced their names back to the land's earliest human settlers.

A map of a small town in Alabama flashed onto the screen. I scrolled through the information. Nearly six thousand people lived in Wetumpka. The name came from the Creek Indians and meant rumbling waters.

There was also a Wetumpka, Oklahoma, because the Creeks had been forced to move west. That population was much smaller, and the location was farther removed from Georgia. Wetumpka, Alabama, felt right to me.

Besides, Angel/Lisa had stated her son was in Alabama when Running Wolf and I encountered her in the dreamwalk. Wetumpka, Alabama, was a few hours from the Georgia state line. It was plausible an Alabama woman could be found dead in Georgia.

But Sinclair County was on the eastern side of Georgia. How did she get all the way over here?

I searched for missing adults. At the first few sites, I didn't notice any people from Alabama, so I searched specifically for missing people in our adjacent state. Bingo. Screen after screen of missing people. I accessed the females. Their stories ate at me. Warrants for child abuse. Abandoned car found halfway across the state. Violent lover. Missing from a tavern.

Man, oh man.

This was hard to see, all these faces and broken lives. I could dreamwalk for each of these people. I could help their families. I could spend the rest of my life looking for missing people. But what if they didn't want to be found? Who was I helping then?

The woman from my dreams, Lisa or Angel or whatever her name was, didn't appear in the pictured women missing, and the list went back ten years.

Maybe I had it wrong. Maybe she didn't live in Wetumpka, but her baby did. Was it possible her family didn't know she was missing? Lisa/Angel could've had a job away from home, a traveling job. I checked missing persons from Tennessee, the Carolinas, and Georgia.

Nothing.

No matches.

I buried my face in my hands. I wasn't getting anywhere. I couldn't make the facts fit the few miserable bits of evidence we had. A woman was dead in Sinclair County. No one in nearby states had declared her missing. The coroner had her body and her vital statistics, but because she'd been shot in the face, law enforcement didn't know what she looked like.

I did.

Too bad I couldn't draw worth a hoot.

Too bad we didn't have cop sketch artists here.

At the tap on my shoulder, I glanced up in alarm. Alpharetta Reid scowled down at me. "People are waiting to use this computer. Your hour is up."

I glanced up at the clock. I'd been here nearly an hour and a half. Where had the time gone? "Sorry. I lost track of time."

I collected my stuff and sat out front, in the butterfly garden I'd created for the library. No butterflies in January, but the fountain and the greenery were pleasing all the same.

Our dead woman had two names, a baby in Wetumpka,

Alabama, and a lover named Jay. She hadn't been reported missing. The coroner said her teeth were of Native American descent.

Had I been wrong to dismiss Wetumpka, Oklahoma? Her teeth didn't lie. Those shovel-shaped incisors were hard facts.

How much should I tell the sheriff and the coroner? There had to be some way I could ask them about my new information. Wait. Couldn't they tell if a woman had given birth? I could ask that question without seeming like a total flake.

Charlotte huffed up the sidewalk and plunked down on the bench beside me. She was garbed in vibrant lilac today. I could almost sniff the purple blossoms. "There you are. Why aren't you answering your cell phone?"

I nodded toward my backpack. "Turned it off while I was in the library."

Her eyes narrowed. "You working the case?"

"Checking some things out."

Lights danced in her eyes. "Gotta scoop for me?"

"No scoops. Only more questions. I can't get a handle on the pieces of this puzzle. I should be able to see it, but I can't get there from here."

Charlotte appeared to be absorbing that for a moment. I noticed she was twisting the life out of her bright yellow purse strap. "What's eating you?" I asked.

My friend stilled. She appeared to be absorbed in the flowing fountain before us.

"Tell me," I urged.

"It wasn't my fault." Charlotte's voice quivered up and down the scale. "I want you to know I had nothing to do with this."

A sinkhole opened in my stomach. "What?"

"Bernard stole my notes. He convinced Kip to let him do a story about the changing of the guard. His story is in today's newspaper. I tried to stop it. Honestly, I did, but they wouldn't listen to me. Bernard can rot in hell for all I care."

I arched my eyebrows and waited.

Charlotte heaved out a troubled breath. "He snapped a picture of you at the jail. When your hat blew off. His story is about how your hair streak publicly marks you as the town's reigning psychic."

CHAPTER 35

"The only good news I have for you," Charlotte said, handing me a newspaper, "is that you're below the fold on page one. Kip put the Native American rally on top. He also printed up five-hundred extra copies of the paper."

"My hair is front-page news?" I couldn't draw in a full breath as I scanned the article.

"Not your hair, per se, but what your hair means. Bernard dug around in the archives and found early pictures of your dad with the same white streak. He even interviewed Mamie Conner at the nursing home about your grandmother."

I glanced up. "Goodness sakes, Mamie's got to be a hundred years old."

"She'll be a hundred and one in August. Her body crapped out, but her brain is as sharp as a blackberry thorn. She says you are a living legend, my friend."

"Crap. I agreed to step into Dad's shoes because his job was killing him. I don't want my new sideline in the newspaper."

"There was nothing I could do to stop it. Kip slotted Bernard's article before I had a clue about what was going on. Both of them are insanely euphoric about it. I'm so mad at Bernard I could just spit. Call up some nasty spirits and sic them on him."

"I wish. It doesn't work that way. We'll have to get our revenge another way."

Charlotte's eyes gleamed. "Yeah. Let's get even."

"Count on it. But first I have to get the word to Larissa and my parents."

"Duh. That's easy. Beam your thoughts over, like you did when Maisie Ryals tried to smash your head with a tire iron."

"That was a special occurrence. I don't want to be Chicken Little."

"Your daughter and your parents would never think that about you. Do it now."

"Bossy britches." She was right. I thought of the right words and sent them out. *Larissa, Daddy, the newspaper ran a story on my hair. Apparently I'm a living legend. Didn't want you to be surprised. I'm okay. Love you both.*

I didn't know the range of my telepathic beam. Last time, I'd reached my daughter from about five miles away. Her school was about that distance from the library. Daddy could be anywhere in the region. Neither of them could broadcast back to me, but if they were in range, they'd receive my message.

At the low-throated diesel rumble on the adjacent highway, I glanced over. Realtor Buster Glassman drove by with Carolina Byrd in his deluxe pickup. Charlotte followed my gaze. "There goes trouble."

A thought tugged at the edge of my memory. "What happened to that article you were going to write with him? How come I never heard about the big lunch date with Mr. Snazzy?"

"He cancelled. He won't return my calls either."

"Curious."

"Tell me about his gambling problems. I can get even with him in print."

"Nah, Buster Glassman is mean. He said he'd crush my business prospects if I crossed him. Remember Janna West from high school? He dated her once, said he screwed her repeatedly. After his lies went around, she tried to commit suicide."

"Janna West. I remember her. Just barely, though. Perky

brunette cheerleader. Her family moved here when she was a sophomore. She went to school with us for one term and then finished school elsewhere."

"So she wouldn't see Buster again." I shuddered. "I do not want to be a Janna West. Neither do you."

"I dunno." Charlotte primped her chin-length hair, light glinting off her glasses. "If Buster blabbed that he'd slept with me, it would do wonders for my dating prospects."

"You don't want those types of dates. Steer clear of him."

"Wonder what he's doing with that Macon woman?"

Lord, I had to love my loyal friend. "He's probably one of the few people she already paid in full. He likes looking like he's got a client in his truck; she likes looking as though she has lackeys at her beck and call. It's a match made in heaven."

"Or hell, depending on your view of the people involved."

"Once Carolina reads in the paper that I'm the resident kook, she'll never pay me. But I've got her weeping cherry and her *Podacarpus*. She won't get them back unless she pays me."

Charlotte pawed the air. "Grrr, get 'em, tiger."

"I'm not going anywhere near her. She can call me if she wants her trees back."

"Where does this leave you with the sheriff? Are you a suspect or an investigator?"

I tucked the newspaper in my backpack and rose. "Heck if I know. That's where I'm headed next."

My friend lunged off the bench, tripping over her feet and teetering wildly until she got her balance. "Wait for me."

CHAPTER 36

We met Carolina and Buster coming out of the Sinclair County Law Enforcement Center. If looks could kill, Charlotte and I would be charcoal-broiled. Carolina ignored my smile and greeting. Buster, always mindful of his sales career, managed a cool nod of acknowledgment. Anger radiated from them in unrelenting waves.

Interesting. What had them madder than feral hogs?

"You thinking what I'm thinking?" Charlotte grabbed my arm and slowed me down once the lobby door closed behind us, with us safely inside and them roaring off in Buster's truck.

I nodded hello to the tired-looking woman built like a fireplug sitting next to the gumball machine. "Depends on what you're thinking."

"I'm thinking the sheriff told them not to leave town, that they are numbers one and two on his suspect list."

"Why stand around in here guessing? Let's ask Wayne."

She released my arm to wave dismissively. "Pooh. You're no fun. Much too serious."

"You'd be serious, too, if you were me. Things are changing in my life. Things I can't control. I have no idea if this roller-coaster ride will stay on the tracks or shoot off on an unknown tangent."

"Whatever." Charlotte rushed ahead and spoke into the microphone to the receptionist. "Tamika, buzz us in."

She did, brightening when she saw me. "Hey, it's our living

legend. Quick. What am I thinking?"

"I'm thinking I'd like to brain Bernard Rivers for writing a story about me." I shook my head. "I don't read minds, sorry."

Wayne rounded the corner. Edgy emotion rolled off him. He pointed at me. "You. In my interrogation room. Now."

Charlotte and I exchanged a sobering glance and started forward. I could say this wasn't my fault, except I didn't know what was wrong. But if there was one thing I'd learned from being married to a take-charge man, it was to hold my peace. He'd tell me what was wrong in no uncertain terms.

To my chagrin, he put Charlotte in one interview room and me in the other one. Great. The old divide and conquer method of interrogation. I shifted in my seat uneasily. Then I stood. No point in giving him the advantage.

Wayne entered, shoulders squared for battle. He tossed the newspaper down on the table. "This is not good."

Thankfully, I'd already scanned the piece so I kept my cool. "I didn't agree to this article, and I'm as surprised as you are. Bernard stole Charlotte's notes, pitched the story idea to Kip, and the rest is history."

"All releases regarding law enforcement personnel must be pre-approved. I do not like to be surprised."

My brows shot up. "Am I on the payroll now? I thought I was a murder suspect."

"I can't rule you out, but you aren't my top suspect."

His admission surprised me. Curiosity plagued my thoughts. "From the dark looks Carolina Byrd and her realtor shot us, I'm guessing they are currently your top suspects."

"Yeah. I rubbed both their noses in it. I like Buster for it, though. Never did like the slippery little bastard. Now he's flashing rolls of cash around the county. Something ain't right there."

I considered his remark. Either one of them could've shot

Lisa/Angel. Maybe they did it together. That brought a smile to my face. "Who else is a suspect?"

"You pretty much nailed my list the first time you were here: the realtor, the property owner, the builder, and the landscaper."

I ignored his landscaper jab. "My money's on the builder. You arrest Duke Quigley for trying to kill me with snakes?"

Wayne's lips tightened. "He's in the wind. But I'll catch him. Only so many places for a cockroach like him to hide."

"He's a cockroach now? Not your good buddy, Dairy Queen?"

"Duke made a mistake. He'll pay for it. For your information, Bubba Paxton filed an incident report charging Duke with theft of church property. We have a warrant out for Duke's arrest. Virg and Ronnie will track him down."

"When you find him, Duke owes me a new tire and body work to fix the floor of my truck."

"I'll make a note of that," the sheriff said.

I drew in a deep breath. Duke Quigley would pay for messing with me. That was good. But it didn't get us closer to solving the murder case. "What about Running Wolf? How's he figure into all of this?"

"I don't have the Native American angle figured out yet. But Running Wolf isn't a person of interest for the homicide."

With this exchange I felt like I was part of the sheriff's team. Not once had he come on to me or suggested inappropriate coworker behavior. It wouldn't hurt to bring him up to speed on my progress. "I have new information. I spoke to the dead woman in a dream last night. Her baby is in Wetumpka."

"What the hell is that?"

"It's a town in Alabama and Oklahoma. The word is an old Indian name. I looked it up online at the library this morning. Due to its proximity to Georgia, the Alabama town is a surer bet."

"How does a baby fit into this thing?"

"I don't know. Except that she's terrified the baby will be discovered. It's a big secret."

"You get her last name yet?"

"Nope. She won't tell me her name. She's trying to protect the baby. I looked through the online missing persons lists in Alabama. I couldn't find her."

Wayne started, then shook his head. "I keep forgetting you know what she looks like. You need to look at our missing persons lists here. They're kept up to date. Someone will report her missing sooner or later."

He was divulging privileged information to me and suggesting avenues to pursue. Time to find out what my services were worth. I cleared my throat gently. "What does a psychic consultant get paid?"

A muscle in his lean cheek twitched. "Nothing if she's a suspect."

"Don't joke with me about this. I've got a stack of unpaid bills on my kitchen counter and months until people start thinking about landscaping again."

"I've used consultants for cases in the past." Wayne named a rate.

I was in the driver's seat for negotiating, only I had no idea what other psychic consultants got paid. But even if I never walked another dog or planted another shrub, with regular casework, at the rate he quoted, I'd be able to pay my current bills and then some. "Sold. Do we sign a contract?"

"Not yet. Your salary is contingent on me solving the case. If we don't solve it, the deal's off."

I let that sink in. "How does this work? Do we touch base each day? Do I follow you around?"

Heat flared briefly in his eyes, but he ramped it down. "Touching base is a good idea."

"What if I have more thoughts about the case?"

"I want to know whatever leads you find."

My fingers curled into my palms. Now that I had a more prominent role, responsibility weighed heavily on my shoulders. "What if I'm wrong?"

"You think all leads pan out? No way. I'll use your info same as I would that of my deputies."

"You believe in my abilities that much?"

He made a palms-up gesture. "The paper says you're a living legend."

"What about—" I stopped myself from saying the Ice Queen in the nick of time. I didn't know if Gail was watching through the glass. "The coroner?"

"Ol' Bo Seavey is in a pile of trouble. He won't be getting his job back. Fortunately, we have someone else who wants to take the job."

"Who?" Please don't let it be Gail, I silently wished. I did not want to have an extended working relationship with her.

"We're keeping it all in the family. Last night the county commissioners appointed your dad the interim coroner. Gail's going to train him before she heads back to Atlanta."

I grabbed the edge of the table and held on tight as the world spun faster and faster.

CHAPTER 37

I drove over to my parents' house so fast, it was a wonder there was any rubber left on my truck tires. Daddy was sitting on the bench outside, as if he knew I was coming. He waved me over.

I checked him out as I approached. He was dressed in his usual garb of faded jeans, old T-shirt, and flip-flops. His long gray hair was pulled back in its customary ponytail. A tendril of Spanish moss hooked over the near edge of the bench. Two calico cats sunned in a nearby pool of light.

Nothing seemed out of place.

Nothing but my anxious stomach.

"What's this about you being the coroner?" I slid in beside him. The old wood creaked under the added weight.

He glanced my way with a friendly smile. "As it happens, I was in the market for a new job."

I couldn't imagine my father pronouncing people dead. "Why that job? Couldn't you work at the bank or the grocery store or the hardware store?"

"I have some familiarity with the dead." He waggled his snowy eyebrows. "Thought this might be a good fit."

I studied him, aghast at his playful attitude. Couldn't he see this job had broken Bo Seavey? I wanted him to enjoy watching Larissa grow up. Couldn't he see that for someone in questionable health being on-call all hours of the day and night was a bad choice?

Except Daddy looked suspiciously healthy. The pallor that

had become his normal color was gone. The deep creases on his face had melted away. Plus, he was smiling and joking around. I couldn't remember a time in recent history when he'd looked so relaxed.

Hmmm.

I hit back with the only other weapon in my arsenal. "What's Mama say about all this?"

"She's warming to the idea."

"But if you have to work hard to convince folks this is the right thing, is it really right for you?"

"I understand your concern. Understand and register it. But I'm certain this is right. And the opportunity opened up when I needed a job. If that isn't fate, I don't know what is. But let's not waste this visit with worries. Tell me about your dreamwalk. Did you help Verbena?"

"You know about that?"

He smiled. "This is a small town."

I frowned. "I had no trouble crossing over, no spatial disorientation at all. It seemed effortless after doing it with Running Wolf. But there were so many spirits. I couldn't find her granny. Maybe if I'd had something of her granny's to hold, I could have had better success."

"If that helps you, ask folks to bring you a personal item."

"I might be successful if I touched the requester during the dreamwalk. I'm not sure. I felt insignificant in the spirit world. Like I was a tiny bit of marsh grass adrift in a sea of spirits. I wanted to help Verbena. I really did. If it weren't for Joe, I would have felt like I'd completely struck out."

"Joe?" Daddy leaned toward me. "What's this about a Joe?"

"He was a guide or something. Very helpful. He offered to take a message to Verbena's granny."

"You said no, right?" Daddy's voice sharpened.

"I said yes. I didn't have all day to thread through throngs of spirits."

Air whistled through Daddy's teeth. "You shouldn't have done that."

My stomach knotted, but I plunged on. "I don't see the harm. Joe volunteered to be of assistance."

"Did you recognize Joe?"

"No. He reminded me a bit of the Chamberlain boy. Exuded goodwill and all that."

"We've got to fix this." Daddy stood. "I hope we're not too late."

I rose too. "Why?"

"Joe isn't who you think he is. He's an unclean spirit. He may have followed you back and entered Verbena."

"They can do that?" My heart sunk as we hurried toward my clean truck. Daddy climbed in the passenger side while I buckled myself in the driver's seat.

"They can do a lot. You can't give them an opening like that. Unless you personally know a spirit and trust it implicitly, don't talk to any of them."

My lower lip jutted like a petulant child. "You talked to them."

"I know a bunch of spirits after doing this for so many years."

I cranked the motor and hurried away. "Why didn't you tell me?"

The Clip 'N Curl was a ten-minute drive, less if I sped. Daddy grabbed hold of the armrest as I accelerated onto the highway. "I thought you knew."

"You guessed wrong. What else don't I know?"

"Dreamwalking isn't an exact science. The rules are different for each situation. I can't cover every eventuality before it happens."

"Seems like an odd way to operate," I said.

He didn't respond. Soon we were at Verbena's hair salon. The front door was wide open. I heard her yelling from the parking lot.

"I told you, and I told you," Verbena hollered. "Don't fold my towels thattaway. Go half and then half again."

"Yes'm," came the barely audible response.

"You over there. Schalinda. Girl, get yo' scrawny butt over here in my chair."

I glanced over at Daddy. "We'd better hurry. That doesn't sound like Verbena."

Daddy nodded in agreement. We entered the shop, and all commotion ceased. Verbena glared at us, fiery eyed.

She shook her finger at me. "You got no appointment. You ain't getting your hair cut today."

Daddy sidled up to her right and gestured me around to the left. "We need to have a word with you in private."

Verbena shook her head. "Can't you see I got customers stacked up in here? I ain't taking no time off to chitchat. I got work to do."

Daddy whispered something in her ear, and she acquiesced. "We'll be right back," he announced to the five customers waiting for hair service.

I had no idea what came next. All I knew was that Verbena was acting strange, and Daddy knew what to do. I trusted that was enough.

We stopped outside under a broad-canopied oak. Strands of moss ribboned down in plump cascades. Daddy stopped beside the tree. "Do as I do." Mirroring him, I placed my hand on Verbena's rounded shoulder and the other hand on the rough-barked tree. Verbena felt cold to the touch. My heart thumped in my ears, in my throat. What had I done to Verbena?

Daddy's voice turned to a low roar. "Get out!"

I said it, too, with as much authority as I could muster. "Get out!"

Verbena twitched and jerked. Her eyes rolled back in her head.

"With all that is within me, I command you to come out of this woman," Daddy ordered, giving Verbena's shoulder a rough shake. "Unclean spirit, be gone!"

I repeated his words and actions, feeling warmth flowing through my hands.

Verbena blinked, and her tensed facial features relaxed. She gazed at us in wonderment. "What am I doing out here?"

"You're taking a break," Daddy said. "Baxley wanted to try to reach your granny again. Have you got anything of hers in the shop?"

"No. I don't. Wait a minute." She nodded her head. "That little picture over my waiting chairs. That used to be Granny's."

"May we borrow it?" I asked.

"Sure. Just a second."

She returned with it a few moments later. Verbena smiled at us. "I don't know what you two just did, but my heart feels so light and happy. Thank you."

"We'll be a few minutes with this," I announced.

"No problem." Verbena jerked a thumb toward her shop. "I'll be tending to my customers. I can't imagine how I got so backed up today."

I glanced over at Daddy. "Ready?" In one hand I held the framed painting of an old woman on a stool gazing at the water; the fingers of my other hand were interlaced with Daddy's. He placed his other hand on my shoulder.

He nodded.

With that, I guided us into the spirit world. Spirits crowded around us, but I focused on Verbena's granny. She'd been a slight woman with completely gray hair. Keeping the framed picture firmly in my mind, I walked right up to her spirit. I relayed her granddaughter's message, and she thanked me.

We turned to go, and there was Joe. His face was a distorted mask of fury. His eyes glowed bright red. "You can't keep me in here."

"I'm not keeping you anywhere. C'mon, Daddy, let's get out of here."

I envisioned the tree where Daddy and I had left our bodies and soon we were back. We blinked our eyes open in the shade of the oak tree. Excitement pulsed through me. I grabbed Daddy in a big hug. "It worked! I found her."

Daddy's eyes gleamed with fatherly pride. "Yes, you did. Now if you could catch that murderer, the town could breathe easier."

"I'll catch the killer; don't you worry about that. I'm going right over and asking the sheriff for the victim's clothing. And I won't be leaving any more messages with Joe or any other unclean spirit. I learned my lesson."

CHAPTER 38

My boots kissed the edge of Sheriff Wayne Thompson's cluttered desk. "I need to examine the dead woman's clothing. As soon as possible." Confidence rang in my voice.

The sheriff stilled and searched my face. He nodded. "I can do that."

I let out the breath I'd been holding. Euphoria cartwheeled through me. This psychic detecting was a snap. I was on such a roll, I'd have this case solved before the school buses left the playground today.

Wayne skirted his desk with a long, prowling stride. I trailed after him, trying to keep a giddy grin off my face. The more of this I did, the easier it became. I'd soon earn the sheriff's approval and start drawing regular wages for my crime-solving efforts.

"What?" he asked as we walked toward the evidence cage.

I shook my head, not wanting to jeopardize my good fortune. After fixing Verbena and getting the message through to her granny, I felt invincible. One more dreamwalk and I'd solve this case. I knew it in my bones.

But I was smart enough to keep my mouth shut. No sense in inviting trouble. I shook my head and kept walking.

"You know something," Wayne said. "I can tell."

"You psychic?"

"Nah. Cop instinct."

Our steps echoed down the tiled corridor. Fluorescent lights flickered and buzzed overhead. Tamika hurried by with a stack of files, a fleeting smile for us.

"You should trust it more often." At his puzzled look, I continued, "Your instinct."

He fished a fat wad of keys from his pocket and unlocked two doors in our path. "Instinct doesn't close cases. Evidence does. Wait here." He closed the cage door, blocking me from physical access to the chaotic shelves of boxes and bags.

At this close range, a Pandora's box of emotions pulsed through the wire cage. Even with my senses buffered, rage, despair, fear, greed, and horror bombarded me. With my well-being foremost in mind, I edged down the hall a bit to reduce my proximity. For good measure, I summoned an invisible cloak of white light and metaphorically wrapped it around me, cloaking me from head to toe. A sense of order returned to my thoughts, but the taint of strong emotion persisted.

Whispers of doubt flitted at the edge of my mind. Sure, I'd helped Verbena, but I'd made a huge mistake first. What if I ran into another unforeseen circumstance? Whose life would I wreck this time? Mine?

"Baxley?"

The sudden male voice startled me from my fugue. I blinked as the familiar sights, slightly antiseptic smells, and the unrelenting hum of the law enforcement center returned to my perceptions. It worried me that I'd been so lost in my thoughts that I'd lost track of my surroundings. That was a first for me.

Wayne stood before me, box in hand. "You okay?"

The despair of Angel's weeping resurfaced in my thoughts as I eyed the box of her personal belongings. Resolve stiffened my spine. This time I wouldn't be put off by her sadness. I would demand answers.

I met his worried gaze. "I'm fine. Where are we going?"

"Interview Two."

Figured. He wouldn't take me to a place where I could be alone with her things. Even if he walked out of the immediate vicinity, he could watch me through the two-way mirror. There would be no privacy.

But I'd just dreamwalked in a public park in front of God and everybody. I could handle one here with Wayne watching. No big deal.

He placed the box on the table, sitting next to it. "Close the door, will ya?"

I pulled the door to. The catch snicked into place. I crossed to sit in a molded plastic chair. Wayne was staying in here with me? Fear surfaced in my head like a mythical sea monster, cavorting and frolicking through my chaotic thoughts. Did I trust Wayne not to mess with me while I was dreamwalking?

I wanted to trust him, but he'd slept with every woman in his path. Except me. And I'd be vulnerable while I was under. "I'd prefer to do this alone."

"Think again. These items are evidence. Police procedures must be followed, particularly the chain of evidence, or a good lawyer will get the case dismissed." He initialed the log and opened the box. Then he handed me a sheet of paper. "Here's the index."

The list was brief. A shirt. A bra. Slacks. Panties. One shoe. Her watch. That was it. Her clothing would be bloodstained. I'd rather not see that again. "Let me see the watch."

Wayne slipped on a pair of disposable gloves and tossed a pair to me as well. "Put these on." He rooted through the box and withdrew a sealed manila envelope.

A protest worked its way up my throat. I softened it in the spirit of cooperation. "I don't know if it will work with gloves on, but I'll try it your way first."

I fumbled the stretchy gloves on, my fingers getting trapped in the wrong places, then getting everything right but having the large gloves dwarf my small hands. "Good thing I'm not doing surgery." Wayne broke the evidence seal on the bag, and the watch spilled out into his gloved hand. He offered it to me. "Do your thing."

Doing my thing had been easy with Daddy at my side and an object from the deceased firmly in my hand. It wouldn't be so easy in this antiseptic room. Plus, disbelief emanated from Wayne. He wanted me to be successful, but he couldn't stifle his natural skepticism. I remembered from our tutoring days in high school he'd always understood things better when he could see them. With my request, I was asking him to take a leap of faith while I did something that couldn't be seen.

He'd already sidestepped protocol to allow me access to the murdered woman's belongings. But he wouldn't derail his career by leaving me alone with the physical evidence. Good cop instinct.

My instincts clamored, too. "Either believe in this process or move farther away from me."

The grin he flashed was all rogue and charm. "You getting bad vibes from me?"

"Something like that."

He retreated to the door, folding his arms across his taut belly. His gold badge gleamed on his belt, his holstered weapon within easy reach. "This is as much space as I can give you."

I nodded and summoned my courage. Most of my encounters with Angel/Lisa had been at her instigation. This time I would ask hard questions and get the answers we needed.

Rubbing my thumb over the drugstore-brand watch, I pictured Angel's decadent bower, and her rumpled sheets. A pathway appeared, and I slipped through the sensory veil.

Lights flashed. Then eerie darkness descended. I whirled like a teacup ride through the spirit world, spinning in a small orbit through ever-widening swaths of souls as I searched for this single spirit, the weeping woman with violet eyes.

Joe the unclean spirit intercepted me, his red eyes boring into mine. "I know where she is. Let me help you."

"Leave me alone." I shouted the words, but they came out as a low whisper. Something was different about this experience, something I couldn't quite put my finger on. I hurried away. After awhile I turned around. To my dismay, Joe was still with me. Joe and a few others. I'd been dragging them behind me.

I confronted them, uncertain of how to proceed, but positive this had to be addressed right now. What would Daddy do? He wouldn't tolerate it, that was for sure. I summoned the surety that I was right, that I needed to banish these beings from my sight so that I could find the murdered woman. I remembered the moldavite pendant at my neck and the amethyst crystal in my pocket. Strength and confidence returned.

Words appeared in my head. I used them. *"I command thee to leave me alone. To trouble me or others no more. Begone. You are not welcome to be with me or to follow me. You may not use me as a portal."*

Joe and his pals convulsed and shouted. They slunk away.

The thick, unwholesome darkness subsided into the gloom I normally encountered here. I breathed easier, hoping the challenge was concluded and that I'd passed.

Now to find Angel.

I summoned the image of the watch. Angel's bedroom appeared before me. She wept as usual. Her sorrow touched me, but I didn't allow empathy to sway me from my plan of action. The way to help her was to get justice for her murder.

I sat on the edge of her rumpled bed. In the pale light, her creamy skin stood in stark relief to the dark furnishings in the room. "Angel, I'm here to help you."

She cradled her face in splayed hands. "No one can help me. No one."

"I can help. I promise. Tell me more about your baby in We-tumpka. What's her name?"

Her long black hair parted to reveal mascara-stained tear tracks on her pale face. "My son. Oh, my poor son. I thought he would be safe. My mother is in danger. My son's life is in danger."

"I don't understand the danger. Tell me your son's name."

"Dyani calls him Little Warrior because his cries are so fierce."

"What do you call him? What's on his birth certificate?"

"I can't tell. She'll know. And she'll hurt my baby."

My maternal instinct swelled. I used it to further my plea for obtaining justice. "I need the child's name. The sheriff can make sure your baby isn't in danger."

"I don't believe you. She knows you talk to me."

That stopped me. Whoever Angel feared knew about my dreamwalking? "How does she know this? Is she a dreamwalker, too?"

"No. She doesn't visit me like you do. But she hurt Jay. She'll hurt Little Warrior, too. I must keep my baby safe."

"Did she hurt you? Did she kill you?"

"She killed me and burned my place. She wiped out all traces of my life. If not for Dyani and Little Warrior, no one would even know I existed. But you could help me. The jewelry Jay bought for me is in a safe deposit box in Macon. Could you tell Dyani?"

"I can once we locate her. Did you live in Macon?"

"Yes."

I hardly dared trust my good fortune. "Tell me about the safe deposit box. What name is it under?"

"Lisa Noble. Box two-five-eight-nine at the Mid-State Bank in Macon. But the key. The key was in my place when it burned."

"Don't worry about the key. We'll figure that part out. How come you go by Angel and Lisa?"

"Angel was my stage name. Angelique is my middle name. Lisa Angelique Noble. That's who I am."

Her words winged through me, lightening my heart. I'd done it. I'd found hard evidence the sheriff could use to solve the case. I patted her hand. "Thank you. I'll work on this right away."

Chapter 39

My physical surroundings swam into focus. Light-green-colored walls. Laminated tabletop. A cheap watch. A pile of discarded gloves. Molded plastic chairs. Fluorescent lighting. Sheriff Wayne Thompson holding my trembling hand.

I tried to jerk it free. He held tight. Primal fear roared through me. I sipped in shallow bursts of air and sought balance in my thoughts.

"Easy there, easy." Wayne spoke in the soft tone one used for injured animals.

His gentleness further confused me. Was I hurt? I glanced at my limbs, all of which were intact. My shirt was damp, and my feet weighed a ton. I tried to speak, but my voice came out as a croak. I caught the sheriff's gaze, willing unspoken questions into my eyes.

"You were out a long time, babe." His thumb stroked my hand. "I was worried. You okay?"

"Water," I managed to whisper.

Water appeared. I drank. We were alone, but I sensed the presence of another, watching from the corridor. I had information the sheriff needed. But how would I honor my promise to Angel to ensure that the news didn't reach her killer's ears?

"What time is it?" I asked.

"After five."

"I have to go." I tried to stand. While I'd been here saving the world, Larissa had been home alone. "My daughter—"

"Shh." He gently tugged me back down with his grip on my hand. "Your parents have her. I got your back."

Comforting and yet worrisome. I'd been dreamwalking for hours? I'd never been gone so long before. All that searching and wrestling with unclean spirits had messed up my internal clock. But the journey hadn't been for naught. The information I'd learned glittered in my thoughts.

I leaned close to Wayne, blinking against his woodsy after-shave, and spoke softly. "I know who your victim is. But we have a problem. Her killer knows someone in your office and is getting information in real time. We have to keep this between us, or a child's life is at risk."

He startled, but he kept his mouth near my ear. "I've got a leak? Who?"

I closed my eyes in relief. "I'm not the answer woman. I've only got one answer for you. But you've got to keep it under wraps until we secure the child. Give me your notebook."

He clasped my hand to his chest and held my gaze. "Does this mean you won't whisper sweet nothings in my ear any-more?"

My good mood soured. "We agreed—"

"Yeah, yeah." He reached for the notebook and handed it over. "You're fun to tease."

I scribbled down the information and handed the notebook back. He scanned it and pointed to the word Macon. "You're sure about this?"

"Dead sure." I watched him put the notebook away, wondering if his thoughts aligned with mine. The only person on his staff with north Georgia connections was the state archaeologist, our temporary coroner, Gail Bergeron. "It's up to you now. I've done my part."

He bagged the evidence, resealed it, and tucked the box under one arm. Locking his other arm through mine, he guided me out of the room. Gail hovered in the hall, wearing her white lab coat over a dark suit and heels, a stethoscope draped around her neck.

"I should check her vitals," Gail said. "She was unconscious for hours."

Until I knew if she was a killer or merely the killer's friend, I didn't want her touching me. "I'm fine."

"Sheriff, I insist. This woman looks dehydrated."

Wayne studied me. "She seems all right to me."

"You may have a liability in this." An elaborate silver pin on Gail's coat lapel caught the light as she gestured. "Baxley could sue the department."

I waved off her protest. "I'm not suing anyone. That's not how we do things in coastal Georgia. I appreciate your concern, but I'm fine. I don't need medical attention."

I would have given anything to read her aura, but I was spent. It was all I could do to keep the negative energy of this place at bay. From the start, my instincts warned me to be careful around this woman. That hadn't changed. Gail would not go quietly into the night.

She couldn't.

She had too much to lose.

Gail had to be the leak.

Or the killer.

I couldn't deal with her in my weakened state. She was right about my exhaustion level. I'd never been out so long before. And I'd burned a lot of psychic energy before I came here today. All I wanted to do was go home and crawl into bed.

"I have to get out of here," I said to Wayne once we'd walked past Gail.

"I'll take you home," he said. "First, I've got to return the evidence. You still like sodas and chocolate bars?"

I managed a weak smile. "You are psychic."

Directing me to his office, Wayne procured a soda and candy bars. "Eat."

I ate as he called his contacts in Macon. The ice-cold drink refreshed me as it sped from lips to toes. The chocolate bars tasted like heaven. I yawned and shivered in the cool room.

He hung up the phone. "Stay here while I return the evidence to the cage. I'll be right back."

I yawned again, wrapping my arms around my full belly for additional warmth. "I'm really tired."

He tossed me a jacket, which I burrowed under. "Ya done good."

"Mmm." I drifted into a light sleep. Demons and angels chased me on a twilight plain. I was tired, so tired. I couldn't run anymore.

"Wake up, sleepyhead." Wayne stroked my hair. "If you don't walk out of here under your own power, Gail's gonna pitch a fit. I had one of my guys ask her something about a case, but I can't promise she'll stay distracted long enough for us to get away. Can you walk?"

I groaned at the thought of walking anywhere. My entire system demanded sleep. But if I had to do this, I would. Daddy had walked out of here a few months ago after a long dream-walk. If Daddy could do it, so could I.

"That's it," Wayne said as I stood. He caught me when my knees buckled. "Never mind." He scooped me in his arms like a bridegroom carrying his beloved over the threshold. "If my wife hears about this, we're both dead."

"Don't tell Dottie." My eyes drifted shut again. "I certainly won't."

CHAPTER 40

Sunlight streamed in my bedroom window. My eyes snapped shut at the startling brilliance. I reached up to cover my eyes, only to discover my head ached, and my skin felt hot to the touch. Downstairs, I heard someone bustling around in the kitchen. The mouthwatering aroma of my mother's soup wafted through the air.

I struggled to rise. "Mama?"

Rapid footfalls sounded on the stairs. Mama appeared in the doorway in a faded jumper and lime-green shirt, gray braid slung over her shoulder, worry stamped on her thin face. "There you are. We've been waiting for you to wake up. How're you feeling?"

"Sorta like that old saying: rode hard and put up wet." I realized I was still in yesterday's clothes. I sat up fast, making the room slide a bit.

"Easy, dear." Mama hurried forward, Daddy and Larissa close on her heels. Larissa carried a small tray with tea and toast. Muffin padded in and jumped on the bed; Precious laid her nose on the covers and snuffled.

I accepted the tray and petted the dogs. "What is all this?"

Larissa settled in next to me. "Food, silly."

"You may be good at dreamwalking, but there are limits to everything," Daddy said. "You shouldn't take such risks."

I could mouth off something witty, but I didn't feel clever this morning. I hurt all the way down to my marrow. A pain reliever was what I needed, but Mama would take offense at the use of non-holistic medicine. I sipped her herbal tea instead.

"Well?" Mama asked.

I cleared my throat. "I'm sorry for worrying everyone. I had another run-in with Joe." Alarm flared in Daddy's eyes. "It's all right. I'm fine, honestly. Just worn out."

He nodded and appeared to be choosing his words. "Wrestling with Joe will do that to ya."

I got the message. He didn't want me to upset Mama and Larissa. "What happened? Last I remember, I was in the sheriff's office drinking a soda."

"Exhaustion, dear." Mama bustled around the room, opening the drapes, putting away the laundry in the basket on my floor. "You must take better care of your health."

I reached down for my cell phone, found it missing from my belt clip. "Has anyone heard from Wayne this morning? We had a breakthrough on the case."

"He said he'd be in touch." Daddy gripped Mama by the elbow. "Let's check on that soup pot, Lacey. Give the girls a chance to catch up."

Mama pursed her lips but left. I munched my toast under Larissa's watchful eyes.

"You really all right?" she asked.

"I could kill for some ibuprofen."

Larissa dug into her pocket. "Got you covered. What really happened?"

I downed the tablets with the rest of my herbal tea. "I found out the name of the woman at Mallow. The sheriff was going to follow up." I touched her shoulder. "Sorry I worried you, pumpkin. I lost track of time while I dreamwalked. It took so long to find her."

"Who's this Joe? And give me a straight answer, not the wandering spirit stuff Pap fed Mama Lacey."

"Dreamwalking has a downside, love. I used to worry about my ability because I didn't want people to know I talked to dead people. But it's not the dead people you have to watch out for. There are other things in that realm. Dangerous things. I don't want you trying it without Pap or me there to help you."

"Did these bad things hurt you?"

Silence crinkled like cellophane. I was at a crossroads with my daughter. I could shield her from the truth, or I could give her small doses of it. Protect her innocence or shatter it.

One fact was undeniable. Larissa was only ten years old. "I want you to grow up and run and play and be a kid in every way. Knowledge exacts a cost."

"I've never seen you so zonked. And you were gone so long." My daughter looked at me with hurt in her Powell green eyes, so very much like Roland's eyes that my breath hitched in my throat. "I couldn't feel you. I thought you were dead."

And just like that, my answer narrowed to one choice. "I'm very much alive, though I pushed the limits yesterday. I won't do that again. It was a special circumstance."

"Promise?"

"Promise." I hugged her close, inhaling her fresh, unspoiled fragrance, very much aware of the fact I needed a shower. The contact warmed the chill in my bones. The sunbeams didn't seem to hurt my eyes so much. My fever subsided.

I managed a half-laugh. "This feels great to sit and cuddle with you, but I've got to get a shower and get going on this day."

"Not until you finish this tea and toast and eat a bowl of soup. Mama Lacey is all set to do her crystal thing. You have to promise to do those things first."

"Deal."

CHAPTER 41

Tamika buzzed me into the admin area. "The sheriff wants you to come on back."

Wayne's voice had been upbeat on the phone. If this was any indication of how my Saturday was gonna go, I had no worries. I strolled down the hall, my mental shields fully engaged, a bounce in my step.

The sheriff stood when I entered his office. "Good work, Powell. We've positively identified our murder victim. Macon PD faxed us her sheet." He picked up the file and read aloud. "Lisa Angelique Noble, of Roosevelt Parkway, Macon. Former exotic dancer. Arrested twice for solicitation. Her apartment caught fire about two weeks ago, but the blaze didn't spread to the neighbors' apartments. The super thought she was out of town during the incident. The property owner plans to tear the building down as soon as the other residents can vacate the premises."

"Did anyone mention a kid?"

"Nope. No kid. Lisa lived alone, except for a gentleman caller, who came at varying hours of the day and night. She routinely traveled for extended periods of time, hence the thought of her traveling these last few weeks."

"Probably visiting her kid. Wetumpka isn't that far from Macon, coupla hours at most. What about the jewelry in the safety deposit box?"

"Can't get into the bank until Monday."

I swore under my breath. If there was a leak here in the Sinclair County Sheriff's Office, the killer could find out about the child before Monday. "That isn't good enough."

"It'll have to do. With all the budget cutbacks, most banks, including this one, are closed on Saturdays."

"You've kept quiet about the child?"

"Yep. No one here knows about a kid. All they know is we've got a dead young woman from Macon."

"Please keep it that way, until we make sure the baby is safe."

The intercom buzzed. "Sheriff, the boys are back with the package you requested. Where do you want it?"

A slow smile spread across Wayne's face. "Interview One. We'll be right there." He stood. "You might find this interview interesting."

I rose, my hand at my heart. "Me? You want me to watch you interview a suspect?"

"You catch on quick. Follow me."

He expected me to heel like a dog? That rankled. But he wasn't hitting on me, and he was treating me like an equal. Progress of a sort.

I peered in the room. Duke Quigley looked small between the massive girths of Deputies Virg Burkhead and Ronnie Oliver. Duke appeared to have a black eye. Grass stains dotted his shirt and torn jeans.

My blood pressure kicked up a notch. "You're right. I very much want to be in on this."

"Follow my lead." Wayne entered the small room.

Duke's head bobbed when Wayne cruised in. His eyes widened at the sight of me. He cursed in a guttural tone. "You! Murderer!"

Virg and Ronnie hung close to the suspect. Was that for his protection or mine?

I glared at Duke. "The only thing I killed, Duke Quigley, was a snake."

"You shot Adam. Blew his head right off. You're gonna pay for that."

"Not hardly. I acted in self-defense. You, on the other hand, acted with malice. I could have died."

"No way. Those snakes ate right before I moved 'em. Plus I milked 'em. They wouldn't hurt nobody."

His words infuriated me. I charged forward. "I have a kid, you moron."

Wayne caught me by the collar of my T-shirt. "Hold up."

I tried to bat his hand away, but his fingers remained snug on the cotton fabric. Outrage simmered in my veins. "Duke tried to kill me."

"You put those rattlesnakes in her truck, Dairy Queen?" Wayne asked.

Duke hung his head. "I did. But she shot my babies. Adam's all blown to bits, and Eve's vanished." His head popped back up. Tears filled his eyes. "Eve don't know the first thing about living in the wild. She don't even know how to hunt. Probably some hawk ate her for dinner."

"Those snakes were the property of Pax Out. They weren't yours," Wayne said.

Duke's chin went up. "I tend to 'em. I care about 'em. They was mine all right."

"Bubba Paxton says he won't press theft charges if you co-operate with us."

"Bubba's a good man, a fair man. But this witch here, she kept me from making my money. No one gets between Duke Quigley and his money."

"Powell can be aggravating, but you can't put snakes in her truck. That's a crime. We've got you cold on that."

Wayne's words stung. I thought he was on my side. Anger

welled up inside me. I was about to lash out at him when I realized he was massaging my stiff neck. What was going on?

"We've got questions that only you can answer," Wayne said. "You spend a lot of time up in Macon, right, DQ?"

Duke's eyes darted from me to Wayne. "I've got cousins in Macon. My ex lives there, too."

"From where I'm standing, you're in a helluva fix, man. You had unlimited access to Mallow, and you have connections to the murder victim's last known place of residence."

Duke swore. "You have any idea how many people live in Macon? I don't know nuttin' about any dead woman. I wasn't trying to kill Baxley. I just wanted to scare her for messing up my pay."

Words boiled out of my throat. "You put poisonous snakes in my truck, moron. You're gonna serve time for that."

"You are indeed going to pay for her damages, DQ. Whether or not she presses criminal charges against you is dependent on your next answers."

"Like what?"

"Did you know Carolina Byrd before she contracted with you to build Mallow?" the sheriff asked.

The builder shook his head. "Didn't know her." Duke studied his work-thickened fingers for a long moment. "Knew her husband though."

Air whistled through my teeth. He was telling the truth. I was certain of it. With Duke's admission, puzzle pieces jelled in my head. Why hadn't I seen these connections before?

"Her husband?" Wayne's voice sounded neutral, as if he didn't care one way or the other. How did he do that? I wanted to snatch Duke up and threaten to choke him until he told me everything.

"Yeah. I used to cat around a bit with Judson Byrd a few years back. He was one helluva party animal. He liked this dancer at a club. Angel. Man, was she hot. I'd have nailed her if Judson hadn't flashed his money around first."

Judson Byrd. He could be Angel's "Jay." If that was true, Angel's son might have been fathered by Judson Byrd. Was the "she" Angel was so terrified of Carolina Byrd?

Carolina was demanding and powerful and commanded a lot of wealth. That didn't make her a killer. I searched my memory for other details I knew about my former client. She had a kid. A special-needs kid. That's why she had so many extras built into Mallow, to accommodate her kid.

"You ever sleep with Carolina Byrd?" Wayne asked.

Duke sneered at me. "Does she have to be here?"

"Yes, she does. Your honesty will determine what she does."

"No. I never slept with my boss."

The air around him shifted and his aura darkened. His nostrils flared, and he averted his eyes, all things he hadn't done during our previous conversations. "You're lying." Confidence oozed through my pores. "You had a personal relationship with her."

He shrugged, looking not the least repentant. "Sue me. She wasn't married then. We didn't break any laws. We hooked up a few times when she came down to see how the house was coming along."

"You still hooking up with her?" Wayne asked.

Duke huffed out a breath. "Nah. She's moved on to Buster. And good riddance."

"Why?"

"She never shut up the whole time. Yammering on and on. It was enough to give me a complex. No wonder her husband had a hottie like Angel on the side. His wife was a she-devil."

CHAPTER 42

"Thanks for coming in on a Sunday." Sheriff Wayne Thompson unstacked his heels from his desk and waved me into his office. For once he didn't leer at my body. Was he finally seeing me as a person and not another conquest? "You were most helpful during the Duke Quigley interview. I'd like you to observe Carolina Byrd while I talk to her. She'll be here in a few minutes."

"Carolina won't like me being included," I warned.

"She isn't in a position to bargain." He studied me a long moment. "How'd you know Quigley was lying?"

I doubted he wanted a metaphysical explanation. "His words felt wrong. That's the best explanation I can give."

"You some kind of lie detector?" His dark eyes took on a faraway look. "You got any idea how valuable that would be in law enforcement?"

I dismissed his remark with a quick flip of my wrist. "Not very. Knowing someone is lying is different from proving it. Besides, I don't always know if a person is lying. Just sometimes. Some people are very good liars."

He nodded. "Here's the thing. Carolina is on her way back up to Macon. I don't have any reason to tell her not to leave town, but if you pick up a lying vibe, I want to know about it. You nod at me or kick me under the table, you hear? We'll explain your presence by saying you're exploring the possibility of a job in law enforcement."

"That's a very good lie. It's close enough to the truth that it's believable. That's why my divination talents aren't a hundred percent."

The intercom buzzed. "She's here," Wayne said. "Remember, you're in observation mode unless I say otherwise."

"Got it." I followed him to the reception area, murmured a polite hello when spoken to by my former employer. Once the niceties were over, she ignored me.

"You said there was news about the case. Are you releasing my property?" Carolina wore a demure mint-green, skirted suit. A silver filigree pen adorned the jacket lapel.

"We have news, but not that kind of news." Wayne waited until both of us selected a chair in Interview Two before he sat. "The victim has been identified. Her name is Lisa Noble. Does that sound familiar?"

Carolina held very still, as if sifting through her brain to remember every name she'd ever encountered. "I don't recognize the name."

"It turns out that she has ties to someone here in Sinclair County," Wayne said. "To your builder, in fact. Were you aware that Duke Quigley often socialized up Macon way?"

She frowned. "Let me think. Oh yes, it's coming to me now. My late husband recommended we hire Duke to build our house down here. Seems they were acquainted."

"Indeed." Wayne leaned forward across the table. "Your builder also knew the victim."

Carolina's head jerked. Her face flushed. "He's not my builder any longer. I fired him last week. On the same day I fired my landscaper." She shot me a pointed look.

I ignored her barb. So far I couldn't tell if she was lying or telling the truth. However, going by her reaction, her last response seemed genuine. Time for me to earn my pay, whatever the heck that would be. I caught Wayne's eye and nodded as imperceptibly as possible.

"Your builder knew Lisa Noble. That seems like a co-incidence." Wayne's eyes narrowed. "I don't trust coincidences."

"I didn't realize until I hired the man that he was ungovernable," Carolina said. "I'm not surprised in the least. The man even made a pass at me. As if someone of my social standing would lower myself to his level." She shuddered. "Did you arrest him?"

"We don't have any direct evidence, other than their previous association, that puts them together at the time of death. But my gut says we're on the right track."

"Don't worry about me, Sheriff. I've distanced myself from the man. Once you arrest him, this nightmare will end and I'll be able to get on with my life." She fiddled with her highlighted hair and looked at Wayne through her darkened eyelashes. "I have complete faith in you. The sooner you arrest him the better for me."

I had no idea if she was lying there or not, but it galled me that she was flirting with Wayne in front of me. Hell, did she want to sleep with any man she came in contact with? And why should I even care? Wayne had the morals of an alley cat. It wasn't like he held the vows of his marriage sacred.

I was supposed to keep quiet, but I needed to shake Carolina's cool façade. I couldn't read her otherwise. "I've been wondering about the victim, Sheriff. Why didn't her family miss her before now?"

Wayne blinked in confusion, as if he had to break Carolina's siren spell to even glance my way. "We're still searching for her next of kin. She appears to have no fixed address; it's possible she lived on the streets."

A flat-out lie on his part and a corresponding nasty glow to his aura. I may not be learning about Carolina's talent for lying, but I could spot a whopper from the sheriff now. Useful information, indeed.

"Neither of you is to mention her name to anyone until we issue an official press release," he cautioned. "Meanwhile, Ms. Byrd, avoid any communication with Duke Quigley."

"Not to worry. I never want to hear his name again. You arrest Duke for this, and I promise to make it worth your while."

We walked her out to the lobby where Gail Bergeron waited. The two of them put their blond heads together and departed. Something else clicked in my head. Carolina's filigreed pin. Gail had one like it, and I was fairly certain I'd seen Muriel Jamison wearing one.

They'd been sorority sisters in college. Perhaps that was the reason for the similar jewelry.

But Lisa Noble had worn jewelry of the same design. What was the connection there?

"Well?" Wayne asked.

"She's very good at lying. The only thing I'm certain of is that she wants you to arrest Duke. Oh, and she wants to sleep with you. That's the absolute truth. The rest was cloaked in shades of the truth."

"I didn't need you for that. I figured that out on my own. What's your gut tell ya?"

I barked out a laugh. "She's up to her ears in this. You have a reprieve because she doesn't know you like her for the crime. I think she did it. I believe she killed Lisa and framed Duke for it. Probably planned to frame me as well by putting my trowel in Lisa's grave."

His brows rose. "Dang, woman. Your gut feeling matches mine. Too bad we can't prove it."

"She's clever. What if we can't tie her to the murder?"

"No matter how clever folks are, there are always loose ends. That safe deposit box might be our ace in the hole."

"I hope so. It would creep me out to know that she got away

with murder and lives here in Sinclair County."

"Don't you worry. I'm on the case."

Despite his assurance, worry hounded me all the way home. How were we going to tie Carolina to the crime? She'd had a week in Macon to cover her tracks. If there were witnesses or evidence lying around, she'd already made them go away.

How did one catch a clever killer?

CHAPTER 43

Lisa came to me that night. Her casual clothes and tied-back hair fooled me at first. If not for the plain dime-store watch and intense violet eyes, I wouldn't have recognized her. This version of Lisa looked like an ordinary young woman.

Her slender hands worried at each other. "Is my baby all right?"

I glanced around the unfamiliar dreamscape. It looked different. Less solid. As if Lisa had somehow met me partway between my world and hers. I couldn't quite catch my breath. My stomach writhed. "Where am I?"

She waved my question away. "My baby? I gave you what you wanted. What about my son? Is he safe?"

I wobbled, clutching my gut. "The bank is closed on Sunday. We'll access your safety deposit box tomorrow."

"Tomorrow is too late!" she wailed.

The room spun. I sank to my knees. "Please, let me go. This place. It's wrong for me. I can't breathe."

As darkness descended, her parting words zinged my ear. "She'll kill again."

When I awoke, the sky had begun to lighten. I clutched the covers to my neck and shivered until I warmed. The more I dream-walked, the more I realized how little I knew about it. Finding someone in a dreamscape was hard enough, but there were dangerous pitfalls like unclean spirits and airless venues.

Precious thrust her nose on the bed, wagging her tail expectantly. I reached out and stroked her intelligent head, ruffling the soft fur of her fluffy ears. A soft whining sound filled her throat.

I knew that cry. She wanted to go out.

My eyes snapped shut in protest. I wasn't ready to face a new day, not with so many unanswered questions circling in my head. Why couldn't I hone in on Lisa's killer? What was I missing? I'd worried late into the night, finally falling asleep after two a.m. Four hours of sleep wasn't enough. I needed to stay sharp if I wanted to catch this killer. But the thought of returning to that inhospitable dreamscape propelled me right out of bed.

Easing past Larissa's room, I padded downstairs in my cotton PJs. Muffin heard the activity and abandoned Larissa's bed, following us outside. The dogs sniffed around the backyard, watering their favorite spots.

Next to the back door was another stack of fresh vegetables and a foil-covered mound. Ever since I'd become the dreamwalker, vegetables had shown up at my door, as if the universe was paying its dues for my services. I could definitely get used to this. I held the thick bunch of greens to my face and inhaled their sun-kissed aroma.

The foil-encased mound was a lump of homemade bread. I pinched off a bit of crust and tried it. Yum. Oat bread.

Muffin sensed he was missing out on food, came up, and begged a pinch. I knelt and gave him a morsel. Only one dog begging? Where was Precious? I stood and scanned the yard. The flat-coated lab was nowhere to be seen.

"Precious?"

Nothing. All I could think of was that rattlesnake. If the snake bit Precious, she'd die before I found her and got her to a vet. Outrage roared inside me. I wasn't losing this client. Precious was my responsibility.

I hustled Muffin inside, thrust my feet into a pair of old boots, grabbed the Glock, and hurried outside, locking the door behind me. I suspected the dog went into the woods, but I checked the highway first to be safe. No dog there.

Lungs burning, I raced back to the wood line behind my house. "Precious?"

No answer. Where was that dog?

I'd promised Louise Gilroy I'd keep her dog safe. Now I'd lost her. I had to find Precious. I called her again. Precious could be anywhere, and if she was on a scent, she'd ignore me. So what was she following? Was someone out here in the woods?

I leaned against a live oak, trying to catch my breath. My extrasensory hearing worked for people but not for animals. If Precious was chasing something human, I could find her. I allowed myself to hope that this was the case. I listened with my extra senses, probing the woods. To my right, a person hurried away from my location. I sensed another person, also on the move, father to the right, only this person seemed to be on an intercept course with the runner.

I considered my choices. I could hide in the house and call the sheriff's office. I could go after the people because that was more than likely where the dog went.

Larissa's safety came first. She was asleep in the locked house. She was fine. I needed to find the dog, and I couldn't take the chance on her finding her way back home. Not with that busy highway in front of my house. It would break my heart if she was struck by a car. I had to go after her.

I angled right along the wood line, looking for a deer path to follow into the underbrush. Found it. Slipped into the shadowed forest. I moved swiftly, trying not to cause undue noise, gun in hand at my side. The fleeing person I was mentally tracking met up with the more deliberate person. The mental signature of the deliberate person reminded me of my watcher. Moments later, the fleeing person went down, and the deliberate person huffed out a breath. The fleeing person didn't move, and the deliberate person, my watcher, melted back into the woods.

Precious barked. And barked some more. I followed the sound of her barking to where Buster Glassman lay hogtied in my woods. His dark clothing was torn; his perfect blond hair and prep school looks were marred by scratches and briars. His glasses lay six feet away from him as if he'd run into a brick wall.

"Good girl." I petted Precious' head. She continued to bark at Buster. He appeared to be out cold. Oh, for a bucket of water to throw on him.

I pinged the area again. My watcher had stopped a distance away. If he were after me, all he had to do was wait here for me. Instead, he'd caught Buster and trussed him up for me to find. I could ask Precious to track the watcher, but the person was quick, effective, and most likely lethal. Knowing his identity wasn't worth the dog's life. I'd keep the dog with me.

Buster moaned.

I leaned down close to his face, noting he lay in a patch of blackberry briars. "What are you doing in my woods?"

"My head," he said. "What did you hit me with?"

I didn't hit him with anything, but it didn't hurt to have him think I was a superhero. "I'm asking the questions here. Why are you watching my house?"

Precious barked as if she'd found public enemy number one.

Buster swore, struggled against his bonds, and swore some more. "Shut the blasted dog up. I can't think."

"Should have thought of that before you came after me. Why are you here?"

Globs of dog saliva flew from the lab's mouth, spattering Buster's back. I made no effort to curb her barking. Buster cringed under the barrage of noise. I hoped he was worried about Precious biting him.

"She told me to come. Shut the dog up, I beg you."

I leaned close to his shadowed face. "She who?"

"Carolina."

"Your girlfriend?"

"Christ. How do you know about that?"

"You'd be surprised at the things I know. Why?"

He remained silent. I nudged him with my foot.

"She doesn't trust you. She asked me to keep an eye on you. That's all. I swear."

His aura shifted. I called him on it. "Liar. Try again."

"I'm not telling you anything."

"No problem. I'll mosey on back to the house and call the sheriff. Precious will keep you company while I'm gone. Oh, and thanks to your good buddy, Duke, there's a mean rattlesnake loose out here. I wouldn't thrash too much if I were you."

With that, I hurried home and made the call. While I waited, I swapped out my PJ pants for jeans in the laundry room. I found a clean T-shirt and donned it. No socks or undergarments in this load of wash. And I didn't want to risk waking Larissa by going upstairs. This outfit would suffice. It wasn't like the sheriff's staff expected me to be model perfect.

Deputy Elwood arrived ten minutes later. "I've got a problem in my woods," I said.

Elwood grinned, showing the gap between his front teeth. He looked like he could bench-press two adults without breaking a sweat. "Good. I eat problems for breakfast."

CHAPTER 44

"I'm fine, Daddy." Clutching the phone to my ear, I hurried up the sidewalk toward the Sinclair County Law Enforcement Center. "Really, I am."

"I know better than that," my father said. "What's going on?"

A light breeze blew, stirring my striped hair, which was still hanging loose. I wore no socks inside my boots, no bra under my T-shirt. Perhaps I should've stopped to fully dress before I followed Deputy Elwood back to the jail.

"I'm going to observe the sheriff question the man we caught this morning. I want to know why he was out there in my woods. That's what's going on."

"You know the man? Is he tied up in that Mallow mess?"

"Yes and yes."

The line hummed with silence. "Is there anything I can do?"

"Y'all got Larissa off to school all right?"

"Did that. Your mom's put a pot of soup on to simmer in your crock-pot."

I stopped before the glass entry doors. "Thanks for everything. I mean that. When this is all over, you and I need to have a long talk."

"Fine." He hesitated. "You sure I can't do something else to help?"

Inspiration struck. I didn't know how Gail Bergeron was tied up in this mess, but I believed she was a conduit to Carolina Byrd. "Can you keep Gail Bergeron busy and away from here this morning?"

"She's involved?" His voice rose with each syllable.

"She could be. I don't know for sure. Best if she's out of the picture."

"I'll ask her to meet me at the funeral home to review my training again. Oh, and Baxley?"

At the tentative sound of his voice, my lungs hitched. "Yeah?"

"Charlotte came by here madder than a wet hornet. Said you were ducking her calls."

I groaned. "I am, and I feel awful about it. I can't tell her about the case. And I don't want to place her in danger."

"Be that as it may, she's on her way to you."

Air eased out of my mouth. "Thanks for the warning."

With that, I pocketed the phone and entered the building. The air of miasma hit me, and I insulated myself from it. This was no time to get overwhelmed by the despair and malaise in the jail.

Tamika buzzed me right in. Her black hair was styled in an elaborate upsweep, her ample curves barely contained in a sheriff's office navy blue polo and snug khakis. She gave me a knowing glance. "You get dressed in a hurry?"

I grinned, knowing she'd spotted my lack of a specific undergarment. "Can you tell?"

"Oh, yeah. And all the guys in here's gonna know, too. The earth is moving when you walk, sistah."

I thumbed my hair from behind my ears, smoothing the hair forward, wishing I had more length to spill down my chest. "Is that better?"

She laughed out loud. "Get on back there before you cause me to bust a gut laughing."

I turned to do her bidding but then thought better of it. "Charlotte's on her way here. I can't tell you what to do, but the less she knows about this, the better."

Tamika winked. "Don't you worry, sugah. I can handle the press."

The press. That thought stayed with me as I made the trek down the corridor to the interview room. Charlotte was the press, an outsider. I was now tentatively associated with law enforcement, an insider within these walls. Officially, we were on opposite sides of the fence. I wasn't sure how that made me feel. Charlotte and I went way back.

One thing was certain. Charlotte would pitch a hissy fit, and I was glad I wasn't Tamika.

Sheriff Wayne Thompson strolled in through the back door. His hair looked freshly showered; his clothes looked freshly laundered. Must have been a good night for him. Not that I wanted details.

His dark eyes warmed at the sight of me. "You just roll out of bed?"

I waved dismissively. "Don't start. I rolled out of bed, chased a pervert through the woods, and now I'm here to find out why he targeted me. I didn't stop to dress for success along the way."

Deputy Elwood exited Interview One. "Got you a present, Sheriff. Found this id-jit hogtied in Baxley's woods."

I waited while Elwood filled the sheriff in. "Thanks. Go ahead and get that incident report written. I'll take it from here."

Wayne turned to me, amusement lighting his eyes. "You are full of surprises. How'd you get the drop on Glassman?"

I lowered my gaze to seem more demure. "Roland taught me some moves." I didn't want to reveal my watcher. If it was my allegedly departed husband out there in the woods, I wouldn't give him up. There had to be a good reason for him to stay away from us.

The sheriff shook his head. "You're my dream woman, babe. Smart. Pretty. Kick-ass fightin' skills. Roland must've been in

238

hog heaven being married to you."

So much in heaven that he hadn't contacted me in two years. My hand reached for the pendant. Wherever he was, I prayed he was safe.

"We had a good marriage," I managed to say.

"Lucky you. And thanks to you we've got a desperate man on the ropes. I'm gonna lean on him until he sings. You ready?"

Incredulity crept into my voice. "You want me to come inside with you?"

"Yep. Do your voodoo stuff. Freak him out."

"I don't do voodoo." I worked to unclench my fists. "Besides, Buster's mad at me for not helping him with his online betting. My presence will be counterproductive."

"Perfect. Angry men make mistakes. Come on."

With that, we entered the small room. Seated at the table, Buster looked lost without his glasses, but he'd smoothed his wild hair down and tucked his shirt back in. He no longer looked like a terrorist.

His spine stiffened at the sight of me. "Bitch."

I projected a calm appearance as if his scorn meant nothing. His dark aura seethed and roiled. Noxious emotions surged through his pores. Anger I expected. Fear, too. But there was something else present.

Dread.

He didn't want his secrets uncovered. A smile flitted through my thoughts.

"Play nice, Glassman." The sheriff took a seat across from Buster. "This woman just took you down. You are in a heap of trouble."

Buster rubbed his raw wrists and glared at Wayne. "Screw you."

"You been Mirandized?" Wayne asked.

The realtor nodded. "Yeah. Write me up and cut me loose.

You can't keep me here."

"You gonna quote the law to me?"

"Hell, no. I just need to leave. I've got somewhere I've gotta be."

"Where?"

"None of your beeswax."

Throughout this interchange, I'd gotten a handle on his voice. His responses so far appeared to be truthful; now I had a good baseline with which to monitor his forthcoming responses.

"But it is my business," Wayne said. "I know about your gambling problem. I know about the payments you've been making to Vegas. The payments never end, do they?"

Buster swore inventively. He pointed his index finger at me. "She told you, didn't she? I shoulda known she couldn't keep her trap shut."

Wayne got in Buster's face. "I know you threatened her when she wouldn't fix your problem. I know you stalked her. Those are criminal activities. Face it. You're a criminal. And, you're a murder suspect. My prime suspect."

Buster surged to his feet. "I didn't kill anybody."

CHAPTER 45

"Sit down or I'll have to shoot ya." The sheriff had his hand on his service weapon.

Buster melted back into his chair, his spine and collarbone losing their rigidity. His eyes rounded. "I didn't do it. I didn't kill anyone."

"I'm not buying it. There are big chunks of money passing through your bank account. Money from an offshore account. You're up to your neck in this."

Buster swore some more. He studied his curled fingers. He looked up, a cunning gleam in his eye. "The money's mine. I earned it."

I was surprised by the truth of that statement. I had no knowledge of the banking irregularities Wayne just revealed, but things looked bad for Buster. He wouldn't be sniffing around my woods again anytime soon.

The sheriff didn't so much as look my way. "That's the thing. How'd you earn it?"

"Family money. Dividends. That kind of thing."

The lie socked me between the eyes. I inhaled sharply. Wayne sent me a warning look, as if he knew it was a lie, too.

"Try again," the sheriff said. "Those payments started a few months ago. Ten thousand dollars, regular as clockwork. Your family doesn't have that kind of money. I know about your daddy's weakness for the flesh. He cleaned out the estate long ago."

My head jerked back to Wayne. He wasn't bluffing. He knew

something awful about Buster's family. A reluctant fascination unfurled in me.

Buster swore again. "It's all his fault. Bastard couldn't keep his pants zipped. He slept with anything and everything and pissed our money away. I've been scrimping ever since. My mother has certain expectations of how she's supposed to live. I can't tell her we're broke."

"But you can scare innocent people like Baxley here half to death. With that new cash flow coming in, I'm guessing you found someone with deep pockets. Either that or you stole the money outright when you killed that girl."

"I did not kill Lisa." Buster enunciated each word with precision.

"Now that's fascinatin'. Her name hasn't been released because we're still locating her next of kin. You're up to your neck in this thing. I like you for the murder."

"You can't pin it on me. I'm not a killer."

"The only way you can clear your name is to tell me who killed her."

Buster's head wobbled from side to side. "I can't."

"You can. Or you can rot in jail. Juries believe circumstantial evidence."

The sheriff's lie flared. I suppressed a smile. I didn't care that he was pressuring Buster. This was kind of fun.

Buster swore. "Nah. I'll take my chances."

The sheriff pounded his coiled fist on the table. "You owe me, sucker. You owe me for all the times my daddy beat the tar out of me for not having the Thompson birthmark. You owe me for my mother's heart being broken when your daddy singled her out, used her, and dumped her when another woman caught his eye. You owe me for keeping her mouth shut because if she'd ever said who knocked her up, my daddy woulda killed yours without blinking an eye."

That truth clunked around the interrogation room for a solid minute, skittering like a wild top into the walls, chairs, and hapless people caught in its path. The truth flashed lightning bright before me, explaining the heartache, the anger, and so much more about Wayne Thompson. He'd inherited his randiness from his biological father. No wonder he knew so much about the Glassman family. He'd hated them for years.

Buster studied the sheriff closely. "We're half-brothers?" His thin voice betrayed his fragile feelings. I sensed that he didn't believe Wayne on one level, but on another, the awful truth ate at him. His father had been a womanizer, as Wayne was now.

"Yep, but you won't get any sympathy from me. I'd just as soon you rotted in jail for the rest of your natural life. You better start talking, or I'll make sure your mother knows the truth about my parentage and a few others in this town besides."

"Others?" Buster's voice cracked. "I have more relatives?"

"Three sisters and two brothers by my count."

"Christ. I had no idea." He paled. "Have I slept with my sisters?"

The sheriff's face remained impassive. "Tell me what you know about the murder."

Buster scrubbed his face with his hands. "She's gonna kill me."

"Life's full of choices."

"You don't understand. If I say anything, my income vanishes. I'll be right back where I started."

"You're extorting the killer? Then it isn't me you have to worry about, dummy. I should cut you loose and see how long you make it. Whatcha say, Baxley? He got a day left? A week?"

My gut tightened at being thrust from the sidelines into the spotlight. "I can't see the future." But I had enough imagination to foresee the future Wayne outlined. Buster's days were numbered.

Buster got a wild look in his eyes. "Oh, God. I can't do this."

The sheriff rose. "I'll get Elwood to start out-processing you. Your death will save the taxpayers the expense of trying your sorry butt." Wayne waved me toward the door.

We hadn't moved two paces before Buster lunged to his feet. "Okay! I'll talk."

The sheriff held his silence. Seconds ticked by.

"Carolina killed Lisa." Buster's words spilled out in a rush.

Wayne glanced at me. I nodded to indicate he was telling the truth. He turned back to face Buster. "I suspected as much, but unless you have evidence, she walks. Why the hell would she kill another woman?"

"She hated Lisa, that's why. She tolerated her husband's infidelities, but she lost it when Lisa bore him a perfect son. Carolina killed her; I swear."

The sheriff frowned and turned to leave again. With his hand on the doorknob, he tossed over his shoulder, "Thought you had me there, didn't ya? Why would she kill the woman and bury her on her own property?"

"She musta thought she'd get away with it." Moisture gleamed on Buster's forehead. "Who knew Baxley would go digging up Carolina's yard? You wanna know who's to blame for this debacle? It's that woman sitting right there."

I did an excellent impression of a doe caught in the headlights as they both studied me. No way was I to blame for this. Outrage boiled out of my throat in a mighty squeak.

My cheeks heated. "If she hadn't made such a fuss about everything being absolutely perfect and withholding my money, I wouldn't have put in the extra effort. But she made sure I'd be on the lookout for plant problems. She wanted Lisa to be found. She wanted someone else to take the blame."

"Bingo," the sheriff said. "Let's beat her at her own game."

Chapter 46

"Finally!" Charlotte's fingers closed around my forearm tighter than a pair of handcuffs. She dragged me outside the Law Enforcement Center into the bright noonday sun. Fury trembled down her arm. Flags of red dotted her plump cheeks.

I fumbled for my sunglasses and wished for my hat. "Hey, Charlotte."

"Don't you 'hey, Charlotte' me. Why did I get stuck in the lobby for hours? Wayne should fire Tamika for insolence. Do you know how rude she was to me? She sneered at me. And I could tell she got a kick out of it. Which made it worse. Why didn't you look out for me?"

I drew in a big breath. Looked like I was gonna need it. "Calm down. So you had to wait a bit. What's the big deal?"

"The big deal is you got inside, and I didn't. You know things about the case. Things I need to know."

"No, you don't need to know." I scrunched up my eyes, wincing inwardly at how tight my voice sounded, grateful for the dark glasses to shield my eyes.

Her hands gestured wildly. "Don't think you can talk your way out of this one. I'm dirt-eating mad. Tell Wayne to fire Tamika. She is mean and spiteful."

"I don't have any control over what his staff does. I'm sorry if you were embarrassed."

"You knew I was coming." She planted her hands on her hips, sunlight glinting on her trendy glasses. "Why didn't you leave word for her to wave me through?"

"You're not going to like this answer, but I want you to hear me out without interrupting." I waited until she nodded before continuing. "I don't want you involved in this. Freedom of the press isn't a bulletproof vest. It can't protect you from a murderer. Until the sheriff catches the killer, this thing could spring wide open. I don't want you hurt."

"I'm an adult. I'll decide what's safe for me. How dare you shut me out? I thought we were friends."

I squeezed my eyes shut. She wouldn't like hearing this either. "I did it for your own good. You're my best friend. You've got a lot more stories to write, a lot more papers to sell."

Charlotte snorted. "Not if Bernard Rivers gets his way. We sold more papers with his hair story than any of the previous weeks with my leads. Kip's gonna reassign this murder story to Bernard if I don't make something happen."

"Bernard won't get any information from me. The sheriff considers this investigation active and ongoing. No way would he leak a word of it to anyone. You'll get first dibs from me as soon as there's info to come out, I promise."

"I want to believe you, I do, but I want to know what you know so bad. Can you tell me if I promise not to tell anyone?"

I died a little bit inside, dreading the strain my new job placed on our friendship. I shook my head. "Sorry. I can't."

Her face fell. "This sucks. I hate this."

"I don't like it either. Come on home with me and grab a late lunch. Mom put a batch of soup on in my crock-pot. It's just sitting there, all yummy, waiting for us to come eat it."

"Your dad make bread?"

"I'm sure he did."

My friend pumped her fist. "I'm in."

★ ★ ★ ★ ★

Two nights later found me sitting in a van hidden near Buster's house. The sheriff's woodsy aftershave filled the tight space. Electronic gadgets abounded. Truly, I'd been surprised that the sheriff had such high-tech equipment available.

Every time I thought I had Wayne Thompson pegged as a chauvinist redneck, he surprised me with intelligence. Maybe womanizing wasn't the only thing he'd inherited from his real dad. Maybe there was more depth to Wayne than I'd ever given him credit for.

"You think she'll show?" I asked.

He nodded. "I heard Buster set it up. She agreed to meet him here tonight."

With Virg and Ronnie on patrol and Elwood and Rogers backing us up, Carolina Byrd didn't stand a chance of getting away. Even so, Buster was probably sweating bullets in there. We'd heard him popping open a can of beer.

My thoughts raced a mile a minute. What kind of woman sets out to kill another? Would she try to kill Buster tonight? "Wonder if she'll wear one of her power outfits to meet with Buster."

"Power outfits?" Wayne's brow wrinkled.

"She's big on suits with padded shoulders, oversized jewelry, and high heels. Or hadn't you noticed?"

He shot me a sly grin. "I noticed she's got all the right parts."

"You would notice that." Still the old Wayne under the glossy veneer of sheriff. "How long will we wait?"

"Shouldn't be too much longer. State Patrol radioed in that her Mercedes exited I-16 and turned south on I-95 an hour ago. Let me check with Virg." He clicked on his radio. "Virg, you got anything?"

"Nope," Virg said. "No killer babes in the car of my dreams. Just Yankees speeding down the interstate to Florida."

"You certain?"

"Sure as I'm setting here."

Wayne swore. "She should be here by now. Virg, you and Ronnie swing around to see if she broke down on the road. Elwood and Rogers, you listening?"

"Yeah, boss?" Elwood said.

"Head on out to Mallow. ASAP. See if she went there instead."

"Roger that."

Wayne settled back in his seat. "I don't like this. She's been a step ahead of us the whole time. I've got a bad feeling about this. You?"

"I feel edgy, no doubt. Thought it was nerves. This is my first stakeout."

"You have nerves of steel." He snorted. "Maisie Ryals still wants to kill you."

"Nerves of bamboo, is more like it. I was plenty scared when he grabbed me, that's for sure."

The sheriff sobered. "Scared is good, babe. Keeps you on edge."

We sat in easy silence, two justice-seekers waiting for the moment to pounce. Wayne hadn't said anything about me bringing my weapon, but I'd tucked my handgun in the waistband of my pants under my shirt, just in case. I'd learned my lesson about killers last time I faced one.

After a while, the sheriff stirred. "You really into this consultant gig?"

"I'm into paying my bills. I'll do what it takes to provide for my daughter."

"You have a flair for this kind of work."

I bit back a smile. "Your cop instinct works just as well. Each time you asked me about Buster's truthfulness, you already knew the answer."

"It's good to have outside confirmation. Plus being a human

lie detector isn't the only asset you bring to the job. Your dreams helped us find out who the victim was, and to locate her family."

"You would have found her eventually. Dyani was worried about her daughter. She didn't know Lisa was missing or dead. If more time had gone by, Dyani would have reported her as a missing person."

"Like I said, you add an extra dimension to the job. What's your read on this stakeout?"

We'd been chatting so comfortably, his request startled me. "I haven't consciously analyzed anything. That burns psychic energy, and I was saving myself for when Carolina showed up. I know you're frustrated and Buster's nervous, but under the circumstances that's to be expected."

He rapped his fist on my forehead as if he were knocking on a door made of tissue paper. "You got anything else in there? Can you do a dream right now and locate Carolina?"

We weren't playing poker, so I didn't see any point in laying all my cards on the table. If it suited his ends, Wayne would push and prod and use me up. I was doing this job on my terms. "Not unless she's dead, and even then it isn't a given. If you want an expert on this kind of thing, we should call my dad."

"Tab made it clear. He's retired from dreamwalking, plus you've got the hair for the job."

I groaned. "My striped hair is a sore spot with me. I'm not a vain woman, but I get headaches if I wear a hat. I swear, it's almost as if the universe wants my hair to be seen."

"Don't discount the value of a good sign." He paused for a moment. "You been getting food at your back door?"

Alarm flared in my body. "How'd you know?"

"I spent some time drinking with old Sheriff McCain. He told me about when Tab first came into his hair, too. How he couldn't understand the food showing up on his doorstep. He finally accepted it. You should, too."

"Where's it coming from? Do you know?"

"Like I said, you should accept it."

"Does this mean Daddy won't be getting food at his back door now?"

"I don't know."

"Hmm." Should I share my unexpected bounty with my parents? I didn't want Mama and Daddy to starve either. I made a mental note to take food to them.

The radio crackled. "Sheriff? We got a problem." Elwood's deep voice blasted through the radio.

"Explain," the sheriff demanded.

"The car's here, but driver isn't Mrs. Byrd. It's her assistant, Donna Webb. She's got a stack of folders for her boss. I double-checked the premises. Mrs. Byrd isn't here."

Wayne swore. "Bring the woman and the car to the jail. We'll question her and search the car."

"Gotcha."

As I listened to the conversation, my unease mounted. Carolina was a step ahead of us again. I discreetly pinged the area. There was no one in close proximity. She wasn't here.

Where was she?

CHAPTER 47

Though it was just past midnight, I felt like I'd been awake all night. I stretched, groaning at my tight muscles, and climbed out of my truck. God, I was tired. The futile interrogation had gone on and on. Carolina's assistant knew nothing about her boss's whereabouts. Neither did Buster nor the sheriff.

We knew nothing.

Carolina Byrd knew everything.

But not for long.

We'd catch her.

I mounted the back steps, scooped up the basket of kale and turnips, and savored their garden-fresh fragrance. I made a note to ask Mama for her kale soup recipe when I picked Larissa up from their house tomorrow morning. I unlocked the door and called the dogs, certain they would enjoy a little late night carousing in the backyard.

There was no answering click of claws on wood floors. The dim light I'd left on over the kitchen sink greeted me with a soft glow. I flicked on the overheard light and placed the veggies on the counter. "Precious! Muffin!" I hurried through the house, flipping on lights as I went.

With each micro-second, my worries compounded. Where were the dogs?

They were in the den, beyond the illumination of the hall light. Both remained unresponsive as I approached. Heart in my throat, I bent down to check for life signs. Muffin had a faint heartbeat, so did Precious. I drew in a shallow breath of relief. What happened to them?

Sensing movement beside me, I rolled right. But I wasn't quick enough to avoid being clubbed on my left shoulder. Pain slammed through me. White dots danced before my eyes.

I scrambled behind a wingback chair and tried to take a breath. My shoulder throbbed. "Who are you? What do you want?"

"You're a dead woman," the husky voice from the shadows taunted. "I'm gonna enjoy killing you the most."

Why, oh why hadn't I pinged my house before entering? I'd put myself at risk. Thank God Larissa was safe at my parents' house. I snatched the Glock from my waistband and gripped it firmly in my right hand.

What was I up against? How many intruders? I scanned the area with my parasenses. Just the one attacker inside my house. One was more than enough to worry about. Rage and fury emanated from this person, all directed at me.

I had plenty of rage and fury of my own. This person had trespassed inside my house, disabled my dogs, and tried to whack my brains out. Not happening.

The fireplace poker struck the wingback chair inches from my head. Gun in hand, I crawled farther down the furniture row, until I was behind the sofa. My nerves revved in hyper-drive. This was bad. So bad. Was I going to die? Fear slammed through me, opening the floodgates on a morass of emotions.

My gut quivered so much I couldn't move. I clung to the safety thought Wayne had given me.

Scared was good.

Scared would keep me alive.

Should I send out an extrasensory summons to Larissa and Dad?

No.

They would come over here to help, even if I only asked them to call the sheriff. Bad choice. I wouldn't endanger my family.

This was my problem.

I'd jolly well fix it, or I had no business doing police work.

With my senses on high alert, I registered a distinctive floral scent. Wait. A memory surfaced. I knew that fragrance. Carolina Byrd wore that perfume. She was here inside my home. She'd incapacitated my dogs. She'd swung that fireplace poker hard enough to brain me. My fingers tightened on the grip of the gun.

Those sweet dogs didn't deserve her malice.

I didn't, either.

Fury mixed in with my fear, a volatile high-octane blend of ugly bravado. It flared from a tiny spark into snapping flames. Cold blue fire seared my entire body, emboldening my tongue.

"I know it's you, Carolina." My voice sounded strong. As if I routinely faced killers. As if I wasn't faced with the horrible possibility of firing this gun.

My assailant shrieked and swung the poker in the direction of my voice. She missed. I thanked God for the sturdy old-fashioned frame of this sofa. I hadn't rearranged this room because this dinosaur was too heavy to move.

"Where is it?" Carolina roared.

I had no idea what she wanted, but I wasn't playing her game. "The cops know all about you, Carolina. About how you lured Lisa to her death."

The poker wacked the sofa while I spoke. A cloud of dust enveloped me, and I sneezed. I needed a better plan than cowering behind my sofa. I remembered what Wayne had said was in Lisa's safe deposit box. That ammunition would hurt her worse than a bullet.

"You little hussy," Carolina muttered. "You've been nothing

but trouble since day one. Sneering at my landscaping ideas, screwing up my plans. Not anymore. The cops will find your lifeless body here in the morning. Right next to your dead dogs."

My breath hitched in my throat. She'd given the dogs a lethal dose? Hate sharpened my focus, fueling me with a singular purpose. Carolina's dark aura seethed with roiling emotion. Understandable.

She was a killer.

She planned to kill me.

I had a different plan.

CHAPTER 48

Energy surged through my body, a lightning bolt of raw power that activated every sense I had. I stood and pointed my gun at Carolina. "Get out of my house."

The poker clanked to the floor, and she leveled her handgun at me. "Not a chance. I already know I'm capable of killing, but you, Ms. Back to Nature, you won't shoot me."

Wary, I edged from behind the sofa, my gun steady, my aim heart true. "Why did you kill Lisa?"

Carolina retreated toward the illuminated hall. "That witch. I didn't mind her screwing my husband. She could have the prick, long as I had his name. But that changed after she bore his perfect son. He threatened me with divorce. I had no choice but to poison him and then bide my time till I could kill his trashy girlfriend. She danced around a pole for money, and he preferred her over me? Give me a break. Once I rid the earth of his bastard spawn, my son will be Judson's sole heir."

"You killed to protect your son's inheritance?" Disbelief tinged my voice.

"I killed her for crossing me. Same as I'm going to kill you. You're in my way. Tell me where the kid is, and I'll only put one bullet through your heart. Screw with me, and I'll empty this gun into your belly."

"You don't scare me. I'm not one of your salaried minions who fawn over you. The cops know Buster was blackmailing you for the murder. They traced the electronic payments. Even if you shoot me, you'll spend the rest of your days in prison."

"The cops." Carolina snorted, pig-loud. "The stupid cops got nothing on me, or I'd be in jail already."

"Don't bet on it. They've got Lisa's safe deposit box. Inside was her son's birth certificate with Judson Byrd named as the boy's father."

Carolina's gun shook. "Liar!"

"Know what else they found? Company shares. Judson signed over his share of the company to Lisa's son. Without his shares, you no longer control the majority of stockholders. You're so busted."

"No! The company is mine. The company is nothing without me."

"Got bad news for you, Carolina. You're fired."

"You can't take my company. I made it the powerhouse it is today."

Carolina stood on the rug with the worn-out backing. I was close enough now. Satisfaction roared in my veins. I twisted down, snatched up the corner of the runner, and yanked the rug out from under her. Not an easy feat, even after all the bicep-building yard work I'd been doing. I threw myself back in the shadowed living room.

Carolina went down, surprise etched on her shadowed face. A thud told me I'd guessed the distance correctly. She'd cracked her head against the marble side table. Her gun roared.

I scrambled to my feet and kicked her gun away from her. She glared at me from the floor. "Don't move," I ordered, flipping on the light. Blood oozed from the side of her blond head. That had to hurt like a bear.

Too bad.

I dialed the emergency number and identified myself. "Intruder in my home."

"Help is on the way," Rhonda, the nighttime dispatcher, said.

"We got an anonymous tip five minutes ago."

I blinked. "You did?"

"Yeah. Elwood and Rogers are en route. The sheriff, too." Rhonda paused. "You get her?"

"I got her."

"Atta girl."

CHAPTER 49

I sipped hot tea in my kitchen. Mama bustled around, chopping kale for the soup pot. The heady aroma of Daddy's homemade bread in the toaster made my mouth water. Larissa spooned down a bowl of oatmeal. Charlotte sat huddled over another cup of tea, writing down my account.

"What about the dogs?" Charlotte asked.

How was it possible my hands were so steady? "The dogs were only drugged not dead, thank goodness. Daddy drove them out to the vet, and they're under observation out there."

"What happened next?" Charlotte asked after I got to the help-is-on-the-way part of the story.

"Next seemed anticlimactic. The EMTs checked Carolina's head and hauled her out of here. Thank God she didn't die." I shuddered. "I wouldn't want her spirit lingering here to torment me the rest of my days."

Interest gleamed beneath Charlotte's narrow glasses. "Could she do that?"

"I was speaking off the cuff. That remark isn't for the paper, and if you write it down, I'll hurt you."

"You're pretty full of yourself."

"Cut me some slack. I'm still wired from confronting a homicidal maniac."

"She killed to protect her kid's inheritance?"

"That's what she claimed, but I don't believe her. Being second fiddle didn't suit her. As long as everything was on her terms, it was fine. Once her husband strayed from her scripted plans, his days were numbered."

"How will they prove any of this?"

"The Macon cops are exhuming Judson's body. If she poisoned him, they'll find it. Plus they have the documents from the safe deposit box. And Buster's blackmail video. And let's not forget she tried to kill me."

"You should have alerted us." Larissa covered my hand with hers. "Pap and I could've come over and taken her out."

I squeezed her hand in gentle reassurance. "That's exactly why I didn't let you know. I wanted you out of harm's way."

"What about that anonymous call?" my friend asked.

I shrugged, hoping to appear nonchalant. "They traced the call to a disposable cell phone. Someone knew what Carolina was up to. Someone ratted her out."

"But not quickly enough," she said. "Help didn't arrive until she'd hit you and fired her gun at you. You're amazing."

"Determined to live is more like it." I sipped my tea, dreading the next question, certain it would come. Sure enough, Charlotte didn't disappoint.

"Who made that call?" she asked. "Your closest neighbor is the post office, which isn't even in the line of sight of your house. I'm assuming Carolina's car wasn't parked here, or you would have summoned help when you returned home. Did someone see her?"

Yeah, someone did. My watcher. He had protected me once again. "That's the only reasonable explanation I know of."

"What about unreasonable explanations? Did one of the spirit people phone from beyond?"

Anger rose, and beneath it, a tempering spirit. I choked out a laugh, hoping to deflect her from pursuing this line of inquiry. "More likely it was Big Brother watching the world through some spy satellite technology."

"Hmm." She scribbled a bit more on her notepad.

I leaned forward. "You're not going to print that, are you? I don't want to jeopardize my consulting job with the sheriff by antagonizing the government. The sheriff's deputies already think I'm a certified flake."

"If that's what they think, they're stupid as a cat chasing her tail. You are brilliant. If they can't see that, they don't deserve you."

"Maybe not, but I want them to pay me for helping them."

"Not to worry. You've got the full weight of the *Marion Observer* behind you. If they stiff you, I'll spearhead the smear campaign to elect a new sheriff next fall."

That was a daunting thought, Charlotte entering the political arena. Sleep tugged at me. I scrubbed my face with my hands. "You got enough to blow Bernard out of the water?"

"I do. And I surely thank you. Bernard will be covering the bridge club before you know it, while I will be exclusively covering the police beat."

Stifling a yawn, I stood. "I've got to get some sleep."

"Not to worry, I am so outta here." My friend gathered her materials and hurried away, light on her feet for a two-hundred-pound woman clad in robin's-egg blue.

Daddy escorted me out of the kitchen. Though I could have made it up the stairs under my own steam, his solid presence comforted me. I averted my gaze from the bullet hole in my hall wall as we passed by. That could have been my head. I'd been lucky. So very lucky. I shivered.

"You all right? We were worried." His brown eyes studied me as we continued to my bedroom. "We could have helped."

The concern in his eyes loosened the tears in mine. I blinked rapidly to keep them from spilling out. "I kept this to myself. Y'all didn't sign up to help the police. I did."

"We want to help."

"And you do. You help me with Larissa, and you're gonna go to the vet to see how the dogs are doing."

"We do those things gladly. You don't even have to ask." He paused. "You could have been my first and last call as coroner."

"You're not taking the job?"

"I'm keeping the job, but if you'd died, my heart would have died with you. Please take care of yourself. You've got responsibilities. Not just to Larissa, but to the entire community. You're the dreamwalker. That matters. To all of us."

"Paying my bills matters, too."

His expression clouded. "Move in with us. Then you won't have bills."

"Daddy, I can't do that. I love you and Mama dearly, but I have to do this my way."

"Understood, but I can't help worrying about you. Our door is always open."

"Thanks." I stifled a big yawn and sat down on my bed. "I need to crash."

"No worries. Lacey's gonna cleanse the house with sage while you rest. Larissa and I will take care of the dogs."

Something nagged my memory. "Daddy, y'all should take home some of the food I've been getting. It's too much for two people."

He kissed my forehead and tucked me in. "Don't worry about that now. Get some rest and we'll talk later."

"Later." I closed my eyes, praying for a restful sleep.

I should have known better.

CHAPTER 50

Lisa charged into my head, hugging me, and squealing like a young girl. In her garb of jeans and a T-shirt, she looked like a young, carefree girl. "You did it. My son is safe. You stopped Carolina."

I sat up reproachfully, exhausted from my crime-stopping efforts. "You could have told me that I was on her hit list."

"It wasn't just you. She planned to kill Buster, too. But you stopped her. I'm so happy. I could dance on the moon."

"Is that possible?"

"Sadly, no. I'm an earthbound spirit now. And I'm not going anywhere. I'm personally overseeing Little Warrior's life."

My hand came up. "Wait just a minute. You can't pester me every time he blows off his homework. I've got a life and a kid to raise."

"Not to worry. I'm going to become your spirit guide. I'll help you, and you'll help me. Deal?"

"How can you help me?"

"I can find spirits for you, check things out for you in distant earth locations. All you have to do is agree to the deal."

"No deal. A spirit named Joe appeared to be helping me, but my agreement with him allowed a dark spirit to enter a nice young woman."

Lisa's essence shifted, darkening then lighting back up. "You need proof? How about I tell you about the person in your woods?"

"The watcher? You know about my watcher?"

"I certainly do. I've got my eye on him."

"So it's a man?"

"Right. And he watches."

"I figured that out for myself. Tell me something I don't know."

"He moves like one of our people, walking soundlessly through the forest."

"Is it my husband, Roland?"

"His name is my bargaining chip. But he is highly trained in fighting arts."

"Knew that, too. He subdued a large man in a matter of seconds. All you got for me is that he's a male with fighting skills?"

"Deal or no deal?" Lisa giggled. "I sound like that deal-making TV program."

After my experience with Joe, I knew better. I sighed. "No deal."

She shrugged. "Your loss. Maybe you'll change your mind. Tell Dyani that I love her. That the moons of love and hate are one, but love prevails."

I had no plans to visit Wetumpka, but life took many turns and twists. "I will, if I see her."

"She will come to you. I'm sure of that."

Lisa faded from view, and I floated on the shore of many dreams. Throughout them all was a tall figure cloaked in shadows, watching.

Waiting.

CHAPTER 51

"You all right?" the sheriff asked when I entered his office two days later.

"Doing good. I'll be even better when you pay me for my work."

"Gotcha covered, sweetheart." He handed me a bulging white envelope.

Surprised he paid without a skirmish, I noticed his payment method was somewhat unorthodox. "You're paying me in cash?"

"I'm paying you with the proceeds of the auctioned items we confiscated from drug dealers. This works better for me, and you won't have to report your income to the IRS."

My head popped back. "That's illegal."

"It's the way of the world, hon." He grinned. "Only illegal if you get caught."

"But I need to deposit this money. To pay my bills."

"Pay your bills in cash. Find a safe place for the rest until you need it."

"This feels wrong."

"I'll be glad to take the money back, in that case. You can work for free."

"Wait. I want to get paid. I expected a paper trail. W-2s at the end of a year, health insurance, that sort of thing."

"This is what I have to offer. Take it or leave it."

"I'm taking it." I stuffed the envelope in my back pocket, hoping that didn't make me a hypocrite. "Where do we stand on Carolina Byrd?"

"She's locked up in jail. The judge refused bail, says she's a flight risk. She won't see daylight for a long time. Count on that."

"What about her husband? Judson. Was he poisoned?"

"Still working that angle. We've obtained Buster's video where she admits all kinds of stuff. It would take a team of brilliant lawyers to get her acquitted."

"She can afford two teams of them. What about Buster and Duke? What happens to them?"

"Duke's out on bail. He'll serve time for the felony, though. Putting poisonous snakes in your truck will land him in prison eventually."

"And Buster?"

"Buster may walk. He cooperated with us, and our prosecutor gave him immunity. Carolina's attorneys may come after him. They'll want to discredit Buster and his video."

I pondered that for a minute. I'd still have to face Buster and Duke in the community. But at least they weren't murderers. Just screw-ups. "What about Dr. Sugar? What will happen to him?"

"Dr. Sugar is tending bar at the Fiddler's Hole."

"No chance of him being reinstated as coroner?"

"Nope. Tab's got the job now. Frankly, it was time for a change."

"I'm not sure I like Daddy being the coroner."

"You're even then, because he tried to get me to stop using you for future cases."

I smiled. I'd always be Daddy's little girl. "Is the Ice Queen gone?"

Wayne nodded to the right. "She's packing up. She wants to talk to you."

"Oh, goody."

"Now, don't take that attitude. Hear her out."

Air huffed out of my lungs. "Fine. I'll listen to her."

"She's been real good to your dad. Don't let her lack of personality cloud your good judgment."

"I promise to be as open-minded as you are."

He laughed. "It's going to be fun having you around here."

"Let me know when you have another case for me." I headed down the wide hallway, wishing I didn't have to speak to Gail Bergeron. But I was an adult. I could contain my distaste for her and be professional. Or at least I hoped I could.

Cardboard boxes were stacked in the office chairs and on top of a utilitarian desk. Gail looked up when I knocked on her open door. In her crisp navy skirt, white blouse, and blue paisley silk scarf, she reminded me of an airline attendant.

"There you are. I wanted to talk with you before I left."

My smile held. "Here I am."

"First, let me apologize. I didn't realize my long-term friendship with Carolina would put anyone in danger. I had no idea she had killed anyone. I'm truly sorry."

I blinked in surprise. She was apologizing? To me?

Gail continued, "I've been reprimanded by my superiors and recalled to Atlanta. But I wanted to explore an idea or two with you."

She'd apologized and gotten into trouble with her superiors. That was a good start at balancing the scales of justice. Carolina had invited Gail here to study the remains of the bodies I'd found, hoping for inside information. She'd gotten it all right. And I'd almost been killed.

She was watching me closely. I should say something. "Like what?"

"Like psychic detecting at archaeological sites. You interested?"

Drat. I was interested. But I wasn't desperate for work.

Landscaping and pet-sitting jobs would come along. Dream-walking paid in veggies, while police work paid in untraceable bills. I wouldn't starve. "It would depend on the time frame. My daughter's in school. I can't commit to tearing off at a moment's notice."

"Wayne tells me you will continue on in your advisory role here," Gail said.

"That's correct."

"Our paths will cross again. Mind you, I'm not giving up on obtaining your services. I am impressed with your conduct and accuracy. A lot of people claim to be psychic. You, my dear, are the real deal."

"I don't make any promises about the information I receive. Some of it helps, some of it does not."

"Even so, you dial it in correctly. That bit you did with Lisa's watch was superb."

"Listen, I don't want to make a big deal about this. I want to lead a normal life. To be another single parent raising her kid in coastal Georgia."

"We share the same goal. I don't want word of your abilities to get out either. If you're swamped with work, you won't have time for me."

I didn't know what to say. She was being nice. And she wanted to hire me. I didn't like her very much, but I didn't have to like her. She'd be gone tomorrow. But Daddy had said kind things about her. I could talk to her about that.

"Thanks for training my father. He's excited about his role as coroner."

"He'll be fine, and light years better than that lecherous drunk who used to have that job."

"Dr. Sugar is an institution around here."

Her lips puckered. "You're better off without him. The world would be better off without that notorious womanizer."

I managed a weak smile. "Have a safe trip."

On my way home, I made stops at the power company and the phone company, prepaying my bills. I opened a savings account for Larissa's college tuition. I plunked in two hundred dollars, and I'd add to it whenever I could. The rest of the money I took home with me and stashed in Grandmother's Bible.

With the money Wayne had paid me, I would have a couple of months of not having to worry about finances. The dogs danced around my feet as I checked my messages. One landscaping estimate request and two pet-sitting jobs were mine for the asking. Hallelujah!

The moldavite pendant at my neck warmed. I'd certainly given it a workout lately. This gift from Roland had come at a time when I hadn't revealed my extrasensory abilities to him. How did he know I needed it? How much did he know about my talents?

And where was he?

CHAPTER 52

Parked vehicles lined the shoulder of Misery Road as far as the eye could see, many sporting Native American dream catchers dangling from their rearview mirrors. The temperature on this late winter day was mild, the mosquitoes hungry.

Larissa and I were coated in insect repellant, so we weren't slapping at the bugs as many of the out-of-towners were. I wore sunglasses to protect my eyes, but my striped hair still defied hats. I got a whopping migraine the minute I tried to put a hat on, so I'd stopped trying.

Not many people pointed at my strange hair anymore. I was old news, and I liked it that way. Especially in a crowd this size.

Daddy was here.

As the new county coroner, it was his duty to oversee the re-interment of the centuries-old bones. For the occasion, he'd put on a new tie-dyed T-shirt, clean jeans, and his trademark flip-flops. His gray hair was clubbed back in a ponytail and covered with a ball cap.

Lucky him.

Though Carolina Byrd was under lock and key, her lawyer had given us permission to bury the settlers' bones at the entrance to Mallow. The new grave site was closer to the road than the original site. If someone else landscaped the entry fence, they wouldn't hit bodies next time. And the historical society planned to erect a marker to commemorate the graves.

Mama finished her conversation with Beulah Woodward and

strolled over to join us. Mama's new shirt color exactly matched Daddy's, and I wouldn't be surprised if she'd dyed them herself, using natural products. Her nut-brown jumper and her olive complexion contrasted strikingly with her thick gray braid. All in all, she looked darned good for a woman approaching sixty.

She slipped several small objects into my hand. My fingers closed reflexively around them, and a sense of peace flowed through me. I looked at the handful of amethysts. "Thanks."

"When this is over, I need to recharge your other crystals," Mama said. "You've worked them hard."

"Thank you for knowing about this stuff. I probably don't say it enough. I appreciate all that you do and are."

"You're welcome, dear." Mama hugged me. "You seem happier these days, less anxious."

I thought about that as I returned the hug. "You're right. There are still things I don't understand, questions I can't answer, but the world keeps turning anyway. No reason for me to bang my head into the wall for answers that won't come."

"The answers will come, dear, in their own time, and maybe not the answers you seek."

"Prophetic and obscure." I grinned at her. "Are you sure you're not a philosophizer?"

Larissa tapped my arm and pointed behind me. "Look, Mom, Charlotte is talking to the TV people."

Looking like an orange sherbet–tinted mushroom in her peachy slacks suit, matching floppy hat, and taupe pumps, Charlotte's bright face beamed. I'd never seen her so happy. The reporter fired questions at her, and she fired the answers right back. *Thatta girl. Reach for that brass ring. Show the world what a star you truly are.*

As if she heard my thoughts, my friend glanced my way and cut her interview short. She hurried to where we stood and linked her arm in mine.

"I might ruin your professional image," I warned.

She waved off my concern, sunlight bouncing off her glasses, warming the freckles across her nose and cheeks. "Who the heck cares what Savannah television reporters think? I'm standing here with my brilliant friend who risked her life to put another killer behind bars. You're my best friend. This is right where I should be."

Her loyalty filled me with a sense of connection. A connection I'd longed for all my life, a connection that had been here all along.

Drums began to beat, and conversations quieted. As Running Wolf and evangelist Bubba Paxton prayed for the cleansing of the land, I opened my senses to the communal coffin before us. The spirits of a woman holding her infant and clutching the hand of her small daughter beamed at me.

"Thank you for bringing us home," Selena Munro mouthed from the veil.

The wind sighed through the pine trees, gusting around us, sending Charlotte's hat tumbling down the road. Larissa ran after it, clutching Muffin to her chest. She'd barely let the dog have a moment of peace since his lingering recovery and had insisted he come here today.

We'd brought Precious along, too. She sat docilely at my feet, sniffing the air. The flat-coated lab had had an easier time recovering from the sedative Carolina had administered, but she was still over-anxious about being left alone.

Running Wolf's melodic voice flowed through me. The land was indeed being cleansed. I slipped away from the crowd on the pretext of walking the dog. We ducked under the gate across the driveway. My senses resonated so clear, so true, it was almost as if I was being summoned. The elevated two-story house came into view, a grand edifice that now had no clear purpose.

I stopped and, though Precious tugged at the leash, walked

no farther. Opening my senses full throttle once again, I sensed the timeless pulse of the land, the ebb and flow of generations over this beautiful spot. Lisa was there, as I knew she would be.

"You've brought me peace." Today she looked more like a sex kitten than a single mom, with her tousled hair caressing her shoulders, a sheer flowing robe, and bare feet. "Thank you for believing in me. Did you see my son?"

"Yes, and Dyani, too. They are standing beside Gentle Dove back at the ceremony."

"I am pleased to see them both looking so well."

Her smugness irritated me. Why was she still haunting me? "Don't you see a light or something? Don't you want to go be with Judson?"

"I'll get to that. But for now, my interest lies here, with my son."

"Your mom will take good care of him."

Lisa shrugged. "Perhaps. But she will do better with me whispering in her ear."

Who was I to give a spirit advice? "Suit yourself."

"I usually do. Someone is coming." She turned her head and faded from sight.

I blinked against the dappled sunlight in the grove of ancient oaks. The landscaping around the mansion looked great, except for the missing shrub. Now that I wasn't destitute, I could be generous. The *Podocarpus* in my greenhouse belonged here.

Sheriff Wayne Thompson swaggered up with Precious on the leash. His gold badge gleamed on his belted twill trousers. "Lose something?"

My mind, most likely. Heat rose up my neck, warming my cheeks. "I guess so. I had the dog a moment ago. She must have tugged free while I was, um, thinking."

A muscle in his cheek twitched. "Thinking in the spirit world?"

I reached for the leash, ignoring the tingle of skin contact with the sheriff. He was still married, and so was I. "Thanks for catching the dog and bringing her back to me."

"No problem." An awkward silence fell between us. Finally, he met my gaze. "Now that you've had a few days to think, you still on board with police work?"

My pulse quickened. "We have another case?"

"Not yet. But it will come. We'll get outside requests, too."

"Gail?"

"And others. With today's television coverage and Charlotte's articles, I predict you will be in high demand."

"They can demand all they want. I want to live simply and raise my daughter. Those are my priorities."

"The town will protect your anonymity, and so will my office, if that's what you want."

An unusual offer, and yet stated so matter-of-factly it fired my curiosity. As we strolled back toward the cleansing ceremony, I asked, "Did you do that for my dad?"

He nodded. "Tab struggled with his gift for years. He's relieved you've stepped into his role. He's a new man."

"That he is." We walked a few more paces, my mind making connections where before there had been none. "Now that I've got an 'in' with law enforcement, can you do me a favor?"

"Sure."

I took a deep breath. "Can you probe into Roland's death? I'm not satisfied with the official version."

He halted. "What's this?"

"The Army lied."

Wayne's aura darkened. He opened his palms and gestured broadly. "No can do. The Army won't let us civilians in."

Liar.

His body broadcast the lie in three dimensions, which brought me up short as well. *Wayne is lying to me.* He knew more about Roland's death or disappearance than he was telling me.

Why would he lie?

It made no sense.

I faked a shrug. "It was worth a shot."

"Darn right. Don't you worry about a thing. Wayne Thompson is on the case. I'm gonna watch over you like a hawk."

A hawk. Funny he should mention a hawk. I'd seen one recently, and it ranged clear across Sinclair County. Like my occasional watcher in the woods.

Another weird thing in a weird world.

I could worry it to death, or I could practice acceptance.

I was happy. Larissa and I were in a good place, a safe place. We were thriving here on the Georgia coast. Like Mama said, time would sort the rest out.

I'd have to be patient.

ABOUT THE AUTHOR

Formerly an aquatic toxicologist contracted to the U.S. Army and currently a freelance reporter, Southern author **Maggie Toussaint** loves writing fiction. She's published five romantic suspense novels and five mystery novels, with *Death, Island Style* and *Dime If I Know* her most recent Five Star releases. *Gone and Done It* is the first installment in her new paranormal mystery series. Her debut release, *House of Lies,* won Best Romantic Suspense in the 2007 National Readers' Choice Awards. She's served as a board member for Southeastern Mystery Writers of America. Visit her at www.maggietoussaint .com, http://mudpiesandmagnolias.blogspot.com/, and http://facebook.com/MaggieToussaintAuthor. Maggie makes her home in coastal Georgia with her husband. When she's not writing books, she enjoys spending time with family and friends.